NOT FOR ME

A Drunk Love Romantic Comedy

Book 1

by

Aria Bliss

Misadventure Press, Gainesville, Florida, USA

Not For Me is a work of fiction. Names, places, characters, and incidents are the product of the author's imagination and are used fictitiously. Any resemblance to actual persons, living or dead, events, or locales is entirely coincidental. Contains adult situations and not intended for young audiences.

Copyright © 2022 by Aria Bliss
Written by Aria Bliss
www.ariabliss.com
aria@ariabliss.com

All rights reserved.
No part of this publication may be reproduced, distributed or transmitted in any form or by any means, including photocopying, recording, or any other electronic or mechanical methods, without prior written permission of the publisher, except by a reviewer who may quote brief passages in a review.

Published in the United States by Misadventure Press, Gainesville, FL.
www.misadventurepress.com
info@misadventurepress.com

Book Layout, formatting, typesetting and cover design by Angelique's Designs, a Misadventure Press Author Service
https://misadventurepress.com/author-services/
Edited by Megan Fuentes https://fuentespens.ink/hire-me/

Limits of Liability and Disclaimer Warranty
The author shall not be liable for your misuse of this material. This book is strictly for entertainment purposes.

FIRST EDITION
ISBN (paperback): 978-1-948169-65-3
ISBN (eBook): 978-1-948169-64-6

Printed in the United States of America

Books by Aria Bliss

A Drunk Love Romantic Comedy
Not For Me: Book 1
Let Me Stay: Book 2

Hearts of Watercress Falls
Healing Hearts: Book 1
Trusting Hearts: Book 2
Falling Hearts: Book 3
Laughing Hearts: Book 4
Forgiving Hearts: Book 5

An After-Hours Affair Collection
In Charge: Book 1
One Drink: Book 2
You're Mine: Book 3
Charm Me: Book 4
Stuck Together: Book 5 (A Holiday Romance)

~~~

Short Stories
Walk with Me

CHAPTER ONE

Heath

I run to move forward. It's as simple as that.

The soft thump of my feet pounding the pavement soothes my mind and calms my nerves. There's something to be said about hearing the low pitch of my sneakers striking the ground over and over again in quick succession.

Hearing my progress—seeing the world pass by around me—eases my tension after a stressful week. It's not enough to know I'm moving forward though. I need to see it, hear it, and feel it.

It confirms I'm alive.

I spent most of my late twenties and early thirties

stagnant—adrift and floating from day to day without purpose. That can happen after the kind of loss I was hit with. I can't let myself go back to that way of life because it wasn't living. Sure, I was still breathing and walking around on this planet, but I was lost.

Running may be a small way to deal with loss, but it's all I have to keep me from falling back into the lifeless holding pattern I was stuck in for far too long. I must keep moving forward.

And right now I'm moving toward the sweetest ass I've ever seen.

I'm used to seeing attractive women running the trails through Central Park. In fact, on a typical Saturday morning, I'll easily pass a dozen or more beautiful women out for a run. I look. I smile. And I keep running.

But I can't seem to take my eyes off the one in front of me today. So much so, I slow my pace to ensure she stays in front of me. It's a difficult task considering her pace is much more leisurely than mine. If I walk at my normal pace, I'd have passed her ages ago. My long legs and natural stride would overtake her with a few steps, and yet I'm holding myself back.

Why? God, I wish I knew.

There's something about her that's keeping me firmly

placed behind her.

Maybe it's her long, blond hair that's pulled back into a high ponytail. With every step she takes, it sways gently—back and forth, back and forth—in a hypnotizing fashion. It brushes across her back, falling just above the line of her sports bra. I picture my fingers grazing the surface of her skin instead of her hair. The tantalizing action of her ponytail sends a wave of heat through me.

Every time her hair brushes across her side, an image of her chest—the chest I haven't seen yet—flashes before my eyes. I imagine she has plump, full breasts that are pushed up by the tightness of her spandex bra revealing just a hint of cleavage. The imaginary curve of her cleavage is enough to remind me I'm still a man with urges.

Who knew a ponytail could be so arousing?

This woman is currently starring in the lead role in my fantasies, and I have no clue what she even looks like.

Dammit, I need to get laid.

It's been a long time since I considered hooking up with a woman, and even longer since I actually followed through with my desires. And this woman's curves have me ready to end my dry spell before I even know her name.

I can't stop my eyes from roaming down to her narrow waist. The waistband of her tight leggings hits just at her hip bone, leaving her entire midsection bare. My hands itch to wrap around her and draw her body to mine until her back is flush against my chest. The very thought of pressing the swell of her round ass against my cock makes me dizzy.

Before I have a chance to pull my mind out of the gutter, she spins on her heels and walks toward me. My eyes immediately shoot to her head, and I freeze. Her round face is outlined by a delicately curved jawline and perfectly balanced features.

Her full lips part and curve up in a wide smile, and for a moment, I panic. I'm certain she's busted me for staring at her. But her eyes never meet mine.

Fuck, she's stunning.

She's talking to her phone, and I realize her smile is not for me. She's fully engrossed with whomever she's talking to. I'm oddly disappointed by that realization.

As she nears, her words become clear. "I wrapped my hand around the thickness of his length. His cock hardened from my touch, turning me on even more. My—"

"What?" I blurt out harsher than I'd intended. Her words shock me like a bucket of ice water over my head, and my lust-filled fantasies vanish.

She stops. Her eyes narrow on mine. We're held in a staring contest for what feels like several minutes. I should probably say something since I'm the one that interrupted her, but my mind is blank. What can I say after catching someone having phone sex? This is definitely a first for me.

With her eyes locked with mine, she lets out a quick huff and continues. "I ached to feel him inside me." Her voice is rough and throaty as she steps closer to me. Her eyes rake down my bare chest to my groin before her gaze settles back on my eyes. I always run without a shirt on, and the glances never bother me. But the way she looks at me makes this interaction feel too intimate, too private, and I feel underdressed. Her aquamarine eyes turn a stormy shade of gray, and I'm mesmerized. They're unlike anything I've ever seen. The lightness of her pale eyes is amplified by a dark ring around the outer edge and her black pupils. As embarrassed as I am by this interaction, I cannot bring myself to look away.

Her lips tick up in a slight grin before she speaks again in slow drawn-out words. "The tighter I squeezed my hand around him, the harder he became. When he groaned out in pleasure, I slowly tugged at him over and over again until he begged me for his release."

Fuck me. Her voice is intoxicating and heady and by far the sexiest thing I've ever heard. She looks down at her phone, hits a button, and smiles at me.

"Well, don't you look yummy," she says in a sweet, almost bubbly tone. The drastic shift in her voice has my head spinning.

"Umm ... I ... Umm." I run my fingers through my hair out of frustration.

A playful gleam lights up her eyes. She said something. I need to answer her, but my brain isn't working, and my shorts are tenting. Between the shock of her words and her undeniable beauty, I'm incapable of forming a coherent thought, let alone words that make sense.

"Umm ..." I mumble again.

"You said that already. Got any other sounds in that gorgeous mouth of yours?" She licks her lips, and my dick twitches.

Holy hell, that one small action is such a turn on. My brain further degrades into oblivion.

And that mouth. No one has ever talked to me like that before. I should be offended, but I'm not. Coming from her, it's the hottest thing I've ever heard. I want to hear more talk like that come out of her mouth.

I flatten my hands to my cheeks and slowly run them down my trimmed beard, attempting to release the tension building inside me. "Who were you talking to?"

Her smile turns mischievous. "No one."

"So, you walk around the park talking dirty to your phone in a sexy voice for kicks?"

"Of course not." She steps closer still and leans in. She's so close, the tip of her nose almost touches my bare chest. She breathes in deep and sighs. "You smell hot—like sex on a stick." Her eyes shift down to my groin, and my body tightens. "Do you always run through the park in nothing but these *really* small running shorts?"

Her eyes study my chest and abs. The heat I felt earlier intensifies. My insides are on fire, and I feel like I could combust at any moment. No woman has ever had this effect on me. *Ever.*

She looks up at my face, her eyes now focused on my mouth. It would be so easy to claim her lips and kiss her hard and deep. But I don't. Instead, I stare at her.

"Your silence and that dumbfounded look on your face is ruining my fantasy." She bats her eyes. "Say something. Anything. I beg of you."

I step back and gape. "I'm sorry, what?"

She tilts her head and narrows her eyes. "Do you need to see a doctor?"

The expression on her face is serious but the tone of her words are playful.

"Are you making fun of me?" I ask.

"Not at all." She pins me with a serious stare. "I'm genuinely concerned about your inability to speak."

"I can speak just fine." My brows furrow, and my forehead creases in annoyance. She's a stranger who incidentally was talking dirty in public for all to hear. I shouldn't care what she thinks of me, but I do. "Why in the hell were you talking like that in public? Did I interrupt your phone sex call?"

Her head falls back, and the sweetest, most arousing laugh exits her mouth. It's deep and raspy and sends a shiver down my spine. It's the kind of laugh that shakes her entire body, including her generous breasts that now bob up and down against the restraint of her sports bra. Fuck, the reality is way better than my fantasy.

"Oh, my God! No! Why would you think that?" she replies.

Is this woman for real? She's got to be messing with me. Regardless, she's driving me a little batty.

My mind keeps hopping back and forth between pulling her into me and kissing her senseless or running in the opposite direction as fast as I can. My body may be reacting to her in ways it hasn't responded to a woman in a very long time, but everything about her is all wrong for me. With a mouth like that, she'd never fit into my world. I need order, solidarity, and reliability. Everything about this woman screams chaos, spontaneity, and mystery. I don't do any of those things. Not anymore.

Despite that, I can't walk away. My curiosity and unexpected attraction to this woman is keeping me rooted to this spot. So, I buckle down and say what's on my mind. "With words like *hard cock* coming out of your mouth, what's a man like me supposed to think?"

Her smile returns, and she points a finger at my chest. "And what kind of man are you exactly?"

I swallow hard. The pain from my erection has nowhere to hide in these thin running shorts. If she looks down, she's going to see the effect she's having on me. My argument about the kind of man I am will be moot. "One who's concerned about hearing a beautiful woman such as yourself talk dirty in a park where bad things have happened to women by creeps who frequent this park."

"Oh, but you're not a creep." Her eyes dance with playfulness as she touches my chest with her fingertip. I tremble. She runs her finger between my pecs and down the taught ridges of my abs, sending a zap of energy to the growing problem between my legs. Thank God her eyes are on mine and haven't moved lower.

My mouth runs dry, and I jump back. I grab hold of her

hand and pull it away from my skin. "What are you doing?"

She frowns and eliminates the distance I put between us. "Confirming you're not a creep."

She stares at me as if daring me to prove her wrong. For a moment, I want to. I want to do equally dirty things to her. Starting with the ones I heard directly from her mouth. But I can't. Because she's right about me. I'm not that guy.

I may be a lot of things—an asshole, a little high-strung, and even cold on occasions—but I'm not a creep. I would never take advantage of a woman. My fantasies remind me just how pathetic my life has become.

She sighs and steps back. Her eyes graze down my body once more. Her brows shoot up when her eyes settle just below my waistband. I look up to the sky, expecting to hear her say something about my very hard erection, but she surprises me yet again. "It's a shame you don't have more profound things to say. With that gorgeous face and this rock-hard body, you'd make the perfect book boyfriend. Now, if only you said sexy, sweet nothings that turned me on."

My eyes widen, and my mouth falls open. "Excuse me?"

She *tsks* and looks at me with sad eyes. "Did my words not make sense to you? Maybe you don't need a doctor, but clearly you're slow."

"What?"

"You say that word a lot," she says in an exaggerated and playful tone. "Am I using big words you don't understand?"

"What? No." Dammit, I can't speak around this woman. Between this ridiculous attraction I feel toward her and the crazy words she keeps saying, I can't think straight. "Who are you?"

"Oh, I'm sorry. Name's Alexis." She offers her hand for a shake with an open mouth grin like this is the most normal meeting ever. "And you are? No, wait." She holds her open palm up to my face. "Don't tell me. I like to give the heroes in my fantasies my own names. Knowing my luck, your real name isn't sexy enough for my book boyfriends, and it'll ruin the experience."

"The experience?" And there she goes again, using that phrase *book boyfriend*. What does that even mean?

"Yeah." She gives me a seductive look. "The fantasy that I'm sure I'll get off on later tonight."

Holy mother of God!

I honestly can't tell if she's serious or just fucking with me. Either way, I think I like it. Maybe a little too much, and if I don't change the subject now, I won't be able to walk home, let alone run. My dick is aching way too much, and the pain growing between my legs is threatening to flatten me to the ground.

"What the hell's a book boyfriend?"

She takes a deep breath and looks up at me with a sparkle in her eyes. "Only the most dreamy and perfect man of every woman's fantasy. They don't exist in real life," she sighs with a slight shrug of her shoulders, "and can only be found in books, hence *book* boyfriend."

"Okay, then." This entire interaction with her has been ... surreal. The more she talks, the less coherent my thoughts become.

"Well, I'd better get back to work. It was nice chatting with you. Even imperfect book boyfriends like yourself make for great inspiration." She presses her hand against my chest, right over my pounding heart, and closes her eyes. Her plump, pink lips turn up in a faint smile. She pauses for a moment and all I can do is stare at her perfectly shaped face and welcoming mouth. My urge to kiss her is strong, and I clench my hands into fists to keep myself from touching her.

As if she's reading my mind, she leans up and shocks me again when she kisses me on the cheek. "Goodbye, imperfect book boyfriend."

She turns on her heel and walks away. I would say she left me speechless, but the evidence shows I've struggled to speak since the first moment I heard her voice.

Despite the awkwardness of this interaction and my strong urge to flee just moments ago, I don't want her to leave. I want to call after her, ask her to stay, and beg her to talk to me some more like that.

She's right about me in more ways than she knows. I'm not the kind of guy that acts on my senseless desires. I'm safe, boring, and no matter how attracted I am to this woman, I'll never ask her out. She's not my type.

Alexis will most certainly make an appearance in my dreams tonight. But that's all I can handle. I don't go out with women like her.

Hell, who am I kidding? I hardly go out at all.

CHAPTER TWO

Alicia

My phone rings just as I shut the door of my apartment. I slide it out of the back pocket of my jeans and answer it. "I know. I'm late, but I'm on my way. I'll be there in a few minutes." The words rush out before I even manage to slide my key into the deadbolt to lock up.

"That's great dear, but wherever you're going, I doubt I'll be there," my mom replies.

"Oh, Mom." I cringe and swallow a groan. "Sorry. I assumed it was Emily calling me."

I really have to do a better job at looking at who's calling before I answer my phone. I know it's wrong to screen my calls from my mom, but she always nags me. Talking to her can be such a killjoy. I'm in a great mood, and I don't want anything to change that. My mind is still reeling over the interaction I had with Mr. Stick-Up-His-Ass this morning, and I want to continue to revel in that hunk of man for a little longer.

If that man had a voice and clever words to match his hot body, I would have been in serious trouble. He's just the right height for my average five foot six—I'm guessing an even six feet tall—and with perfectly toned muscles. Every curve and ridge of his chest is defined and made for touching and licking. His body is what book boyfriends are made of.

"Well, I'm grateful to Emily for unintentionally being the reason you *finally* answered one of my phone calls. You've been ignoring me, and it's very upsetting."

"I'm not ignoring you. I've just been busy."

"Not too busy for Emily, I see."

"Mom, don't." I squeeze my eyes closed and take in a deep breath. Getting mad will only make things worse. "You know I'm busy and value my downtime with my friends. Please, don't give me a hard time about that."

"If you answered my calls more often, I wouldn't have a reason to give you a hard time. I'm your mother. I need to speak to you on a regular basis, or else I worry."

"I see you every Sunday. You shouldn't have time to worry." I cringe as soon as the words come out. That's the wrong thing to say to Mom unless I want this conversation to go poorly.

"Alicia, you have no idea what it's like to be a mom. When you finally give me grandchildren, you'll understand a mother's worry. Maybe then, you'll be kinder to me."

I set myself up for that one. Knowing Mom, she called me with the intention of talking about my poor life choices and the fact that I'm still single at age twenty-seven. But I didn't have to make this conversation easier for her. She does a fine job making me feel like shit without my help. "You know I didn't mean it like that."

"With the way you are sometimes, sweetheart, I can never tell."

"Sorry. How have you been?" I try not to ask her that question too often either, but I'm desperate to get her mind off my accidental insult. She always takes my comments personally, and after twenty-seven years, I should know better.

"I'm good, sweetheart. I ran into Mrs. Rinehart last week. Do you remember her?"

"Of course. I haven't seen her since high school. How's she doing?"

"Good, good. Her son, Phil, just moved back to New York after spending a few years in California. He's single and would love to take you out for dinner soon."

And here it is. The reason for her call. She's not worried or concerned about my wellbeing. She wants to set me up on a date. "I'm not interested in going out with Phil, or anyone for that matter. Thanks, but no thanks."

"Sweetheart, you can't hide behind your computer screen forever. You need a real man, not just those fake ones you write about."

"You mean my book boyfriends?"

"Yes, those things," she says with a hint of disdain.

"I *love* my book boyfriends. They're so much better than real boyfriends. Real boyfriends disappoint. Book boyfriends always come through in the end, and despite their flaws, they're perfect."

"No one is ever perfect, dear. When are you going to stop with this fantasy comparison and start living in the real world?"

"I do live in the real world." I say a little too harshly. I take a deep breath to calm myself before I continue. "That's why I'm not dating. Men suck and always let me down. I don't have time for that kind of letdown in my life right now. Besides, I have plenty of time to find a man later."

"No, you don't. You're not getting any younger. I want grandbabies, and you're my only child. If you keep putting men off, you'll be too old to have kids by the time you decide a man is worthy of your time."

I punch the button to call the elevator, then bang my head against the wall while I wait. This conversation never changes. "You make it sound like I have one foot in the grave. I'm *not* interested in dating right now. I will *not* go out with Phil or any other man you decide to set me up with. No way, no how."

"Don't take that tone with me, Alicia. I will not tolerate your disrespect."

"I'm not disrespecting you. I'm putting my foot down. It's *my life,* and I'm happy. I don't need a man mucking it up."

"One day you're going to wake up sad and alone. I don't want to have to be the one to say I told you so."

I pinch the bridge of my nose, feeling the start of a headache. "Then don't. Let it go."

"Just meet Phil for dinner. What's it going to hurt?"

"No, Mom. I'm going to go now. I'll see you tomorrow for dinner, and don't forget about my book launch party on Friday. I love you."

"Alicia, don't yo—"

I hang up the phone before she finishes that thought. The woman can be so infuriating sometimes, and I don't have the patience to deal with her interference in my love life.

Why can't she just be happy that I'm happy? I don't need a man to be happy. In fact, having a man in my life would make me very *unhappy* right now.

Relationships take work and compromise. My schedule is hectic and sporadic. I like to write when inspiration strikes, which is nearly all the time. If I was dating someone, he'd expect me to make time for him, work normal hours, and turn off my computer so I can pay attention to him. Even then, he still might not be happy. I don't want or need that right now. Why can't Mom accept that and leave it be?

BY THE TIME I arrive at the restaurant where I'm meeting Emily and Trent for lunch, my mood is in the crapper. I'm forty minutes late, and still frustrated over my mom's meddling. Now I have to deal with my friends giving me a hard time for being so late.

I have no one to blame but myself. I'm always late. I try to do better, but no matter how hard I try, I fail. As Mom always says, I'll be late for my own damn funeral.

Another reason why I don't need a man in my life. My inability to be on time has always caused problems with the guys I've dated. It's a stress I don't want or need.

I see my friends glaring at me from a table in the back of the restaurant. *Yep, they're pissed.* If I upset *them* by always being late, I can only imagine how angry a boyfriend would be. Especially after my ex-boyfriend, Jeremy.

I immediately dampen that thought. *Not hopping on that thought train today.*

Passing the hostess stand, I head back to face the music.

Emily, Trent, and I have been my best friends since college. Emily now co-runs a popular bar and event space with her three older brothers, and Trent is a food critic. They both have busy schedules and cherish this time we get together. Me being late is like a slap in the face.

When I reach the table, I sigh. It's even worse than I thought. They already ordered and have eaten half of their lunch. "Sorry I'm late. Mom called and held me up."

"No excuses, babe." Trent points a finger at me with raised brows. "We hardly see you anymore and when you're this late, it upsets us."

"Especially when you live fifteen minutes from here," Emily adds, her words laced with annoyance.

"I know, and I'm sorry. It doesn't matter what I do, I

can never get myself out the door on time. You guys know this about me."

"Yeah, but it doesn't change how it makes us *feel*." Emily sits back in her chair and crosses her arms over her chest. "We love you and understand your life is a bit *unconventional*, but when you're this late, it's disrespectful."

"I'm sorr—"

"Nope." Trent holds his hand up to stop me. "No more I'm-sorry's. Just work on it. You can do better than forty minutes, babe, and you know it."

"Okay. You're right. I'll work on it." I roll my eyes and try not to sound angry at Trent's demand even though I am. He's not wrong to ask. I can argue with them about this all I want, but it won't do me any good. I made a deal with them months ago. They agreed I could be five or even ten minutes late without a penalty. Clearly, I broke that.

"Thanks. We appreciate that." Trent smiles and takes a bite of his food.

Emily, not one to stay mad for long, immediately asks, "Was your mom bugging you about dating again?"

"Yeah, apparently the son of one of her friend's just moved back to New York. She wants me to have dinner with him."

"Your mom's friend's son, uh? Sounds like a match

made in heaven." Trent laughs.

"It's not funny." I glare at him over my open menu. "If Mom had her way, I'd be married to Phil by the end of this month. And it's already the twentieth." I peruse the sandwiches and decide on my lunch just as the waitress comes up to take my order.

Emily shrugs. "Maybe you should meet this guy. You might hit it off."

"No, thanks. I do *not* need a man trying to control me again. It's bad enough that I upset you two when I'm late. Can you imagine how I'd make a man feel? That's a disaster in the making."

"Not all guys are bad, babe." Trent reaches over and squeezes my shoulder. Trent knows better than anyone how much my ex-boyfriend hurt me. He's the only one who saw what Jeremy did to me. The day Trent barged through my apartment and pulled Jeremy off me was the last time he hit me. It's been almost four years, and I haven't let a man close since.

"I know. My decision not to date has nothing to do with my past." *Liar.* "I'm happy with my life. I don't want the complication of a man. Is that so wrong?"

"No." Emily smiles, but doesn't do a good job at hiding the sadness that fills her eyes. "We want to make sure you're okay. You know, not screwed up in the head because of that jerk. You've turned into an unromantic, cynical romance writer. We're worried about you."

"And I love you for that. Both of you." I take a second to look them in the eyes. "But I'm not cynical, nor am I unromantic. I'm an extremely romantic person. I just don't want to date right now. Maybe I should lie to Mom and tell her I'm seeing someone."

"Then your mom will want to meet him." Trent shakes his head. "Remember how she was when you mentioned me as a friend? She hounded you for weeks, insisting on meeting me because she was determined to make sure we were dating. She practically planned our wedding before she'd ever met me."

I chuckle. "Oh, my God. How did I forget about that? She swore there was no way we could just be friends."

"Yeah, because men and women can't be friends." Trent narrows his eyes. "What was it she said?"

"That we're either fucking, thinking about fucking, or will be fucking very soon." Emily and I say at the same time. Laughter erupts around the table at the memory of hearing my sweet, innocent, church-going mom use such language. It's one of the few times I've ever heard her curse.

Trent's handsome smile grows. "Yeah, I love you, babe,

but more like a sister than a lover."

"Right back at you, bro." Trent's a good-looking man and very charming, but there's never been any chemistry between us. Emily and I have received our fair share of dirty looks from women when we all go out together. Especially from the girlfriends he introduces to us. They're always jealous and insist there's something going on between one or both of us.

Emily claps her hands and squeals. "I know. I know. You should tell your mom you're dating my brother. That way, when she insists on meeting him, you can actually produce a body."

"Emily." I shake my head. "I'm not going to date one of your brothers."

"Well, not for real. Just pretend. Our mom is always trying to set Heath up, and he hates it. He's lied to her for the past couple years and keeps telling her he's dating a new girl. He's made up so many names that he's struggling to keep them all straight. But if you pretend to date him, problem solved."

"Why have I never met Heath?" I ask.

Emily cocks her head to the side and gives me a curious look. "You've met him before."

"Not that I recall. I see Luke and Dexter every time I

visit the bar, but never Heath. He's like the mystery brother that lurks in the shadows. I'm beginning to wonder if he's nothing more than a figment of your imagination."

Emily's shoulders shake in laughter. "Trust me. He's not imaginary. He was a pain growing up. He just doesn't hang out at the bar like Luke and Dexter, but he's there a lot. Mostly stays in the back office, I guess." She snaps her fingers and grins. "Wait! He was at the grand opening a few years ago. I know you met him then."

"Oh, God. We were all so drunk that night. I don't remember who I met."

Emily grabs my hand and squeezes. "Oh, come on! You have to do this. Our family vacation to the Hamptons is coming up soon. You could go with us. If you pretend to date Heath, I'd get to spend two weeks with one of my best friends."

"Are you insane? I have a book launch next week."

"After supporting you through a gazillion book launches, I know you have a few weeks off before your tour starts. Our vacation is right in the middle of that. You won't be missed, and you know it."

I shake my head, refusing to give in to her. "Your mom hates me. There is no way she'd accept me as one of her precious sons' girlfriends."

Emily's jaw drops and her eyes widen. "Mom doesn't hate you. She just doesn't really know you. It's not like you spend a lot of time with my family."

I groan, knowing that's a dig. I love Emily like a sister, but I've never been comfortable in her world. I've turned down every family event and vacation she's ever invited me to. It's not that I don't like her family. I just don't fit in. I'm from Brooklyn; she's from the Hamptons. My mom barely made enough to cover rent growing up and her family, well ... Let's just say they're wealthy.

I can't tell her any of that without hurting her feelings, so I come up with a different excuse. "Luke and Dexter know me. They'll know it's a lie. It'll never work."

"They'll have to be in on it. We all will. Your mom is child's play compared to our mom. Trust me, they'll play along. The only reason she's not setting the rest of us up on dates is because she's too preoccupied with Heath. He's the oldest. He just turned thirty-six, and she wants him married."

"I don't know." I play with the straw in my drink. Lying to my mom is one thing, but I'm not sure I can lie to her mom. "I don't want to lie to your parents and risk them *actually* hating me forever."

"They never have to know. You help Heath. He helps

you. It's a win-win. And you'd get a free two-week vacation in the Hamptons."

"Can I come if I pretend to be your boyfriend?" Trent looks at Emily with a serious expression then waggles his brows.

"Ha, ha. Very funny. I'm not the one on Mom's radar. I won't need to worry about her setting me up until all my brothers are married. I'm safe for a few years."

"You say that, but from the way you talk about your mom, she could turn on you at any moment." I toss her an evil grin, but she ignores me.

"Just meet Heath and talk to him. If you two decide to help each other out, great. If not, fine. But you'll never know if you don't talk to him."

I shake my head. "This sounds like a disaster in the making." And I avoid disasters at all costs.

"Please." Emily clasps her hands and bats her eyes at me. When I don't respond she leans forward and starts laying it on thick. "You've not vacationed until you've vacationed in the Hamptons with the Rockwells. We'll have so much fun. You've been working so hard and deserve a break. We can go shopping, get massages, and lay out at the beach. Just say you'll meet Heath. I'll set it up. You two can talk and decide if it's a go. No pressure."

This is such a horrible idea, and she knows it. Lying to family never works, but I can tell by the look on her face she's not going to give up until I agree to meet with him.

"I don't know—"

"Please." Then she pulls out the big guns. "You can people-watch for hours on end. I bet you could get enough inspiration in those two weeks for an entire book!"

She knows me too well. I drop my head back and groan. "Fine. I'll meet him. But I'm not promising I'll agree to fake dating him. That's a lot to ask. Even for a romance writer like me."

Emily squeals again and bounces in her seat. "Yay, this is going to be so much fun."

I look to Trent for help, but he shrugs and gives me a *what are you going to do* look.

Fake relationships never work. Not in real life or in fiction. In fact, in fiction, they lead to love.

And I do not want love.

So, I'll meet Heath, then politely decline.

CHAPTER THREE

Heath

My chance meeting with Alexis on Saturday morning disrupted my entire weekend. Normally, I enjoy quiet weekends alone hanging out at my apartment, going to the gym, watching a late-night movie, or inviting my brothers over for a beer. Long ago, I settled into the homebody lifestyle of a family man. Only I never got the family.

I generally don't have a problem with my quiet life, but I've craved the company of my siblings and a sociable day at work all weekend long. After my run-in with Alexis, I found myself wanting that comfortable companionship a relationship offers. I haven't wanted anything remotely close to that in a long time.

Something about her ignited a spark in me that I can't put out. I can't stop thinking about her, and it's killing my focus.

I hope a day in the office brings me back to reality. Losing myself in my work always makes me feel better when I start down a negative path. We've got a lot going on at the bar this week, and I need to stay on task.

Alexis's blunt honesty and her ease at saying exactly what she wanted without fear of judgment continues to baffle me. But it's so much more than that. Even now, two days later, my body reacts to the mere thought of her. My dick gets hard when I picture her full lips turned up in that gorgeous smile of hers. The memory of her sweet, yet seductive voice whispers to me like a soothing symphony. It both calms me and excites me.

Then immediately fills me with guilt.

Knowing I'll never give my heart to another helps me control my wayward thoughts about Alexis. I've already had my chance at love, and I lost it. I have no business thinking about another woman that way. Not now, not ever.

"Hey, big bro, what's up?" Luke, my youngest brother by five years, plops into the chair opposite my desk with his typical shit eating grin on his face. It quickly disappears. I must be doing a shitty job at hiding my haggard state. "Why do you look so down?"

"It was a bad weekend." I lean back in the chair and stretch my arms above my head. I've been sitting at the desk in my office for far too long without moving. I meant to take a walk around the bar before our business meeting, but I lost track of time.

"Wanna talk about it?" Luke asks.

"Nah, it'll only make me think about it more. Plus, we have business to discuss. Where's Emily and Dex?"

"We're here," Dexter says as he and Emily enter the office and take their seats at the small round table in the corner. Luke turns his chair to face them, and I get up to take the remaining seat next to them.

We opened The Rock Room three years ago as a family business. Our personalities and skills complement each other, which made running a business together an easy decision. The hardest part was choosing the type of business. Like smart, sensible people, we put a bunch of ideas in a hat, and the first draw won.

Dexter, Luke, Emily, and I are all equal partners in the bar. I manage the finances and act as the overall business manager, Dexter manages the staff, Luke takes care of our food and drink menu, and Emily is our event planner.

The space we lease has two private rooms that allow us to schedule private parties and events. In the main room we host happy hours on the weekdays. It's also large enough to host live bands on the weekends when we don't have private events scheduled that lease out the entire space.

I start the meeting as I always do, giving everyone the rundown of our finances and areas I'm looking to improve our overall bottom-line. "Luke, on nights you bartend, can you keep a closer eye on the staff? Our profit margin on liquor has declined the past few months from where it's held steady the past two years. Costs have remained the same, so I want to make sure we're not giving too much of it away."

Luke nods. "That problem may have been resolved already, but I'll keep my eyes open."

Dexter, my younger brother by two years, jumps in. "Yeah, we had to let Ben go. Luke caught him giving his friends free drinks. And he had a lot of friends. I have a round of people lined up for interviews next week to replace him." He hands me a piece of paper.

"What's this?" I take it and stare at his chicken scratch. "Come on, Dex. How many times do I have to ask you to type this shit up? I can't read any of it."

I toss the paper back to him.

"You know I can't type worth shit," he asserts.

"You also can't write worth shit." I bark back. Dexter huffs as he wads up the paper and slouches in his chair. "What does it say?"

"Call order for the staff in case anything goes wrong while we're on vacation." Dexter glares at me. "I'll type it up for you."

"Thanks." I gesture to Luke. "How are things with the kitchen and bar?"

"Good. I'll email you the supply list for next month by the end of the day." He grins at Dexter. "And add me to the schedule for Thursday and Friday to bartend. I feel like working those nights."

It always amazes me that Luke takes so many shifts bartending. He doesn't have to, but he loves it and can't imagine doing anything else, so we let him. He's trained in culinary arts and sets our menu. I'd never tell him because it'd inflate his ego way too much, but he's a fucking fantastic chef. Like, drool-worthy food.

Emily does a fantastic job at booking great bands and events that draw in the crowds. Her connections and networking talents are a large part of why we're so successful.

Then there are times like now, when I want to strangle her, because she overbooked us. Inside I'm panicking, imagining running out of food, or not having enough staff on hand to manage two large parties. Our reputation, and our bottom-line, depends on our ability to make customers happy. All it takes is one screw-up and we could be out of business. Maybe I worry too much, but it's my job to worry.

We have an engagement party Friday night that rented out the entire bar for a private celebration for one of our regulars. The party has been on the books for months, and I can't for the life of me understand how Emily could make such a critical mistake.

"Zoe and Wyatt's engagement party is Friday. They requested the entire bar. Why do I also see a book launch party on the schedule at the same time?" I look around the room, making eye contact with each of my siblings.

Dexter and Luke look clueless. Emily stares back at me with a huge grin on her face like she enjoys messing with me. "Emily, why would you do that? Zoe rented the entire space. With her guest list, we're going to be slammed. Her party alone could get us in trouble with the fire marshal."

"Chill, Heath. I cleared it with Zoe first. When we got the final guest count from her, she said she didn't need the second room. My friend from college, Alicia Sanders, has a new book releasing tomorrow. I offered our bar for her launch party when her original place fell through."

"You offered her the bar even though we were booked?"

I run my fingers through my hair and stifle the growl building in my chest. "Why would you do that?"

"Give me some credit, Heath. I only offered it *after* Zoe said she didn't need the room. Besides, that room is the perfect size for Alicia's event. She has a lot of friends who love to drink. It'll be good for business."

"Really? A book launch party? It sounds cheesy." I scoff, maybe a little too harshly, as I think of Alexis and her book boyfriends.

"Shows what you know. There's nothing cheesy about one of Alicia's parties. I know my events, and this one will make us money."

"Do we have the staff to handle both events?" I look to Dexter for an answer.

He tosses me a single nod.

I look at Luke. He shrugs his shoulders with a faint grin.

"You all knew about this, didn't you?" I ask, my anger spiking.

"If we told you in advance, you would've tried to stop it." Emily snaps. "Alicia is my best friend, and I want to do this for her. It's a big deal. She was overjoyed when I told her we could handle it."

"Fine," I say through my teeth. "But next time, have a

little faith in me. I would've been okay with it."

"Yeah, right." Emily challenges. "You're never okay with anything that you can't control."

"That's not true." I glance around the room. The look on each of my siblings' faces tells me they know I'm lying. "Okay, fine. I would've argued against it at first, but I would've come around once you made a reasonable case. I'd rather know about these things in advance than be surprised like this at the last minute. You know I hate surprises."

"Oh, we know." Dexter chuckles.

"Anyway." I glare at my brother. "Anything else we need to discuss for this week?"

Everyone shakes their heads. "Good. I guess that's it. Let me know if you need any help from me to prepare for Friday."

I start to stand when Emily's hand rests on my arm. "Actually, there *is* something else we wanted to talk to you about."

I sit back in my chair and glance around the room. Neither of my brothers can look me in the eye. "What's wrong? Is someone sick?"

"Oh, God no. Nothing like that," Emily says quickly. "We wanted to talk to you about an idea we have to help keep Mom off your back this summer."

I let out a low groan and drop my head to my chest. "Can we *not* talk about Mom and her crazy plans for my future?" This is what I hate most about being the first born.

"You know she's lined up like seven dates for you over our two-week vacation, right?" Dexter leans forward and squeezes my shoulder. "You should listen to Emily. Her plan just might work."

I lift my head and shift my eyes toward the window. There is no way I can handle Mom's dates. "Or I could just not go. Stay home this summer."

"Mom will kill you if you try that." Luke laughs. "Remember the summer I took off for Cancún and missed the family vacation?"

"Yeah," I answer.

"That was almost ten years ago. She still hasn't forgiven me. Every few months she calls me to remind me of my mistake via an hour-long lecture. There is no way her oldest baby boy can get away with missing the traditional family vacation."

Luke's right, but there's no way I'll survive two weeks in the Hamptons with Mom setting me up with every available woman within a reasonable age to me. Knowing Mom, seven dates is just the start.

"We all know how hard this is for you," Dexter says.

He has always been my biggest supporter and confidant. "But unless you want to entertain Mom's dates, you need to listen to Emily."

"Fine," I growl. "Let me hear it."

Emily beams and turns to face me. "You and my friend, Alicia, share a similar problem."

I furrow my brows. "The one with the book launch party?"

"Yes, her."

I stifle a groan.

Emily takes a deep breath. This means she's about to get on a roll, and it will be next to impossible to stop her. "As I was saying. You two share a common problem. *Meddling moms*. Her mom is always trying to push her to go on dates the same as our mom does with you. If Alicia doesn't produce a boyfriend soon, she'll be doomed to way too many unwanted dates with all the Phils of the world. And if you—"

"Who's Phil?" I ask, thoroughly confused.

"Ugh, don't interrupt me. Phil doesn't matter, not really. He's just some random guy her mom wants her to go to dinner with. Next week, it'll be a Steve or a John or a Tim. The point is, there's an endless supply of men available for Alicia's mom to set her up with. Same as there is an endless supply of women for our mom to set you up with. Dexter's not joking when he says Mom has set up a lot of dates for you." She pauses her tirade to clear her throat and give me a nervous look. "Including one with Tiffany."

"I am *not* going out with Tiffany." I quickly add. "I cannot stand her. Mom knows that."

"Unfortunately for you, Mom is past the point of caring. She's desperate to see you happy and will set you up with any woman to prove her point. Even Tiffany."

I groan and look to the ceiling like all the answers I seek are plastered there to guide me through this disaster. Tiffany is obnoxious and only cares about marrying into money. *Not interested.* "Why does Mom assume I'm not happy?"

Dexter gives me a pointed stare. "Dude, you're miserable. We all know it."

"*Anyway.*" Emily drags out the word to bring the attention back to her. "As I was saying, you can either go out on all those *lovely* dates Mom has scheduled for you, or you can bring a girlfriend on vacation instead."

"Um, I think you're forgetting a key component in that equation." I give her a hard stare. "I don't have a girlfriend."

Emily has lost her mind, and from the looks on my brothers' faces, they have too.

"I know that dumbass." She gives me the look only a younger sister can perfect—one of utter annoyance and frustration. "Stop interrupting me so I can properly explain the plan. Back to my friend, Alicia. She needs a boyfriend. You need a girlfriend. So, we propose that you two pretend to date to get the moms off your backs."

My jaw falls open. There's no way I heard her correctly. "You want me to take a woman I don't know on our two-week family vacation and pawn her off to Mom and Dad as if she's my girlfriend?"

"Yes, but you know Alicia. You've met her before."

"No, I don't." My sister has truly lost her mind.

"I mean, you don't *know her* as well as Dex and Luke, but you've definitely met her before."

"When?"

"She comes into the bar all the time," Luke says. "You had to have met her at some point."

"But I don't hang out in the bar. I'm always in the office unless you need my help with an event."

Emily grabs my hand. "She was at our grand opening, and I know for a fact that I introduced you two."

I close my eyes and think back to that night. It had been a packed opening. More people showed up than we anticipated. I met a lot of new people that night, and I did remember Emily introducing me to a few of her friends. "I remember a few introductions. Maybe I remember her, but I don't think I've seen her since then."

"It doesn't matter. Meet her for lunch or coffee one day this week. Make sure you don't hate her, and she doesn't hate you."

"Why would she hate me?" I ask like that's the most appalling thing my sister could ever assume about me.

She shakes her head and rolls her eyes. "Let's face it, Heath, you're not everyone's cup of tea. If you both agree, then fake date for a few weeks. Problem solved."

Emily takes a deep breath and smiles. I can't help but laugh at her confidence in her plan. It has so many flaws that it'll never work.

"Surely, Mom and Dad know Alicia. How do you propose we handle that?"

"They've met her a few times, but Alicia's never really spent much time around them. But that doesn't matter. We can tell Mom I set you two up, and you hit it off. No biggie."

"'No biggie,' she says." I shake my head. "Emily, you can't possibly be serious. You've had some crazy ideas over the years, but this has to be the craziest."

She pouts. "Why is it crazy?"

"You're encouraging me to lie to Mom and Dad. They'll be furious when they find out, because they *will* figure it out. Crazy schemes like this never work."

"It'll work, trust me." Emily sighs. "Just meet with her. Talk to her and see if you two get along. Dex and Luke love her. She's their favorite friend of mine."

I look at Dexter and Luke. They both nod in agreement.

"She's cool, bro," Dexter says. "And funny. And beautiful. You really can't go wrong."

"And since Alicia is one of my best friends, you don't have to worry about keeping her entertained the entire time. She can hang out with me as much as you want her to." Emily grins from ear to ear.

"Are you more excited about having your friend on vacation with you or helping your brother out?" I ask.

"Both." She wiggles in her chair, clearly too excited about this prospect. "It's really a win-win. And another win because you'd be helping Alicia out, too."

"How exactly would I have to help her?" I ask.

"She might need you to go out to dinner once with her mom just to prove that you do indeed exist. That's all."

"That's all, huh?"

"Yep. When can you meet her for coffee or lunch?"

I shake my head, knowing full well I'll regret this. "How about Wednesday, late morning, at Coffee Stop? Ten o'clock?"

"Perfect. I'll text her now." Emily is giddy that I agreed

to this nonsense.

This is a monumentally stupid idea, but at least if I get busted, my siblings get busted with me. We'll all get into trouble together. Just like when we were kids.

CHAPTER
FOUR

Alicia

With my coffee in hand, I grab a small table near the side entrance of Coffee Stop. I may have agreed to entertain Emily's crazy plan to get my mom off my back, but I need a quick out in case her older brother and I don't get along.

I'm sure Emily is right, and I've met Heath before, but for the life of me, I can't remember him. I can't recall Emily ever telling me much about him either. I love Emily to death, and her brothers, Luke and Dexter, are cool as hell. They're like the big brothers I never had and didn't know I wanted.

Luke and Dexter are typically at the bar on the nights I come in. Dexter is broody and way too overprotective. He's always watching out for me the same as he does for Emily. Anytime he thinks some guy might be getting a little too drunk and handsy with me, Dexter shows up to intervene. He does it in a way that diffuses the situation without anyone knowing what he's doing. He has a knack for sensing exactly what people need. I guess that's why he manages the staff.

Luke's the fun one, always getting everyone drunk. Every time I meet Emily and Trent at The Rock Room, he feeds us new shots and drink recipes he's been working on. Most of them are pretty damn good, and if it weren't for Dexter stepping in, Luke would have us drunk off our asses every time we're there.

But Heath is never there. I'm not even sure what role he serves at the bar. Maybe I should've asked Emily a few more questions about him before I agreed to meet him.

All I got from her was Heath is an older version of Dexter in both looks and personality. Dexter is certainly handsome with his dark hair, green eyes, and physically fit body. If Heath looks like that, I can handle pretending with him for a while.

But it's not Heath's looks I'm worried about. It's his personality that has me concerned. Dexter is nice enough and knows how to have fun when the occasion arises, but he has a cold sternness to him that's sometimes off-putting. He's broody as fuck.

The few times I recall Emily complaining about Heath, she called him stubborn and inflexible. Not exactly the qualities I look for in a man. If I'm going to date someone, I'm more into the fun-loving, goofy, never takes anything too seriously kind of guys. Like Luke. He's way more my type than someone like Dexter.

Maybe if this doesn't work out with Heath, Luke will pretend to be my boyfriend. Hell, he might even get a kick out of getting a rise out of my mom almost as much as me. I can see it now, both of us telling crude jokes and showing way too much PDA. It would drive Mom crazy.

I smile and shake my head. Driving Mom crazy is not the end goal. I need to get her off my case about dating. Period. As much fun as it would be, a man like Luke would not accomplish that goal. Mom wouldn't see Luke as *marriage potential*, and most likely, she'd be right. Luke is as serious about dating and settling down as I am.

No, I need a man who can make Mom envision me walking down the aisle and into his arms. I can see that quality in Dexter, even if he does brood a little too much. If he and Heath are a lot alike, then he just might do the trick.

Assuming I can stand to be around him.

Checking the time on my phone, I still have twenty

minutes before Heath is supposed to meet me. Just enough time to finish working out a few specifics for my next book idea.

My fun and entertaining run-in with the hot jogger on Saturday inspired me to write an opposites attract love story. Mr. Stick-Up-His-Ass, as I've come to call him, is by far one of the best-looking men I've ever met. But God, was he uptight. He didn't say much, but his expression and shock at every word that came out of my mouth spoke volumes about what he was thinking. He was judgmental, pensive, and way too strait-laced for my taste. Give a man like that a few redeeming qualities, and he'd make for a great book boyfriend in an opposites attract romance.

Combine those qualities with a leading lady cast alongside him that will make him uncomfortable, create tons of awkward situations, and I have an instant bestseller.

I open the voice recorder on my phone to make a list of characteristics for my two love birds.

"Him—pensive, judgmental, and uptight. Her—carefree, easy-going, laid-back, and highly improper. Awkward situations to include things like—"

"Well, at least this time your language is clean."

A rough, deep voice draws my eyes up. My mouth gapes open as my eyes meet the deep green gaze of none other than *my* Mr. Stick-Up-His-Ass.

I lick my lips and curl them up into a seductive grin. His eyes widen and his frown deepens. Such a Mr. Stick-Up-His-Ass response. I love real-life book research, and this man is the perfect case study.

Without caring if he notices, I let my eyes roam down his large, muscular form. Damn, I thought he was hot when he was all sweaty and in nothing but a pair of running shorts. He looks even yummier cleaned up and fully dressed. His dark hair is cut short with a close shave around his neck and ears. It's parted on the side and perfectly combed over without a hair out of place. His hard jawline is barely visible beneath his dark trimmed beard that is starting to show a tad bit of gray around his soft pink lips.

Might I add, his very kissable pink lips.

He's wearing a crisp, light purple button up shirt with the sleeves rolled up to his elbows. I'm impressed to see such a manly man wearing purple. Not only does it scream confidence, but it also brings out the bright green flecks in his eyes. His arms are crossed over his chest and the position accentuates his defined biceps. *Fuck, he looks strong.* I bet he could nail me against the wall with very little effort. The thought sends a shiver through my body.

He's wearing black dress pants that hang low on his

waist and hug his hips before falling loose along the length of his legs. While not as obvious, I can see the outline of his very generous dick that I got a glimpse of on Saturday through his running shorts.

His attire gives away nothing and yet teases the eye enough to trigger a girl's imagination.

This man is too hot for his own good. *Would it be wrong to ask him to turn around so I can check out his ass?*

"Do you always talk to your phone?" he asks, pulling my eyes back up to his. Only now he's smiling, and his brows are raised. He caught me staring at his dick, and he looks intrigued. I'm already smiling but it spreads wider across my face. Maybe he's not as uptight as I first thought.

"So, you can talk and formulate complete sentences." I tease.

"Yes." I can't be sure, but I think he's fighting back a laugh. "Now, answer my question."

"I do, actually. Do you have a problem with that?" I lean forward with my elbows on the table and rest my chin on the back of my hands. I suck my bottom lip between my teeth and wink. His eyes dart to mouth and his jaw twitches. I can't wait to see how I can push his buttons today.

"Not at all." He drops his arms and pulls out the chair across from me. "May I sit for a moment?"

I try to swallow the laugh that threatens to erupt and end up snorting instead. This guy is too much. One second, he looks pleased that I'm checking him out and the next he looks mortified that I respond with a flirtatious look. If I wasn't experiencing him firsthand, I'd swear men like this didn't exist. But here he is in all his handsome and uptight glory. He most certainly makes for perfect book research.

His politeness and manners are commendable, but it's so not what I'm used to from men. Add in his awkward curiosity about the way I talk to my phone and there's no way I can let this go. "Of course, I'd love to see how I can shock you today."

He sits in the chair with his back straight and crosses one leg over the other before he rests the edge of his forearm on the table. He looks like he's sitting down for a business meeting, not a casual run-in with a crazy girl that gets a kick out of talking dirty to strangers. "You think you shocked me on Saturday?"

"Oh, I know I did." I lean in even closer and hold my gaze on his. He squirms in his seat, and I smile knowing he's uncomfortable with my forceful eye contact.

He brings his fist to his mouth and clears his throat. "So, you never told me what you do that requires you to talk dirty to your phone."

I shrug my shoulders. "You never asked me."

"I did, but you never answered."

"No, you asked if you interrupted my phone sex." I sit back in my chair and take a sip of my coffee. "And the answer is no, I was not engaging in that respectable activity."

He snorts, and my smile grows. "Now I know you're messing with me. I suspected as much on Saturday, but your confidence threw me off."

"Are you sure about that?" I ask in a teasing tone.

"No, but I'm holding out hope." He grins—a full face grin that brightens up his deep green eyes. It hits me right between the legs. I clench my thighs together to keep from squirming in my seat. "I'd much rather believe a beautiful woman such as yourself purposefully tried to shock me for a laugh rather than know you were engaging in phone sex in public."

Well, I'll be damned. Maybe he does have a sense of humor. That makes this all the more interesting. We watch each other for a moment, neither of us breaking eye contact. He's still grinning, and I can't tell if it's because he's genuinely interested in me or preparing for whatever outlandish thing I might say next.

"Go ahead. Ask me what it is you really want to ask." I do my best to sound calm and hide the fact that he's turned me on.

"And what is it I want to ask you?" This time he's the one to lean on the table and look at me with a flirtatious grin. There's a sparkle in his eye, and there's something about the way he grins that makes me think he doesn't smile like that for just anyone. My panties get a little wet. *Fuck me.* When was the last time a man made me wet just by looking at me like that? Too long ago.

Matching his move, I lean forward until we're only a few inches apart. My face is so close to his I can feel his breath brush across my nose. It feels intimate and suggestive for two strangers who know very little about each other. It also makes my question all the more uncomfortable. "You want to ask me out on a date."

He chuckles, but doesn't retreat. *Interesting.* "Really? And what gave you that impression? For all you know, I have a girlfriend."

Our eyes are locked in the sexiest stare down in the history of the human race. My heart is pounding, and I have to concentrate on my breathing to keep my lungs under control. I dare to lean in even more. The slightest bump, and our lips would touch. I'm pushing my research further than I ever have before. I really should stop, but I can't.

I speak my next words at a whisper. "If you had a

girlfriend, you wouldn't be here talking to me."

His eyes shift to my mouth, and his green eyes turn three shades darker. For a moment, I think he's going to kiss me and wouldn't that be a surprising turn of events. But instead he says, "I could be a total loser who cheats. You don't know me."

He's right, I don't know him. I don't even know his name. He's just some random guy who presented me with an opportunity to fuck with him for book research. Not once, but twice.

Jesus, do I wish he'd kiss me right now, though.

We both hold our ground, and no matter how hard I will him to eliminate the last bit of space between us and let me taste his gorgeous lips, he doesn't move.

I sigh and lean back in my chair. "We already established you're not a creep. You're not a cheater either. You're one of those guys who's loyal to a fault. And you probably have some stupid six date rule, too."

He swallows, and his Adam's apple pushes out like the air got caught halfway down his throat. He raises his brows and his forehead wrinkles. "Six date rule?"

I lick my bottom lip before biting it, and he flinches. An action I've learned gets him every time. The sexual tension between us builds, and I'm more turned on by Mr. Stick-Up-

His-Ass than I've been by a man in a long time.

Maybe ever.

This exchange is getting a little too real, and I'm starting to lose focus on my research. I want to shock him, not date him. I need to regain control and focus, so I choose my next words carefully. "You know, you have to take a lady out for six dates to wine and dine her before you'll take her home and sixty-nine her."

"God, Alexis." He lets out a low grumble and slouches in his chair. My words cut through the tension like a knife just like I hoped they would. "Why did you have to say it like that?"

"Aw. You remember my name." I fucking love that he remembers my name, but it's doing nothing to help calm my libido. I pick up my coffee and hold it over my face. If the warmth spreading across my cheeks means what I think it means, I'm blushing.

"Of course, I do. You made quite the impression." He speaks with such conviction. He almost sounds insulted that I suggested he wouldn't remember the name I gave him.

I toss him a teasing grin. "Well, I do aim to make lasting first impressions."

He narrows his gaze and straightens in his chair. He's watching me closely as if it's him that is now choosing his next words wisely. "Is this your way of trying to secure a date?"

"No." I drop my smile, genuinely surprised by the direction he took this conversation. Most men focus on the sexy talk and never even mention dating. "Why would you think that?"

He shrugs, and whatever uneasiness he may have felt moments ago is gone. He looks completely in control of his emotions, and now I feel uneasy. "Why else would you bring up some silly dating rule? Sounds like a roundabout way to hint at a date to me."

Fuck. That's not what I'm angling for at all. I need to turn this around, and fast. I only said that to mess with him. There's no way I can leave here with him thinking I want a date. That will never do. "Maybe I was just trying to get a rise out of you."

His expression doesn't change. He just stares at me like he doesn't know what to do with me but also doesn't believe a word I've said. It's unnerving, and I don't like it. "Maybe." He shrugs. "Or maybe you use humor and shock value to hide what you really want. In this case, that would be a date." He tosses a playful grin my way. "With me."

Well, shit. This didn't go as planned. It's past time for me to excuse myself from this conversation. Book research gone awry is not good for my creative process.

"Hmm, maybe one day you'll find out." I swallow the last of my coffee, slip my purse strap over my shoulder, and stand to leave. I pause and stare at him like I'm studying his face. "It was ... *delightful* running into you again."

I turn to leave when his hand wraps around mine. A bolt of energy rushes up my arm, swirls around my insides, before it settles between my legs and explodes. I'm forced to straighten my back to keep from falling over from the intensity of his touch. His expression doesn't change. If he notices the effect his touch has on me, he doesn't react.

"Why are you leaving?" he asks.

Good question. Why am I leaving? I'm leaving because my book research has backfired, and I'm very quickly losing control. I can't let that happen. No matter how attracted I am to him, I'm in no position to go out on a date. But I can't tell him any of that. So, I say, "It's past time I go."

Something that looks a lot like disappointment crosses his face. "I'd like to see you again." As soon as the words leave his mouth, he flinches. His hand tenses around mine further causing havoc on my insides.

His declaration surprises me and leaves me with an unsettling flutter in my gut. What surprises me even more is that I *really* want to see him again too. That never happens.

He's looking at me with a hopeful gaze and waiting for me to answer. But I'm at a loss for words. That's something else that never happens. I can't tell him the truth, and I can't seem to get my legs to walk away. It's a conundrum I've never been in before. So, I leave it up to fate.

"If we're meant to see each other again, fate will bring us together." I say this in the sexiest voice I can muster and hope he doesn't see the hidden truth behind my words.

He squeezes my hand before he lets it go and nods with a sideways grin that reveals a dimple in his cheek. It's cute as hell, and in this moment, I really do hope fate intends on bringing us together again.

I step out the side door and shake my shoulders at the warmth that rushes through me. Both his smile and his scowl intrigue me, but it's his touch that left a mark on me. It ignited a fire in my belly that's still burning strong. I grab my phone and start recording every single thought and feeling I have with regards to the very surprising Mr. Stick-Up-His-Ass.

I'm wearing a smile and there's a lightness in my step as I walk down the sidewalk back to my apartment. Seeing him was unexpected and enjoyable. I wonder if he runs in the park every Saturday. Maybe if I walk on ...

"Oh, my God. What's wrong with me?" I shout as

I'm struck motionless by the ridiculous thoughts swimming around in my brain. I can't think like this. Not about a man like him. My lifestyle and career choices would drive a man like him insane. I'm crude and loud and behave inappropriately in almost every situation. He's uptight and professional and reserved. I live in the moment, go with the flow, and can't stand to adhere to schedules. Hell, it's why I'm always late. He's probably one of those people who intentionally arrives early everywhere he goes to make sure he's not late. My constant tardiness would surely push him over the edge. Which means, if I ever see Mr. Sexy-As-Hell-Stick-Up-His-Ass again, I need to run the other way.

That man is *not* for me.

Besides, I'm supposed to fake date Emily's brother. I can't find a real date and leave Heath hanging.

"Fuck," I shout again, and this time, a few people walking close by give me dirty looks. I forgot about Heath. I was at Coffee Stop to meet Heath, not flirt with the uptight and amusing man from the park. I completely lost all focus around him. Another reason I need to get him out of my mind.

Emily is going to kill me.

I check the time. If I go back now, I'll be ten, maybe fifteen minutes late. That's good for me. Knowing Emily, she warned Heath of my incessant tardiness. I should just go back.

But what if Mr. Sexy-As-Hell-Stick-Up-His-Ass is still there?

No. I can't go back. Walking back in to meet a fake date in front of a man I was dangerously close to kissing less than thirty minutes ago is not my idea of a good time. Talk about *awkward*. I'll just have to make up an excuse for Emily. She'll understand. If she doesn't, well, there's not much I can do about that.

CHAPTER **FIVE**

Heath

My mind should be focused on the woman I came here to meet, but all I can think about is Alexis and the fact that I asked her if I could see her again. What the hell was I thinking? I would've followed her and argued against leaving our next meeting up to fate if I weren't here to meet Emily's best friend. Emily would never forgive me if I bailed to chase after another woman.

Besides, who the hell leaves major life decisions to fate? Fate didn't dictate my life. I did.

I plan out every detail of every day. There's way too much at stake to not plan. The success of the bar would be in jeopardy if I didn't manage it the way I did. I meticulously weigh the pros and cons of every decision I make—from which bands we agree to book, to alterations made to our drink menu, to all financial expenditures, even all staff hires. It's not that I don't trust my siblings to do their jobs. I do. But my siblings sometimes make rash decisions that, if I didn't step in and evaluate more thoroughly, would result in the bar losing money. We wouldn't have stayed in business after our first year if it weren't for my constant analysis.

I can't imagine leaving anything in life to fate. If I left the bar to fate, I'd do a lot more than break myself.

I'd let my siblings down.

Leaving life to chance is foolish and, well, irresponsible.

The fact that Alexis willingly left our next meeting to fate should have been all I needed to hear to know that woman is *not* for me.

Then why can't I get her off my mind? I've thought of her often since our chance meeting in the park on Saturday. *Fuck. Chance meeting? Run, dude. Forget about this woman.* I'm here to meet my sister's friend. *This* meeting was planned, and this location was carefully chosen for my comfort. This is how I do things.

There may be an insane amount of chemistry between Alexis and me, but it would never work out between us. That's obvious by the way she blurts out the first thing that pops in her mind, no matter how inappropriate it is. She screams free spirited. She seems like the kind of girl that goes with the flow and lets life take her wherever it leads without a care in the world. Yeah, I don't operate that way.

Pushing Alexis out of my mind, I order a cup of coffee and slide into the seat Alexis just vacated. Her behavior may be unconventional and deliberately shocking, but she knows how to pick a seat. This spot is perfectly positioned to watch every person who walks through the door. I'll see Alicia before she has a chance to see me. Assuming my memory of her appearance is correct, she has long dark hair, brown eyes, and is no taller than my baby sister. If I don't like what I see, I can duck out the side exit since it's directly to my right.

I check the time on my phone, and it's a few minutes past ten. That's a strike against her. Promptness is important to me. If she's going to pretend to be my girlfriend, she's going to have to do better than this. This is a surefire way to piss me off.

My urge to get up and leave is strong. Instead, I pick up my phone to check the status of my latest investments hoping that will calm my frustration while I wait.

I shouldn't have let Emily talk me into this. Yes, I want to get Mom off my back, but I'm not this desperate. Who pretends to date someone anyway? Certainly not me. I can only imagine what kind of woman Alicia is if she needs to pretend to date someone too.

Why can't she get a real date? What's her excuse?

There has to be something wrong with her if she's willing to let a man she doesn't know pretend to be with her. Plus, she's way too young for me. She's the same age as Emily for Christ's sake. I couldn't possibly have anything in common with someone that's almost ten years younger than me.

Shit. I rub my eyes, already feeling a tension headache coming on. That means Alicia is the same age I was when I lost Lauren.

Nine years, three months, and twelve days ago.

I haven't stopped keeping count of the days since. I know it's weird and maybe even makes me seem a little crazy, but numbers soothe me. It's one of the reasons why I handle the finances for the bar.

Losing Lauren was the darkest time in my life. In the first few months that followed her death, I isolated myself and refused to see anyone. When I finally surfaced, Mom tried to get me to see a therapist, but that wasn't happening. I didn't need to talk about my feelings. I knew how I felt. I didn't need a damn therapist to help me figure that out. I just needed time.

Looking back, if I had appeased Mom, I might have saved myself a lot of trouble now. Maybe then she wouldn't be so worried about me. Maybe I wouldn't be sitting here waiting on a girl—who I don't remember—that is now twenty minutes late.

On a sigh, I toss my empty coffee cup in the trash and head out the same side door Alexis left earlier. I should have followed her. At least then, I would have been entertained.

THIRTY MINUTES LATER, I'M walking through the front door to The Rock Room, my anger increasing by the minute. Nothing pisses me off more than wasting my time. And my sister and her friend, Alicia, just wasted an hour of my busy day. I still have so much to take care of before our double-booked events on Friday night.

I'm still trying to calm myself down from that bit of news. Emily knows how much I hate surprises, and even more so when they affect my work.

The last time she booked two events on the same night, we were understaffed and failed to keep up with the needs of all the guests. I had to discount both parties' bills, and we barely made a profit. Consider the added stress, and I might as well say there was no profit. She swore she'd never do that to me again. Yet here we are.

I come to a halt just inside the main room of the bar. My siblings are gathered around a cluster of drinks—most likely a few new concoctions Luke whipped together.

Emily's the first to see me, and her eyes widen in surprise. "You're back already?"

"Next time you get the bright idea to set me up with one of your friends, don't. Just don't." I walk past her, in need of some alone time to focus on work and recenter myself before I interact with anyone else today. I don't play well with others when my frustration spikes like this. To say I can be an asshole is an understatement.

"Oh, my God. What did she say?" Emily hops up from her barstool and blocks my path.

"She didn't say anything because she didn't show up." It's a damn good thing we're not open yet. I hate losing my cool around patrons.

I start to step around Emily, but she grabs hold of my arm. "What do you mean she didn't show up?"

"Seriously?" Do I really have to explain everything? Saying someone didn't show up is self-explanatory, right? I glare down at Emily, and she pulls her shoulders in. "I waited twenty goddamn minutes. She didn't show. I left."

Emily huffs and gives me one of her *I can't believe*

how impossible you are looks. "That's all? You should have waited longer. Alicia is al—"

"No." I pull my arm away from her and head to my office. Unfortunately for all of us, Emily doesn't let it go.

"I'm sorry, Heath." Emily's on my heels. "Alicia promised me she wouldn't be late. She's always late. It's like her brain is incapable of seeing time. I should have warned you, but I didn't want you to say no. You two would probably get along great if you gave her a chance. She may be a little capricious at times, but—"

I turn and give my sister a hard look that causes her to stop and stumble back. She's talking a mile a minute, and I don't think I can listen to another word. "Capricious. You really think I'd get along with someone you define as *capricious*?"

Emily rolls her eyes and sighs. "Maybe capricious isn't the right word. Alicia is fun. She has the biggest heart. You *will* like her if you give her a chance."

I straighten my back and exhale slowly. I can't do this. I'd rather deal with Mom than even consider giving Alicia another chance. Mom, I can handle. But this, whatever *this* is, is way outside my comfort zone.

"No." I spin around and continue toward my office. This time, Emily doesn't follow. But she does continue telling me what she thinks.

"I'm sure Alicia has a good reason for being late. I'll talk to her. But you better prepare yourself to see her on Friday night since her book launch party is one of our events. And you better be nice to her. She's my best friend."

"No problem. I don't plan on talking to her," I yell back.

"Heath!" My name snaps from her mouth so fast, I can't help but turn around. "I've got one word for you." She rests her hands on her hips and gives me a smug look. "Tiffany."

I suck in a deep breath, and my nostrils flare. She's playing dirty, and it pisses me off even more.

What I really want to do is slam the door in my sister's face. But I don't. That would only make her mad and probably result in her barging into my office to continue telling me what she thinks. Instead, I slowly shut my door and drop against it.

Emily means well. I know that. And so does Mom. Why can't they just let it go? Let me live my life. I'm *not* unhappy. Just the opposite, in fact. I don't need a woman in my life to be happy. I'm healthy. I love running the bar with my siblings. We're successful, and we *mostly* get along and have fun working together.

Maybe one day I'll figure out how to convince them I'm fine. Until then, I'm going to be dodging a lot of dates Mom sends my way.

CHAPTER
SIX

Alicia

The early stages of starting a new writing project are my favorite. Creating new characters, giving them names, teasing out their personalities, and deciding how I'm going to tear them apart before I build them back up is exhilarating.

Thanks to my recent interactions with my newest and most surprising book boyfriend, I've found the perfect character to work with. I can't resist building on the two meetings I've had with Mr. Stick-Up-His-Ass in my current project.

Correction. Mr. Sexy-As-Hell-Stick-Up-His-Ass.

I close my eyes and picture his face. His deep green

eyes look down at me in a hard stare. His hair is a little messy up top like it was the day I met him in the park. I imagine what it would feel like to run my hands through his dark locks and wrap my fingers around it for a gentle tug. He's slick with sweat from his morning jog, and small droplets drip down the base of his neck.

His sharp jaw twitches under my heated gaze, and it takes every ounce of strength I have to not reach out and touch him. What I wouldn't do to feel the scratch of his beard against the soft skin of my neck as he peppers kisses from my ear to my collarbone. The touch of his lips sears my skin and sends a jolt straight to my core.

His large hands are smooth and soft against my bare midriff. My breathing quickens. My heart pounds so loudly in my ears I can't think straight. But when his fingers toy with the elastic on my sports bra, I—

My eyes shoot open, and I stare at the notes on my computer. My body is clammy, my mouth is dry, and my panties are wet.

Shit, shit, shit.

I push away from my desk and rush into the kitchen to get a drink of water. I down a full glass in one long drink and refill it before leaning against the counter.

That never happens. Sure, I picture my heroes in

my mind and imagine what it would be like to touch and kiss them as I'm putting the image into words. But I never *actually* get excited like this.

I'm not just excited. I'm horny as fuck.

I rub my hands over my face and vow to never ever see Mr. Sexy-As-Hell-And-Now- The-Object-Of-My-Fantasies-Stick-Up-His-Ass again. This fantasy is getting a little too real.

A knock on my door startles me, and I let out yelp.

"Jeez, get a grip," I mumble to myself.

With my hand to my chest, I head to the door. It's not even 10:00 am, and everyone who knows me knows not to interrupt me before 3:00 pm when I'm writing.

Before I even get the door open, Emily pushes past yelling at me. "What the hell is wrong with you?"

I shut the door with a sigh. I expected to see Emily before the day ended—I just didn't expect her to show up this early. When I turn around, she's glaring at me with her arms crossed over her chest.

"Hey, Em. What's up?" She's *really* mad. Heath must've been pissed that I stood him up yesterday. I can't say I blame him. It's one of the reasons I don't date. Emily knows this.

"Don't *hey, Em* me. You know why I'm here. How

could you, Alicia? You promised." She drops her arms to her side and pouts. Emily is the only grown woman I know that still pouts like she's five years old. It's ridiculous, sometimes frustrating, but also adorable.

I drop into the corner of my sofa and pull my knees up to my chest. "I didn't mean to miss the meeting. I was—"

"You mean you didn't even bother to show up. I just assumed you were late. I can't believe you." Emily throws her hands over her head and leans against the wall opposite where I'm sitting.

"Em, sit down and let me explain." I pat the sofa next to me, but she doesn't move.

She glares at me. Her eyes narrow and her anger dances like flames in her bright green eyes. I lace my fingers together and hold them to my chest. "Please."

She rolls her eyes and sighs. "Fine."

She pushes off the wall and plops down next to me on the sofa. I take her hand in mine and she tenses. I don't think I've ever seen Emily quite this angry. I hate that it's directed at me. The Rockwell siblings are thick as thieves. No matter how much they annoy each other, they're the first to step up and defend each other too. "I was there. I swear. Twenty minutes early in fact."

"Then how did you miss each other?"

"Well." I take a deep breath and brace myself for her reaction. "I met this guy. And—"

"What the hell, Alicia?" She yanks her hand from mine and sinks further into the side of the couch. "How could you meet another guy after you promised to meet my brother?"

I stare at her and do my best to hide my own frustration. I understand why she's so upset, but she's not giving me a chance to explain before she cuts me off. "Will you stop? I'm trying to tell you what happened, but you have to stop interrupting me."

"Fine."

I take a deep breath and exhale slowly. "Like I said, I arrived early so I wouldn't be late. No wait." I pause while I debate on how much to tell her. "I need to start with Saturday."

"Saturday?" She raises a brow and looks like she's about to yell at me again.

"Yeah, Saturday." She's not going like what I tell her, but it's the only way she'll understand. "Remember how I said I started walking and dictating my writing to my phone?" Emily nods but doesn't interrupt me again. "I was walking in the park on Saturday morning. I might've been dictating a sex scene."

"Alicia!" She clasps her hands to her mouth and gasps.

"You can't do that in public."

I chuckle. "Oh, but I can. And I did." My smile grows. She rolls her eyes in a dramatic motion and huffs. Her shoulders relax and she fights a smile. "Anyway, I was dictating this scene when this hot man covered in sweat and wearing nothing but these tiny running shorts walks past me. He hears me, stops, and questions me. He was uptight and seemed upset that I was talking like that in public. He accused me of being into phone sex. It was a funny interaction. Great book material, you know?"

She tries to stifle a laugh but ends up snorting instead. "Okay, sounds funny. But what does that have to do with standing up Heath?"

"Like I said, I arrived twenty minutes early. I was minding my own business, drinking my coffee, and taking notes on my phone when Mr. Stick-Up-His-Ass sits down at my table."

"Mr. What?"

"Mr. Stick-Up-His-Ass. That's what I call him. It's quite fitting. Well, actually now I call him Mr. Sexy-As-Hell-Stick-Up-His-Ass because let me tell you, this man is fucking hot."

Emily slaps my arm, and her mouth falls open. "You like this guy."

I gape at her like she's just committed a cardinal sin. "God, no. He is so not my type." Sure, we had chemistry, but I do *not* like him. "But holy hell. He just might be the sexiest man I've ever met. Tall, broody, uptight, but knows how to stare down a woman to make her all warm and tingly inside."

Emily narrows her eyes on me and slowly shakes her head. "You're describing him like you like him."

"I'm a writer. Describing people is what I do."

"Whatever." She waves her hand at me like she's brushing me off. "How did this guy make you miss my brother?"

"You know me." I pull my feet underneath me and sit cross legged on the couch. "I like to mess with people, and I didn't hold back with this guy. I mean, he was *perfect* book research material. On Saturday, he'd been so easy to rattle. But yesterday, I couldn't shake him up. Instead, I sensed he was going to ask me out, which he kinda did. So I bolted. By the time I remembered why I had been there in the first place, I was standing outside my building. There was no way I could go back knowing Mr. Sexy-As-Hell-Stick-Up-His-Ass was probably still there."

"Alicia." Emily relaxes and the last of her anger fades. "You do know how crazy that sounds, right?"

"Yeah, but even I couldn't make this shit up."

She *tsks*. "Of course you could. You're a writer, remember?"

I force out a harsh sigh. We could go in circles about this, and I'm not in the mood. "Listen, I'll apologize to Heath. I really didn't mean to stand him up."

"You'll do more than apologize. He'll be at the bar tomorrow night during your book launch party. You will beg for his forgiveness, and do whatever it takes to convince him to still fake date you for our summer vacation. He thinks he can deal with Mom and all the dates she's lined up for him, but he's underestimated how far Mom will go to see him married."

I cringe. "Is it really that bad?"

She drops her chin and looks at me with raised brows. "Two weeks, seven dates. And all with women Mom loves and Heath hates. It will kill him."

I haven't even met Heath, and I feel sorry for him. "I'll try. But I can't make him agree to it."

"No, you can't. But after he meets you, he'll agree to it. I just know it."

Emily's smile grows and she shrugs her shoulders in glee. While I'm glad she's no longer looking at me like she wants to strangle me, I think I prefer the angry look to this overly cheerful version. She looks like she's got something up her sleeve, and I'm the pawn in her next play.

CHAPTER SEVEN

Heath

There's God-awful country music blaring from the speakers and the main bar area is packed with guests for the engagement party. It's an odd crowd—an even mix of rugged cowboys and designer-dressed businessmen and women. I guess this is what happens when a city girl marries a Montana cowboy.

The book launch party doesn't start for another hour, and Alicia hasn't arrived yet. The only people here to prepare for that event are the author's personal assistant and a couple friends.

Luke's behind the bar working alongside three other bartenders to keep up with the crowd. Dexter's walking around greeting the guests and making sure the waitstaff has the food set out and hors d'oeuvre trays are circulating. Emily's overseeing the set up for the book event party. She hasn't popped her head out of the side room since they started about an hour ago.

Everything seems to be under control. My siblings are in their elements and having a great time. Me, I feel like a fish out of water and would rather go home. But I promised to help when we have large events like this.

I turn to leave the bar to check on Emily, but I'm knocked back when I run into someone.

"I'm so sorry." On instinct I grab hold of the person I ran into and freeze. "Alexis?"

The most frustrating and intoxicating woman I've ever met is staring up at me. She looks just as surprised as I am. Despite my pep talks to convince myself to forget about her, she's stuck with me. Excitement builds inside me, and a nervous sensation fills my chest. At least I think it's nerves. Regardless, now that I've found her, I don't want to let her slip past me again.

"That's three times in one week. I guess fate meant for us to meet again after all." Her voice is a little breathless, and she's staring at me with those pale blue eyes of hers.

"Fate." I chuckle. "Yeah, I guess so."

Her eyes dart around like she's looking for someone. "What are you doing here?" she asks.

She's fiddling with a strand of her long blond hair and nibbles on her lower lip. God, I love it when she does that. It's sexy and makes my dick perk up. I can't stop staring. "I work here. How about you?"

"I'm here for the book launch party."

"Oh, do you know the author?"

She brushes her hair behind her ear and scans the room again with a nervous laugh. "You could say that."

"Are you looking for someone?"

Her eyes meet mine, and I can't interpret the wave of emotion that flashes within. "What's with all the sexy cowboys? Kinda odd for New York City."

My attention diverts to my hands, and I realize I'm still holding onto her. I let go and step back a couple feet before answering. "It's an engagement party. A city girl got engaged to a Montana cowboy. They decided to hold the event here."

"Wow." I keep my eyes on Alexis as she scans the bar again. Her eyes widen and her lips turn up into a grin as she takes it all in. She looks like a little girl given free rein in a candy shop. I find myself wishing she looked at me like that. "This is a smutty romance writer's wet dream. It's the perfect event to share with a romance novel book launch."

I snort and shake my head. "Why am I not surprised you like smutty romances?"

She shrugs and brings her eyes back to mine. "So who's the lucky girl?"

My chest tightens. I don't know what it is about this woman, but my body does weird things around her. It's been years since urges like this overwhelmed me. All I want to do is pull her close and discover what her body feels like next to mine. Naked. I want to press my lips to hers, swipe my tongue along her lip, and lose myself to the taste of her. This is unfamiliar territory for me, and I'm starting—

Fuck. She's looking at me with a questioning gaze, and her breath hitches.

I clear my throat and look around the room until I spot Zoe. "The woman right over there." I point at Zoe who has her arms wrapped around her fiancé. "That's Zoe, and the tall Montana cowboy she's wrapped around is her fiancé, Wyatt."

"Well, she could've chosen worse, I guess." Alexis chuckles and shakes her head. "You mean to tell me all these sexy cowboys are from Montana?"

"Yeah. Zoe's giving up her city life for a pair of boots and a cowboy hat. I can't say I see the appeal, but to each their own."

"Are you kidding?" She snaps her eyes back to me, fans herself off, then lets out a long, exaggerated breath. "All I want to do is whip out my phone and interview every one of those sexy men for research. This room is too good to be true."

God, I hope this is an act. I hold my breath as I wait to make sure I didn't say that out loud. When she doesn't react, I slowly start breathing again. I'm not a jealous guy, but dammit, I only want her to react that way about me.

"How about a drink instead?" I point to the bar behind us and find Luke watching us, beaming with curiosity. I glare at my nosy brother and order a drink. "Whiskey on the rocks and whatever Alexis wants."

Luke raises a brow before he glances at Alexis. She leans against the bar and tosses him a wink. "Hey, Luke. I'll have a glass of Cab."

"You know Luke?" The words come fast and a little defensive. I hardly know this woman, but I hate that she knows my playboy brother. Worst case scenarios run through my brain about how well they might know each other. Women always fall for Luke's charm, and it often doesn't take long for them to also fall into his bed.

Luke's laughter drowns out the background noise. "Relax. It's not what you're thinking."

There's a mischievous glint in his eyes that causes my pulse to kick up several notches. I lean against the bar and narrow my eyes. "And how do you know what I'm thinking?"

He reaches across the bar and pats my shoulder. "Because I know you well." With a wink and a smile at Alexis, he grabs a glass. "Let me get those drinks."

Alexis slips onto the barstool next to me. She's quiet and not really looking at anything in particular. A sense of awkwardness builds between us unlike either of our last chance meetings. *Chance.* There's that damn word again.

I look toward Luke, willing him to speed up the drinks. I need something to take this edge off.

Before I'm able to grab my drink, Wyatt leans beside me and squeezes my shoulder. "Thanks for doing this. Zoe couldn't be happier with all the support you've given. She's really gonna miss you guys."

"Anything for Zoe." I nod. "She's a keeper."

"Yes, she is. That little lady owns me, and I love it."

A genuine smile takes over my face. I remember feeling like that with Lauren, and it's an awesome way to feel. Love is a wonderful gift, and anyone who finds it is damn lucky. I had it once, and it felt damn good while it lasted.

Luke returns with our drinks, and Wyatt places his own order. I'm about to say my goodbyes and excuse myself when

Zoe rushes up behind Wyatt and wraps her arms around his waist. He smiles. "Hey, love. Your drink is coming."

"Thanks, but ..." Zoe leans in close to Wyatt's ear and whispers. His eyes darken before he tosses his head back and groans. Zoe takes him by the hand and leads him away from the bar, their drinks forgotten. Suddenly, the bar feels like it's squeezing in on me, and I'm struck by how much I miss that kind of affection.

Alexis gasps. When I turn to her, she looks like she's admiring a sweet puppy. She lifts her glass to the happy couple before they disappear down the hallway and says, "That right there is what sells smutty romance books."

"What do you mean?" I'm not sure why I asked that question because I saw it too. Hell, I used to have it.

Alexis sighs. "Did you see the way he looked at her? And then how he responded to whatever she whispered in his ear? That's the look every woman dreams of seeing from the man she loves."

"You don't say." I take a sip of my whiskey to hide the smile trying to show itself. It pleases me to hear her talk about love in such a sweet and romantic way. I thoroughly enjoy her dirty talk, but this is so much more endearing.

"You want to know how to love a woman? Read a romance novel."

I burst out laughing. "Yeah, that will never happen."

"Then I hope you have more friends like that to teach you because you could handle learning a thing or two about what a woman wants."

"What makes you think I don't already know what women want?" I hear a snort next to me and find Luke watching us with an amused look on his face. "What are you laughing at?"

"Oh, my God. There you are. You're late for your own—" Emily stops, her eyes darting between Alexis and me. A wide smile slowly forms on her face before her eyes settle on Alexis. "Thank God you two are talking. Please tell me you're getting along."

Luke's laughter draws our attention to him. "Oh, there's something going on here, but I can't say what exactly." Luke leans forward on his elbows like he's settling in for a good show. Emily rests her hands on her hips, shifting her eyes between us.

"What?" Alexis and I say at the same time.

Alexis looks at me with a furrowed brow like she's studying me. After a few seconds, her eyes widen and her jaw drops. "You mean to tell me Mr. Stick-Up-His-Ass is Heath? Your brother?"

"You tell me. Is this the guy from the park?" Emily

points at me but keeps her eyes trained on Alexis. She waggles her brows and does a little shimmy. "I thought you bumped him up to Mr. Sexy-As-Hell-Stick-Up-His-Ass?"

The color drains from Alexis's face, and my sister looks happier than I've seen her in months. I glance over at Luke. He's laughing so hard tears start rolling down his cheeks. I feel like I'm the butt of some horrible joke, and I'm too slow to figure out the punchline. I glance back at Alexis, and she looks like she's ready to bolt.

"Who are you?" I ask.

She leans toward me and rests her hand on my forearm. A rush of heat runs through me. Even in my confused state, her touch makes me hot. "I swear, I didn't know who you were. If I did, I never would've talked to you that way. I'm so sorry."

I hold my eyes on her. She looks sincere. Hell, she looks mortified. Gone is the controlled, confident woman I met in the park. The woman before me looks timid and scared. I tilt my head toward the ceiling and concentrate on the meaning behind her words and how they relate to my siblings' actions. As the truth starts to unravel, I slowly return my gaze toward Alexis. "Let me guess. Your name isn't Alexis?"

"Alexis Stone is my pen name. My real name is Alicia Sanders. I've been best friends with Emily since college."

She cuts her eyes in Emily's direction. "Why didn't you tell me he had a beard? Had I known, I would've seen the resemblance to Dex."

Emily shrugs, and I stumble back a few steps. This is way more than I bargained for. I run my fingers through my hair before I pick up my glass of whiskey. I down it in one gulp and hand it back to Luke for a refill.

I can't do this. I've fantasized about having Alexis—or should I say Alicia—in my bed. I can't fake a relationship with someone that I've already imagined naked, pinned beneath my body with my cock buried deep inside her.

She's my baby sister's best friend. Thinking about her naked feels wrong on so many levels. I have to end this before it goes any further. But the horrors of this moment only get worse when I spot Mom walking toward us with a determined and purposeful look on her face.

"Fuck. What's Mom doing here?" Moments like this, where I've lost control and can't see my way out, are what my nightmares are made of. I want to run and hide, but I have no choice but to stay put and deal with whatever outcome transpires.

I straighten my back and catch Emily mouthing something and pointing at Alicia but can't make out what she's saying.

"Heath, sweetie. I'm so glad I caught you." Mom pulls me into a hug and kisses my cheek.

"Mom, what are you doing here?" She never visits the bar. The fact that she's here on a Friday night when she knows we always host events is more than a little shocking. She's the last person I want to talk to right now, but I can't escape. I'm surrounded by women with my back against the bar.

"I need to speak to you about our vacation, and you never returned my call."

"I didn't realize it was that big of a deal considering I'll see you Sunday for family dinner."

Mom places her hands on her hips and scowls. "If you listened to my messages, you'd know I have to finalize these dates. We leave in a week."

My hands tense and I curl them into fists. I grit my teeth in an attempt to not yell at Mom. I know she means well, but I can't go out with any of these women. "There will be no dates."

"Yes, there will. I've lined up several nice women for you to go out with. I just need to confirm a few details with you."

"No," I say with as much authority as I think I can get away with. "I'm not going out on a single date while we're gone."

"Well, why on earth not?

My eyes are locked on Mom's, and I'm momentarily at a loss for words. For the longest time, my go to excuse has been that I'm dating someone else. Clearly, she's not accepting that answer anymore unless I produce an actual girlfriend. I thought fake dating Alicia wouldn't work out, but there's no time to find someone else. Would Alicia still agree to it? I swallow hard. I guess there's only one way to find out.

"Because that would be cheating."

"Oh, Heath. You really should've seen that therapist like I asked. Lauren has been—"

"Mom!" I cannot let her finish that statement. Honestly, how could she think I was still that messed up? It's been ten years since I lost Lauren. I certainly didn't think of dating as cheating on her memory. "I told you, I have a girlfriend."

Mom rolls her eyes and huffs. "Not with this again. I've heard this lie from you too many times. Either produce a body or you're going on these dates. Tiffany is anxious to see you again."

I'm about to tell Mom exactly what I think about Tiffany and every other woman on her date list when a pair of warm hands slide around my waist. My arms shoot out to my sides, and my body stiffens at the unexpected touch. Alicia is tucked into my side. I hesitate, not sure how to react to this sudden show of affection, but then I let my arm wrap around her and accept her embrace.

The confident woman I met in the park is back, and I like it.

She looks up at me with a smile before she turns to my mom with a hand held out. "Hi, I'm the body you want this guy to produce. Remember me?"

Mom doesn't take her eyes off me as she shakes Alicia's hand. I can't tell what the look means. Is she mad? Does she see right through the lie?

With Alicia by my side and the lie initiated, I go with it. "Mom, this is my girlfriend, Alicia. I believe you've met before."

A slow smile spreads across Mom's face as she shifts her gaze to Alicia. "Yes, I know Alicia. Not well, unfortunately. I must say, this is quite a surprise. I wonder why it is I'm only now hearing about this."

Alicia laughs and rests her hand on my chest. Heat permeates from her touch and seeps through my shirt to the skin below. My chest burns and my lungs feel heavy.

She looks into my eyes, and every breath I take feels forced and difficult. And when she speaks, her sweet voice pulls me in. "I don't need to tell you how reserved Heath can sometimes be. He's insisted on keeping me to himself until we knew where this was going."

Her hand slides up my chest until her fingers find the edge of my shirt, then she traces the ridge of my collarbone. It's an interesting and surprising move on her part. It feels so natural and normal, I can't tell if she even realizes her hand moved.

My brain stops functioning and my own hand moves. I cup my hand around her neck and brush my thumb along her jaw. She gasps at my touch and leans in closer. It's like we're connected by a string that keeps getting shorter and shorter, pulling us closer.

Before I can fight against this pull, our lips join.

CHAPTER
EIGHT

Alicia

One minute I'm jumping out of my chair to help Heath. Next, I'm wrapping my arms around him. The look on his face when his mom started talking about dates was one of pure horror. I couldn't in good conscience sit back and watch this poor guy suffer through that. My mom is the same way, and I know how out of control it feels when she's pushing me to go out with men I've never met or don't like.

So, I came to his rescue.

But I didn't plan on him leaning toward me, drawing me in until our lips connected. I inhale at the softness of his lips between the gentle tickle of his beard. It sends a shiver down my body. His hand is firm against my neck, and I can't pull away. Even if I could, I'm not convinced I would. His hold around my neck tightens and makes me want more of him. His kiss turns hard and demanding, and his beard scratches my face. It's a stark contrast to his soft lips, and I love it. There's something sensual and arousing about it, and I want to know how his beard feels on other parts of my body. This kiss is intense—it's fire—and it gives me a hint of how strong and incredible he would be in bed.

As quickly as his lips found mine, they're gone. I open my eyes, and he's staring at me. His own gaze filled with lust, want, even need. It isn't until I hear someone clear their throat that I remember where we are and that we're not alone.

I tear my eyes from his, embarrassment washing over me. Not only is his mother and sister staring at us like we've lost our minds, but I hear Luke behind us cackling. Every eye within ten feet, maybe more, is on us.

But that's still not the worst part.

Standing just behind Emily with her mouth agape is my own mother, and she's not alone. A tall, slightly awkward looking man I don't recognize is with her, and he looks sad and disappointed.

I press my hand against Heath to put some distance

between us, but he pulls me closer. It's confusing and exciting, and dammit, it makes me want to wrap my arms around him and kiss him again.

Heath speaks, and his voice drags me out of the daze he put me in. "Like I said, Mom, this is my girlfriend."

"Girlfriend!" My mom's high-pitch voice squeals, and my eyes snap to her. "Since when?"

I open my mouth to speak, but nothing comes out. This is all happening so fast. I didn't come here tonight with the expectation of explaining a boyfriend to Mom. Because I didn't have one.

I'm too busy trying to process the fact that Heath is Mr. Sexy-As-Hell-Stick-Up-His-Ass to deal with Mom. *Oh, my God.* I've been having inappropriate thoughts about Emily's older brother. I've daydreamed about lots of sexy times with him behind closed doors. And that kiss. I want more of that kiss. But I can't have that. *That* is not the plan.

"Well?" Mom puts her hands on her hips and huffs. "Are you going to answer me, young lady, or stand there playing dumb?"

"Sorry, Mom. What?" If she asked me a question, it didn't register. My brain is mush.

"This man says you're his girlfriend. When did that happen?"

"Oh." I look up at Heath hoping he has the answer, but he gives a slight shrug and remains silent. "It's ... It's new."

"Well, I'd say so. When I spoke to you on Monday, you said you had no interest in dating, and not five days later, I find you kissing this man. Explain yourself."

Heath tenses next to me as I struggle to come up with an answer that will satisfy Mom. "Well, it kinda just happened. Heath is Emily's older brother. We were recently reacquainted with each other. When I spoke with you, we hadn't decided to date yet."

"Well, I have never been so ... so ..." Mom gives a loud grunt and stomps her foot. "You should have told me. Now what am I supposed to say to Phil?"

"If that was Phil you walked over with, I'd say Phil figured it out all on his own." I point behind Mom where Phil is exiting the building. "I also think it's time you *stop* setting me up on dates."

Mom's eyes widen, and her jaw drops. I may argue with Mom in private, but I have always given her nothing but respect in public. I'm definitely going to hear about this later.

"Okay then." Emily claps her hands, attempting to ease the tension building around us. "As much fun as this is, Alicia, you're officially late for your own party. Why don't you finish up with Heath, then head over." She turns to Mom and smiles. "Mrs. Sanders, I could really use your help with the book display. Do you mind helping me while Alicia wraps this up?"

Mom looks from me to Heath and back to me again before she nods. Emily loops her arm through Mom's and waves goodbye. As soon as they're gone, I look at Heath's mom. She's watching me with a careful gaze. When our eyes meet, she narrows her stare. *She doesn't believe us.* Maybe if my mom hadn't shown up or if we'd met earlier this week like we planned, we could've pulled this off. Any second now, Heath's mom is going to call us out on our little charade, and this will be over.

But that doesn't happen because Heath speaks first. "Mom, Alicia will be joining us next week in the Hamptons. I hope you don't mind."

His mom flinches, but only slightly. If I hadn't been watching her so closely, I would have missed it. Her lips turn up into a faint grin before she shifts her regard toward Heath. "Why would I mind? I'm delighted to have Alicia join us. We have more than enough room, and it's past time I got to know her better."

Heath smiles, and his hand squeezes my waist. "See, I told you Mom wouldn't mind."

"Yes, you did." I paste on a smile and pat his chest. "Mrs. Rockwell, would you please excuse us for a moment? I need a minute alone with Heath before I go."

"Of course. I need to get going anyway. Heath, I'll see you on Sunday. It was a pleasure seeing you again, Alicia. I look forward to the Hamptons." With a slight nod and a tight smile, Mrs. Rockwell leaves.

Once she's out of sight, I pry Heath's hand off my waist and push him away. His touch is making me think about all sorts of inappropriate things I'd like him to do to me, and I can't have that.

He leads me to a door off to the side of the bar and waves me in. As soon as I hear the click of the door closing, I ask, "What the hell was that?"

"Umm." He slips his hands into his pockets and falls against the door. The look on his face is a mix of uncertainty, guilt, and something I can't quite pinpoint. "That was us lying to our mothers."

"Oh, I got that part." I walk up to him and poke him in the chest. I immediately regret touching him. My face heats, and I try to convince myself I'm angry, but I know that's not it. "Why did you kiss me?"

He leans into my touch and lowers his head until his eyes are level with mine. His green eyes darken to the shade of a forest before they shift to my mouth. "I'm pretty sure you kissed me."

I swallow hard, the burning desire to feel his lips against mine strengthens. "No. You clearly kissed me."

His mouth turns up in a crooked grin. "You're the one who slid in beside me, put your hand on my chest, then tickled my neck with your fingers." His voice is deep, husky, and it sends a wave of lust crashing through my body. "I also wasn't the one who pushed up on her tiptoes and planted her lips on mine. That was all you."

I step into him without thinking. My mind is a swirling mess of desire and frustration. "You were the one that held me close with a grip so tight, I couldn't break away even if I wanted to." Our lips are almost close enough to touch. All I'd have to do is lean in the last inch, and his mouth would be mine. "Then *you* leaned down and kissed me. Are you going to blame *me* for that too? I had nowhere to go."

He opens his mouth to speak, then stops. His eyes search my face, shifting between my eyes and mouth. It's hot and arousing, and it takes all my strength to stand my ground.

I step back and end up stumbling over my own feet. He pushes off the door and grabs hold of my arm to keep me from falling. His touch is surprisingly gentle, and it makes me want to fall into him. Instead, I brush his hand off me and move out of his reach.

"Look." Heath steps toward me. "This has been a week of ... well, I don't know what I'd call it. A series of misunderstandings, maybe. If you had given me your real name, I might not have jumped to conclusions about you when I saw you in the coffee shop. But—"

"Wow. Are you really blaming me for everything?" My question comes out a little too defensive, but I'm desperate to obliterate the chemistry between us. He still looks like he wants to kiss me again. If that happens, I may never escape this pull he has on me. "I didn't know who you were when you stopped me in the park. You were just some random guy. I wasn't about to give some strange man running around the park—shirtless, I might add—my real name."

He huffs and it's followed by a low growl. "That's not what I meant. I'm not trying to blame you for anything. I'm simply stating that had I had the correct information when I saw you at Coffee Stop, I probably would have put two and two together and figured out who you were."

"Well it's too late for all that now." I cross my arms over my chest. His piercing green eyes lock on me and the room closes in. I feel like I'm being crushed. "Can you stop looking at me like that?"

"How am I looking at you?"

"Like you want to ... I don't know ... Strangle me?" That's a lie. I know what the look in his eyes mean, but I can't bring myself to say it. If I do, then I'd have to admit that this *thing* building between us is real.

It's faint, but he jerks back, and his gaze softens. "That is *not* what I'm thinking, and you know it."

The air cracks between us, and I swear I see sparks. If I don't get out of here soon, a lot more will happen than kissing.

"I have to go. I'm beyond late for my own party." I start to push past him when he grabs hold of my arm. When I look up, his face is only inches from mine. He's too close and yet not close enough.

"We're not finished here. We need a plan."

On a long exhale, I nod. "I'll get your number from Emily. We can meet sometime this week."

"Fine." He lets me go, and I walk out the door. When I'm halfway across the room, I glance over my shoulder, and he's watching me. I can't see his eyes in the dim light of the bar, but I feel the full intensity of his desire. It shoots right through me and ignites my own burning need to be close to him.

If I have to spend two weeks pretending to date this man, I'm toast.

CHAPTER NINE

Heath

I'm waiting for Alicia again at Coffee Stop to discuss a plan that meets both our needs for this fake relationship. She's already ten minutes late, and I can't shake this feeling that she won't come at all.

The truth is nothing could've stopped me from meeting her again. Not after that kiss. It rocked me to my core and squashed every thought I had about running the other way. Even though I denied it to Alicia, I initiated that kiss. That was all on me. When she looked up at me, her eyes full of heat and desire, there was no way I was walking away without kissing her.

I'd been fantasizing about what it would be like to kiss

her ever since I met her in the park. When she stepped into me, I couldn't stop myself. I had to know what her lips felt like against mine.

Now that I know, I want more.

Alicia is hesitant about this whole thing, but she still agreed to meet me. I get it. Fake dating someone isn't my idea of a fun time either. Partaking in deception and lies is enough to stress anyone out, let alone when it involves our parents.

But this charade is already in motion. We can't turn back now.

Here I sit, picking at the paper sleeve wrapped around my coffee, waiting for her to arrive. I'm excited to see her again, even though the logical side of my brain is still yelling at me to run away. Whatever this is with Alicia is nothing more than lust. Right?

But I already feel like I'm getting attached to her. And I don't get attached. Not after Lauren. If things had gone differently with Lauren, I would be married with kids right now.

If Lauren hadn't gotten sick, this summer would have been our ten-year wedding anniversary. I'd been damn lucky to have her love. It was the kind of love that only happens once in a lifetime.

It wasn't that I didn't want to love again, or that I was against it. I had my chance and that was that. I'd long ago gotten over the loss of Lauren and made peace knowing I wouldn't get the life I planned with her. I don't expect to ever find that kind of love again. No one could possibly be that lucky twice.

Then Alicia waltzes into my life and challenges everything I've accepted about my future. She's someone I want to get to know better. I want to learn all her quirks, habits, likes, and dislikes. I want to slowly discover what excites her both inside and outside the bedroom.

I know she feels this connection between us too. I see it in her every time she's near. But something is holding her back. I can feel when she pulls away or tenses under my touch. But her hesitation isn't as strong as her attraction, and I'm hoping I can use the next two weeks to convince her I'm worth a real date.

A real date? Where the fuck did that come from? I haven't been on what I'd call a date since the last time I made the mistake of letting my mom set me up. That was four years ago. Ever since then, I've made up girlfriends to keep Mom off my back. I've had the occasional casual hookup, but even that's been a long time. Hell, I can't even remember the last time I picked up a girl.

Maybe that's my problem. I just need to get laid.

I'm sitting in the same seat Alicia sat in last week when she walks in. I see her before she sees me. A tingling sensation builds inside me, and I clench my hands into fists trying to make it go away. There's no denying she's beautiful. My eyes are sending triggers all through my body telling me I like what I see. Her long blond hair is down and hangs in large curls around her shoulders, hugging her breasts. My mind, and other body parts, immediately imagine grabbing a hold of those locks while pounding ... *Fuck, I have to stop thinking about her like this.*

She glances in my direction, and waves with a tight smile before heading to the counter. My eyes roam down her body, following the lines of her curves. Her short sleeve blouse is tailored to hug those curves perfectly. She's wearing dark jeans that fit snug and just below her waist. I catch a glimpse of her bare skin where her shirt hem just meets the waistband of her jeans. My mouth runs dry. My thoughts turn positively dirty, and my dick twitches. I have got to get a grip.

When my eyes lock with hers, she's watching me watch her. Her eyes widen, and the light reflects off her blue irises. They look a deeper shade than they did before, causing my own need for her to strengthen. She rolls her eyes as if telling me this will never work, but it has the opposite effect on me. I want her more.

"Is Coffee Stop our place now?" Alicia asks as she pulls out the chair and sits.

"No. I just thought this would be easy."

"The park, then. That's our spot. I mean, it *is* where you first came on to me with all that sexy talk." Her words are laced with accusation, and from her tone, I'd say she's purposely trying to get a rise out of me.

She leans back in her chair and drapes her arm over the back. She looks like she'd rather be anywhere else other than here with me. If she's trying to piss me off, it's not going to work. Two can play this game. "Are you having a bad morning?"

Alicia shakes her head and chuckles. "Have you ever had a sense of humor, or have you always had a stick up your ass?"

I narrow my gaze and she laughs harder. She's avoiding my question with insults, and that's when I know I have her. It's a defense mechanism she's using to try and push me away. I want to ask her why she's doing it, but I decide not to. I suspect it's because she feels what I feel, and it scares her.

Instead of arguing with her, I throw it back. Let's see how *she* likes being in the hot seat. "Don't forget about sexy as hell."

Her mouth drops. "What?"

I smile and, for the first time since she sat down, it isn't forced. "Emily said you upgraded me to—how did she put it? Mr. Sexy-As-Hell-Stick-Up-His-Ass."

She rolls her eyes and shakes her head. She does that a lot with me. I find it adorably frustrating. "There's a lot more to a person than looks."

I chuckle. "Tell me about it."

The barista calls her name, and she gives me a smug grin before she stands to get her coffee.

I drag my hands through my hair and drop my head back. Maybe we're too different for this to work. Maybe it's best to call it off now before the lie gets any deeper. Maybe it'll be enough to let Mom think Alicia is coming with me. At least then she can't finalize any of those dates. If they never get scheduled, then they can't happen. Right?

"When do we leave for this fun-filled, romantic vacation in the Hamptons?" Alicia asks with a hint of irritation.

I snap my head up, and she's staring at me. I hadn't heard her sit back down and that bothers me. I've never gotten so lost in my thoughts that I lost focus on my surroundings.

God, she's a beautiful woman, but that mouth of hers drives me insane. In more ways than one. The words that come out are one thing, but I haven't been able to stop thinking about that kiss. That unexpected kiss that drew me in and made me want her more.

"Well?" she says, her annoyance evident in the way her eyes look up at me.

I huff, close my eyes, and count to ten. Her purposeful attempts at trying my patience are starting to work. "Must you say it like that?"

"Like what?" She leans back in her chair and sips her coffee.

"Like you have better things to do than waste your time on someone like me. Or like nothing in this world is worth taking seriously. If this is how you're going to act, then maybe we should call it quits."

"Oh, come on, Heath. Relax." She sighs and rolls her eyes, *again*. "Maybe you should stop taking everything so seriously. Lighten up."

"You want me to *lighten up*? We're lying to our parents about our relationship. It's not something I particularly feel good about. Nor do I want my mom to find out. She'd never forgive me."

"Then why did you agree to do this?" she asks.

I lean forward on my elbow and rub my hand over my face before resting it behind my neck. I hate lying to Mom, but I also know I won't survive the family vacation if she thinks I'm single. "Because I can't go on all those dates Mom has planned. I can't do it."

"Then just don't go," she says, like it's so easy. I wish it were. Unfortunately, the only thing that will convince Mom I'm fine is a girlfriend. I don't know why she refuses to take my word for it. Losing Lauren was hard, and I'd be lying if I said I didn't wish it had turned out differently or that it still didn't hurt. Because I do and it does. But it's been ten years. It doesn't affect me the way Mom seems to think it does. I hate that the only way she'll believe me is if I'm dating someone.

When I look up, Alicia is watching me with raised brows. There's a fire in her eyes similar to what I saw when she stepped up to rescue me from Mom. Then it hits me that she doesn't really know Mom. "How is it you don't know my mom all that well?"

She shrugs. "I've only ever met her a few times."

"How did that happen? You and Emily have been close friends since college, right?"

"Yep, freshman year." Alicia leans forward and gives me a thoughtful look. "Emily has invited me to several of your family events over the years, but I've always turned her down."

"Why?"

"I guess you could say the Hamptons lifestyle isn't really my thing. I'm a Brooklyn girl."

I eye her carefully. I want to ask her to elaborate on that, but I don't. My family may be rich, but we'd never judge someone for where they came from.

If she met Emily her freshman year of college, maybe she doesn't know about Lauren. Lauren and I were supposed to get married the summer before Emily started college, and therefore, before she met Alicia. I assumed Alicia knew about Lauren, but I might be wrong.

Not wanting to go down this path, I redirect the conversation back to the present. "Listen, if I show up at the Hamptons alone, Mom will find a way to make sure each of those dates happen. Trust me when I say the girls she picks out for me are not my type."

She snorts. "And you think I'm your type?"

She's not my type, but she's definitely someone I want to get to know better. "I haven't decided what you are. You're certainly opposite from me in almost every way, but you do possess qualities I like."

"Oh, yeah?" She rests her elbow on the table and drops her chin in the cup of her hand. "Now, this I've gotta hear." A light sparks in her eyes and the same aquamarine color that struck me in the park stare back at me. I'm tempted to tell her how beautiful they are and focus on all the superficial things about her that make her attractive. But her beauty is not what I like best about her.

Instead, I tell her the truth. "You're smart, kind when you want to be, funny, and loyal to those closest to you. You don't take shit from anyone. Except I suspect maybe on occasion your mother. While she may drive you crazy, you respect her and would rather lie to her about a fake boyfriend than hurt her feelings by refusing to succumb to her meddling."

Her eyes widen, and she looks at me in surprise. "That was ... unexpected. I don't know what to say."

"What did you expect?" My lips tick up, and I fight off a smile. It pleases me that I surprised her.

"You know, I don't know." She blushes. "But it wasn't a compliment."

"Well, it's all true. Maybe if you gave me a chance, you'd find out I'm not quite the asshole you think I am."

"I don't think you're an asshole." Her playful pretense is gone. I can't tell if she's offended or just taken aback by my accusation. "A little uptight, and in serious need of a sense of humor, but not an asshole."

"I can work with that." I lift my coffee to her and nod.

"We leave on Monday if you're still game."

She hesitates.

"I wouldn't go through with this if I thought there was another way. I really need your help, Alicia." I am desperate for her to say yes, but I don't want to pull the pity card and tell her about Lauren. This is my chance to finally get Mom to realize I'm okay. That my life, although not what she wants for me, is okay, and I'm happy.

"Please?" I keep my cup raised, hoping she'll join me.

Alicia stares at me and maybe senses my reasons are far deeper than I'm willing to share, and she raises her coffee. With a nervous smile, she says, "Yep, you bet."

Not exactly the enthusiastic response I hoped for, but I'll take it. She agreed, and at this juncture in our fake relationship, that's all I can ask for.

CHAPTER TEN

Alicia

I can't remember the last time I've been this nervous. I've changed my outfit three times, and I can't stop checking my hair and make-up. I finally settled on a pair of black jeans and a red, short sleeve sweater that hangs past my hips. It fits snugly and shows off my narrow waist. Trent always says this looks great on me. If he likes it, I figured Heath would like it too.

It shouldn't matter, but I want to impress him.

I hate that he's evoked this need in me. He's not my boyfriend—and he never will be—but I want him to like me. I keep trying to convince myself it's because of Emily and his brothers, but that's a lie.

I have a feeling there will be a lot of lies I tell myself over the next two weeks.

Two weeks.

I've lost my mind. There's no way we can pull this off for two full weeks. I'm completely on edge, and I can't stop shaking. Since when do I get nervous like this? It's been a long time since I dated anyone seriously. I've been on enough first dates—courtesy of my mom—to know how to act, but those don't count.

Heath shouldn't be any different than any other guy Mom has set me up with. Except he *is* different. He's my best friend's brother. If I screw this up, I could screw up my friendship with Emily. I'd be lost without her.

Then again, this is her harebrained idea. If this blows up in our faces, she's the one to blame.

My bags are packed and have been by the door for over an hour. I didn't want to be late and give him a reason to look down on me. He didn't say anything about how late I was for our meeting at Coffee Stop earlier this week, but from what Emily told me, it had to have irritated him. According to her, he's notoriously early, and being late is a sure way to poke the bear. If I'm not ready when he arrives, it'd be a strike against me. I don't want to start off our two weeks together that way.

Arg! Why do I care?

I grab my laptop and curl up on the couch. Writing typically calms my nerves, and I hope to find that calm before Heath arrives. I lightly tap at the keys, trying to find words worth putting down, but I've got nothing. My mind is clogged with thoughts of Heath.

I drop my head back on the couch and groan. I close my eyes and an image of Heath surfaces. His arm is around me, and his eyes are focused on my lips. God, that kiss. I can still feel the softness of his lips tucked between the roughness of his prickly beard. I suck my bottom lip between my teeth and imagine how his hands feel as they—

There's a knock at my door, and I jump. My laptop slips off my lap, and I scramble to catch it before it hits the floor. I let out a deep sigh and cradle it to my chest, relieved I didn't drop it.

There's another knock at my door, but this one is louder. I slip my laptop into my bag and check the time. It's a quarter to ten which means Heath is fifteen minutes early.

I open the door to find him tapping his foot with a frown. "Why the long face? Since you're early, it's me who should be frowning."

His foot stills, and he jerks his head back. "I'm not frowning."

"Seriously." I chuckle. "Should I get a mirror?"

He rubs his eyes and smiles. "Sorry. I didn't mean to frown. I guess I'm just nervous."

"Ah, that's okay." I give him a playful shove. "I tend to have that effect on people."

That earns me a smile and a slow rake of his eyes down my body. "You look nice."

"Thanks." The compliment, combined with the look in his eyes, causes my face to warm. I step aside to both hide my face and let him into my apartment. As soon as he passes through the door, my own nervousness bubbles up inside me. I don't invite men who aren't my close friends into my apartment. Ever. He's now in my home, and I'm more than a little uncomfortable with it.

He lets out a low whistle as he looks around my large open concept living space. "Wow. This is nice. And upscale. I didn't realize authors made this much money."

"I do well for myself." I gather my purse and laptop case before heading into the kitchen to grab a water bottle. "I guess you could say I do better than most."

"I'd say. When you gave me your address, I was expecting to find a small studio, but this place is huge. I must admit, I'm surprised. It's just my style."

"Whoa! Are you saying we have something in

common?" I tease. With my hands on my hips, I smile. I love my apartment. The simple, sleek, modern open-concept design is perfect for entertaining a small gathering of friends. The main living area is a single large room with the only division being the large island separating the kitchen. The walls are painted a soft pale gray, and the furniture is a darker charcoal gray with dark wood accent tables. But I have splashes of color everywhere. I let the art, accent pillows, and decor add brightness and life. It works.

He glances around with an approving nod. "It would appear so."

"Miracles do happen." He looks at me with a heated gaze. The same butterflies I felt when he kissed are back. Damn, how does he do that to me?

I turn my back to him, open my refrigerator, and grab a second bottle of water. "Do you want one?"

"Thanks." When he reaches for it, his fingers brush across mine. It's brief, but his touch is enough to send a shiver up my arm. "You ready?"

"Yep, all packed." I rush past him and grab my keys from the side table. "My bags are by the door."

Without a word, he picks up my bag and suitcase and heads out. I let out a long breath and close my eyes. I have to get it together. Heath and I are not compatible, but for the life of me, I can't figure out why my body doesn't understand that.

WE'RE ABOUT THIRTY MINUTES into our three-hour drive, and we've hardly spoken a word to each other. While the silence leaves me uncomfortable, Heath seems perfectly content. From what little I know about him, this shouldn't surprise me. He's a man of few words. The first day I met him in the park, he hardly said anything while I babbled on and on, playing the role of a naughty girl from one of my books.

At the time, I wasn't sure if he was surprised into silence or if he just didn't speak much. I now know it's because he's the silent type. He's probably content without talking the entire drive, but I can't take it. Besides, we need to know more about each other if this is going to work.

"So, what does your mom know about our relationship?" I ask.

He shrugs and glances my way. "Not much. Only that we just started dating a few weeks ago."

"That's not very long. Don't you think a vacation like this is a little ... I don't know ... Fast?"

"Oh, I think it's way too fast." He lets out a nervous

chuckle. "If we were dating for real, there's no way I'd invite you along for my family vacation yet. But it's the only way Mom will get off my back."

"If you think it's way too fast, won't she as well?"

"Who knows what Mom thinks anymore?" He opens his mouth like he has more to say, but he stops himself and sighs.

I wait and watch, but he only stares out the windshield tapping his fingers on the steering wheel. I can't tell if his tapping is a nervous habit or a sign of confidence. He looks confident, slouching in the driver's seat with an easy smile on his face. Suddenly, it makes me even more nervous than I already am. Aside from being Emily's oldest brother, I don't really know anything about him.

"Maybe we should share a few things about ourselves. You know, typical first date stuff or things your mom would expect us to know about each other."

"Okay, that's probably a good idea." He says as he slides his hands around the steering wheel and grips it at the bottom. He looks so at ease, like he does things like this all the time. "I've got a question I've been wanting to ask you."

I smile, glad that he's given this some thought. "Okay, shoot."

"You're not dating yourself, and Emily said you had no

interest in dating. So, why do you write romance novels?"

My smile drops. I close my eyes and feel my body slump. I hate this question. It makes me uncomfortable. Emily and Mom hound me with this question all the time, especially Mom. But no matter how many times they ask, my answer remains the same. "Because happily-ever-afters make people happy. I love making people happy."

He raises his brows and frowns. "But *you* don't want to be happy?"

I cross my arms over my chest and shift my body to face him. "What makes you think I'm not happy?"

"If anyone knows you can be happy without love, it's me. But aren't you afraid your readers will think you're a fraud?"

"Why would I be a fraud?" The words come out in a high-pitch squeal. He looks at me out of the corner of his eye, and I swear he smirks.

"You're selling books about hope, love, and happily-ever-afters. A perfect love story where the boy always gets the girl in the end and vice versa. Yet you don't want that kind of love for yourself."

I shake my head and try to tamp down my frustration. Why does everyone always assume my love life must be perfect because of my writing? The two are so unrelated.

"Love found in fiction isn't real life. That's why it's called fiction."

"But it's based on real-life possibilities." He glances at me. His gaze is piercing and knowing. He holds his eyes on me for a few seconds too long before he looks back toward the road.

"I suppose, but that doesn't mean those things really happen. The stories may possess a kernel of truth, but the characters I create are pure fiction. Book boyfriends do *not* exist. They are the most fantastical characters ever created."

"Book boyfriends?" He furrows his brows, but he doesn't look at me. "Those are the dreamy, perfect men you were telling me about that day in the park, right?"

"Yyyeeeaaah." I drag out my response. "You remember?"

A faint smile tugs at his lips. "I listen."

"Hmm." I regard him. Most guys aren't interested in my ramblings about writing. I love to talk about writing and my process, and once I get started, it's hard for me to stop sometimes. Most guys just appease me by pretending they're listening when they're just letting me talk and waiting for a break in the conversation to change the subject.

"So, tell me about these book boyfriends." He says, pulling me out of my thoughts.

"You really want to know?"

He glances my way. "Yes. I wouldn't have asked if I didn't."

I drop my arms to my side and smile. "Well, they are complete fantasy. Like the most perfect guy imaginable. Perfect body, perfect personality, the absolute perfect man for the woman. Sure, they're flawed, and they have issues to work through. That's part of the story. But they always come through in the end and do the right thing for the women they love. They're unbelievably sexy and are capable of handing out orgasms like free candy. After spending years writing men like that, it's next to impossible to date real-life men because there's no way they can live up to the fantasy in my head."

"Handing out orgasms like candy?"

"In. Every. Book. Book boyfriends can make their women come two to three times in one night. Speaking from experience, that never happens."

He turns and holds his gaze on me again. This time there's heat and maybe a hint of desire in the way his eyes hold mine. I squirm in my seat. "Maybe you've just never found the right man for you."

I swallow hard and pull my eyes away from his. This is the last thing I want to talk about with him. "Doubtful. It's more likely that men capable of pleasuring a woman to that extent just don't exist."

"Sounds like a challenge." His voice is low and husky and its way past time to end this conversation.

"Don't get any ideas, big boy." I attempt to lighten the conversation with a playful laugh, but it ends up sounding forced.

"Big boy?" He tosses me a crooked smile. A hint of his dimple peaks through his beard. My heart rate picks up and, *oh, my God*, this has gone too far.

"All right. This conversation is getting derailed. Tell me something about you that I should know."

He stares ahead, still tapping his fingers against the steering wheel. He looks so relaxed and happy while I'm over here panicking.

"Okay, I've thought of something." He shifts in his seat. "I'm a huge fan of PDA."

"Excuse me?" My voice cracks and ends on another squeal. I shrink back in my seat a little, hating that he keeps doing this to me.

"PDA. Public display of affection."

"I know what it is." I bark back, struggling to keep my mouth from falling open. There is no way I heard Mr. Stick-Up-His-Ass correctly. I cannot imagine this man being okay and comfortable with PDA. "What exactly are you saying?"

"I'm saying when I'm with someone, I have no problem showing my affection publicly."

"Are you saying PDA is expected from me over the next couple weeks?"

He glances at me with a blank expression. "Is that going to be a problem?"

"Um, yeah." My eyes start to burn with how hard I stare at him. He can't be serious. This has to be some type of payback joke he's playing on me for the way I acted when we first met. But there's nothing teasing about his expression. Heath Rockwell is dead serious. "No! I can't do it ... I mean ... Don't you think that's something you should've told me *before* I agreed to this?"

"I didn't think it would be a problem considering you wrapped your arms around me and then kissed me in front of my family." He shrugs. "Not to mention how comfortable you seem to be with talking about sex."

"Oh, my God. We are *not* having sex." My mouth falls open in shock, and he laughs. A full belly, bringing tears to his eyes laugh. I'm staring at him like he just grew two heads, and he thinks it's funny. It takes every ounce of my energy to stop myself from punching him in the arm.

"Relax. I didn't say we were." He manages to catch

his breath and slow his laughter. "But my family will know something is off if we aren't openly affectionate with each other."

"Define openly affectionate." The smirk on his face breaks through my self-control, and I slap his shoulder. He's enjoying my freak out a little too much when all I want to do is hop out of this car and hitch a ride back to the city. "Heath, tell me."

He reaches over and takes my shaking hand in his. I start to pull away, but he gives it a gentle squeeze. He smiles, but it's not to tease me like he was a moment ago. This smile puts me at ease.

"Hand holding." He laces his fingers with mine. "Definitely hand holding. Kissing, but nothing too intense. And snuggling."

"Snuggling?" I raise my brows.

"Yeah. Curling up next to me on the couch while we watch a movie. Or sitting on my lap if we get one of the plush chairs instead. I won't ask you to spoon with me while we sleep, but I probably miss spooning more than anything about not having a woman in my bed."

"Whoa, whoa, whoa." I jerk back, and my hand slips out of his. "I already said we weren't having sex."

He reaches over and takes my hand back. This time he

lifts it to his lips. "Spooning doesn't require sex. But we will be sleeping in the same room. I'll do my best to stay to my side of the bed, but please don't hit me if you wake up and I have my arms wrapped around you."

My mouth drops. I'm speechless. I want to yell at him, tell him there is no way he can *spoon* me while we're sleeping, but nothing comes out. In part, because now I can't stop thinking about what it would feel like to have his large arms around me. Or how his rock-hard abs—or other hard parts of him—would feel pressed against my back.

My mouth runs dry, and my heart pounds in my ears.
Shit, I can't do this.

Why did I think this would be easy, and why did I assume I'd be in my own room? I'm such an idiot for not asking these questions before I agreed to this fake relationship. It hasn't even officially begun, and it's already a fiasco.

"Hey." He tugs at my hand then laces our fingers together again. I meet his stare and his expression is serious. No more joking or laughing at my expense. "Don't worry, it's a king size bed. You'll have plenty of room on your side. And I really will try to stay on mine."

He turns his focus back to the road. I stare at him for a moment before I shift my gaze to my hand. The hand he's still holding. A part of me wants to pry my hand out of his, but another part of me—a part I don't want to acknowledge—really likes how this feels. I can't remember the last time a man held my hand. Even Jeremey never held my hand and that ended years ago.

I sigh, drop my head to the side window, and watch the landscape pass by while I try like hell to forget about how good his hand feels wrapped around mine.

Fake dating Heath is supposed to be easy. Yet somehow, the simple act of holding my hand complicates everything.

MY MOUTH DROPS ALL over again when Heath pulls into the driveway of his parents' Hamptons house. I knew Emily came from money, but this is a freaking mansion. Not one of those McMansion homes in an upscale community for new money, but an honest-to-God, old-money massive mansion with a security gate, extensive grounds, beach access, and a garage larger than my entire apartment building. That's an exaggeration, but my point is it's huge and completely ridiculous.

"You all right?" Heath squeezes my hand, and I jump in my seat. I look at our hands, fingers still intertwined, and feel at ease. He held my hand the rest of the car ride, and I let him. I shouldn't have, but I couldn't bring myself to pull away. It felt too good to let go.

"This ... This house is huge," I finally manage to say.

"You knew my family was from money, right?" The look of concern on his face is endearing, and it makes me smile. Heath may be uptight and come across as stiff, but he's got a soft side too.

"Yeah, but this is not what I imagined. This is like real money."

"As opposed to fake money." He chuckles and kisses the back of my hand before he lets go. "Stay put."

The touch of his lips on my skin warms my face. I'm grateful he steps out of the car before he sees my cheeks blush. If he keeps acting sweet like this, these next two weeks are going to be interesting. I think I prefer the uptight version of Heath. At least with Mr. Stick-Up-His-Ass, my heart is safe. But with Mr. Sexy-Sweet-PDA, I'm treading in dangerous waters and will certainly drown.

He walks around the front of the car and opens my door. He takes my hand, lifts me out of my seat, and pulls me close. When his arm snakes around me and his hand presses flat against my lower back, I suck in a breath. "What are you doing?"

"We have to make this look real, remember?" He leans down and gently brushes his lips against mine. It's soft and light and hardly much of a kiss but it still makes me weak in the knees. "Ready?"

His breath is warm against my cheek. He smells a little like cinnamon, coffee, and something sweet I can't quite place. Unable to formulate words, I nod, force a smile, and remind myself that this thing with Heath isn't real.

That fact is reinforced when he leads me toward the front entrance, and his mom is standing on the front porch smiling at us.

Let the games begin.

"What was that?" Heath asks.

"Oh, nothing. Didn't realize I said that out loud." I take a deep breath and remind myself I already know his brothers and sister. This should be a walk in the park as long as his parents don't end up hating me.

As we near the front door, Heath releases my hand, wraps his arm around my shoulder, and tucks me into his side. "Hi, Mom. You remember Alicia, but I guess I should give you a proper introduction."

"Of course, I know Alicia." His mom beams. She reaches for me and pulls me into a tight hug. "We've met plenty of times, but I'll gladly accept this new introduction. I'm so glad to finally get to know you better."

"Thanks for opening your home to me, Mrs. Rockwell.

I look forward to getting to know you better as well."

"Please, call me Elaine." She squeezes my hand and leads me into the house.

I feel my eyes widen, and I pinch my lips closed to keep from gawking. The grandness of the outside of the house has nothing on the inside. The foyer is open for three floors and a massive chandelier hanging above my head sparkles and shines like it's never seen a speck of dust.

"Yo, bro." Luke rushes down the stairs from the second floor and pounces on Heath in more of a wrestling hold than a hug. "Think you can peel those lovesick eyes off Alicia long enough to get the bags?"

Heath groans and narrows his eyes on Luke. "Be nice."

"I *am* nice." He pats Heath on the chest and turns his grin to me. "Hey, Alicia. Good to see my brother didn't bore you to death on the drive."

"Not at all. I think he managed to speak about ten words or so. Does that sound about right, Heath?" I toss Heath a teasing smile and Luke and Elaine laugh. Heath shifts his eyes to me and tries to stop the smile that tugs at his lips, but he fails.

"Sounds right to me." Luke chuckles. "Then again, my big brother always did prefer action over words."

"Ha, ha. Very funny." Heath shrugs Luke's arm off

his shoulder before he heads back to the car. Luke waggles his brows at me with a devilish grin before he chases after Heath.

"Come, let's join the others in the kitchen. Lunch is almost ready," Elaine says.

I watch Heath and Luke for a moment before I turn and follow Elaine through the house. Every bit of the nervous energy I felt this morning is back.

CHAPTER ELEVEN

Heath

Alicia has been in the bathroom for over an hour. I'm not sure if she really takes this long to get ready or if she's hiding from me.

I'm guessing it's the latter because she doesn't strike me as a woman who primps for hours. It could also be nerves. Emily hasn't arrived yet. She had a water pipe burst in her apartment and has been delayed dealing with that mess. I'm sure Alicia was counting on Emily for support.

Maybe I came on too strong with my PDA. I wasn't lying to her when I said I'm an openly affectionate person. I didn't say that to her as some ploy to get closer to her. It's the truth. Mom would instantly know something was wrong if we never touched or kissed or cuddled.

But I'd be lying to myself if I didn't at least admit that getting closer to her sounds good. Better than good. It sounds fucking fantastic.

I didn't expect to feel this way about her. The same tingling sensation that always excites me when I'm attracted to someone rushes through me when Alicia is nearby. But it's more intense. It's the main reason I couldn't let go of her hand during the drive over. Her hand felt too damn good in mine. Like she belongs next to me.

I've only kissed her a couple times, but holy mother of God. Kissing her is like breathing in my last breath. If I stop, I might not survive. And I have no idea what to do with that knowledge. Kissing Lauren didn't make me feel like that.

I can't be thinking these thoughts. This relationship isn't real. It has an end date. We've only got three weeks of pretending to get through. After this vacation with my family, I owe her a dinner with her mom where I convince her Alicia and I are a very happy couple. That's it. Then we go our separate ways.

Alicia is not mine. She's given me no indication that she wants more. I'd do well to remember that.

Unless I can convince her, we need more time.

The bathroom door finally opens, and I jump up from

the bed where I'd been sitting for the last thirty minutes.

"Hey," I say.

"Hey." She gives me a nervous smile as she walks to her suitcase. She's wearing a simple lavender dress with capped sleeves. It fits snug to her waist and then flares out into a flowy skirt that stops just above her knee. She looks gorgeous. "Have you been waiting for me this entire time?"

"Nah." I lie. She doesn't need to know I've been sitting here for thirty minutes fantasizing about kissing her again. "I figured I'd walk down with you if that's okay."

"Of course." She smiles, and looks more at ease now. "I am posing as your girlfriend, so that does seem like the normal thing to do."

"Right." I hate how awkward I feel around her. Maybe it's because all I want to do right now is pull her into my arms and press my lips to hers. "I love this dress on you. Lavender is your color."

"Thanks." Her smile grows, and she looks happy. It's not faked or forced or uncomfortable like so many she's given before. It's genuine, and in this moment, I decide to find more ways to make her smile.

"Ready?" I offer her my arm. To my delight, she takes it. Together we walk down the stairs to the dining room to join my family for dinner.

DINNER IS UNEVENTFUL.

For my family, that's a miracle.

No one hounds me or Alicia with questions about our relationship or how we met. Instead, we take our seats, pass around the food and dig in. My brothers are surprisingly quiet.

Mom hasn't even brought up my lack of dating and past single status. That's typically her favorite conversation and the first thing she hits me with. I guess in that regard, Alicia's presence is working.

"Any changes in this year's schedule?" Dexter asks.

"No, I don't think so," Mom replies. We've taken these family vacations for years, and it's pretty much always the same. "We'll hang out here and relax most of this week. Take the boat out on Thursday, the party is Saturday, you'll have your annual bar crawl, and we'll end with the golf outing at the country club. In between, we'll grill and enjoy the beach."

Dexter nods. "Sounds about right."

"When is Evan arriving?" Dad asks. "Shouldn't he be here by now?"

Dexter takes a drink of his beer before he answers. "He can't make it until Saturday. He had to go out of town for business, but he'll be here all next week."

Mom lets out a low huff and glances around the table with sadness in her eyes.

"Mom, what's wrong?" I ask.

"I hate that Emily and Evan aren't here. This is the first time in years they've missed our first vacation dinner. I want all my kids here with me."

"Mom." Luke chuckles. "Evan isn't your kid."

"I know that, but he practically grew up with you boys. He's like a son to me." Evan is Dexter's best friend and has been since kindergarten. Evan's family isn't wealthy like ours but managed to snag a scholarship that allowed Evan to attend the same private school that we did. Dexter and Evan became instant friends and have been inseparable since.

"How about you, Alicia?" My mom looks at her with a small smile. "Do you have siblings?"

I'm suddenly hit with a moment of panic. I don't even know the answer to this question. We've talked about a lot of things, but her family is not one of them. Real girlfriend or not, I should know this.

Alicia puts her fork down and wipes her mouth. "No, I'm an only child."

"That had to be a quiet upbringing," my dad deadpans as he glances around at his sons. Mom slaps his arm lightly, and we all laugh. We know he's joking, but we weren't exactly a quiet bunch of kids.

"You would think, but no." She smiles, and the look in her eyes makes me think she has fond memories of her childhood. "I had my mom and an entire neighborhood of kids my age and countless second mothers to keep me company. Our community is still very close."

"What about your father?" Mom asks.

"He died when I was very young." Her smile drops, and she shifts her eyes down. She lifts her fork up and scoots her food around her plate but doesn't pick anything up. I reach out and rest my hand on her thigh. She stiffens slightly. I hold a smile on my face and lightly squeeze hoping she relaxes. I didn't think before I touched her. It was a gut reaction.

"I'm sorry to hear that." My mom offers. "That had to be tough."

Alicia shrugs again and tosses me a faint smile as she relaxes next to me. "It probably was at first, but I was so young. I don't really remember. I went through a phase where I wished I had siblings. But Mom never remarried." She pauses and turns a playful eye toward Luke and Dexter.

"But then I met Emily and her crazy brothers. Made me glad I didn't have overprotective brothers to interrogate every man I date."

Everyone laughs. Poor Emily has never been able to bring a boyfriend home without all of us glaring with an implied death threat.

"Don't think we won't do the same for you, Alicia." Dexter points at me from across the table. "The only reason we haven't kicked this guy's ass is because he's our brother."

Luke grins at me, but there's no laughter in his eyes. "Hurt her, and you're a dead man."

I raise my brows and shift my gaze between my brothers. This isn't at all how I expected them to act. I expected my brothers to be relentless with their teasing and jokes about my fake relationship with Alicia. My siblings know this isn't real. Hell, it was their idea.

My brothers know Alicia better than me, and they genuinely like her. They mean it when they say they'd protect her same as they would Emily.

Their lack of harassment is not a sign that they're giving me a break. They never give me a break. They respect her, and I can see why. She's sweet, kind, and very funny. It's clear to me now that I got a heavy dose of her funny and sarcastic side when we first met in the park. I like that side of her, too. It's feisty and sexy. Now I'm seeing her kindness. It's doing nothing to remind me that this is all fake.

I like her. Like, really like her.

And I want to get to know her better.

The fact that my brothers think so highly of her only feeds my growing feelings for her. It's confirmation that she's a good person and worth getting to know.

But she's Emily's best friend, and she's made it perfectly clear that she's not interested in dating anyone. It's why we're fake dating in the first place.

Conversation shifts away from Alicia. Dad peppers us with questions about the bar, and Mom makes small talk with Alicia about her food likes and dislikes. Mom loves to cook and will change her entire menu if Alicia doesn't like something she has planned. Thankfully, it sounds like Alicia will eat just about anything.

We finish up and start to clear the table. Despite Mom's objections, Alicia is helping her clean up. She's ignored every one of Mom's protests, and I can tell Mom secretly loves that Alicia is helping anyway. It's a task Emily typically helps with, but since she's still MIA, I'm glad Alicia offers. It's respectful and kind. It shows me she's comfortable around my family.

"Any word from Emily yet?" I ask as I help clear the

plates.

"She called before dinner. She's gonna wait and head out in the morning." Mom sighs and her shoulders slump. Nothing upsets Mom more than when something keeps one of her children away. It can seem overbearing at times, but we know it's because she loves us. "Her landlord was able to turn off her water before too much damage was done, but the flooding reached the carpet. They had to remove her furniture and arrange for someone to come in for a deep clean. By the time they were done moving all her furniture to an empty apartment, she was exhausted."

"I wish she called. I would've helped her," I say.

"You know Emily. She's more stubborn than any of you." Mom smiles and takes the plates from my hands. "We'll save the cleanup for later. Let's join your father and brothers in the study for drinks."

I nod and kiss her cheek. I glance over at Alicia and find her watching me with a smile. She quickly shifts her eyes back to the table and continues stacking dirty dishes.

"Are you sure?" I ask. "You hate leaving a mess."

"Yes, dear. I'm sure." Mom turns to smile at Alicia. "I'd like to get to know Alicia better. I can't believe she's been friends with Emily for so long, and she's just now spending time with us."

We join the others in the study. I pour myself a glass of scotch and take the large chair opposite my father. Mom pours herself and Alicia a glass of red wine before she sits on one end of the empty sofa. I expect Alicia to sit next to her, but she surprises me when she sits on the armrest of my chair and rests her elbow on my shoulder. I glance up at her and meet her smile. I rest my hand on her knee, and I swear I feel her tremble, but when I look up at her she looks calm and happy.

"So, Alicia," Mom says. "Tell me about your writing. You write novels, correct?"

"Yes, ma'am."

"That's a tough profession." Dad interjects. "I can't imagine success has been easy to obtain."

"Henry." Mom scolds. "From what I understand, Alicia's a huge success."

Dexter snorts from the side table where he and Luke are playing cards. "That's one way to put it. How many books are you up to now? Forty-seven?"

"How do you know that?" I ask. I know she's published a lot. Her success is evident by the apartment she lives in, but I don't like that Dexter seems to know more about her work than I do.

"She comes into the bar to celebrate every time she

finishes a new book." Luke grins at me. "You'd know that if you bothered to hang around after hours."

"Not all of us can—"

Alicia squeezes my hand on her knee and smiles. "Heath works hard. It's not like he's had a reason to celebrate with me until now. I'm sure that will change moving forward."

"Have you really published forty-seven books?" Mom asks.

"Yes." Alicia beams. She clearly loves talking about her work. It's hard not to smile with her. "Just celebrated the last one on the night Heath introduced me to you."

"Anything I would have read?"

"Do you read romance? I write under the pen name Alexis Stone."

Mom's jaw drops, and I try to hide the cringe I feel coming on. My parents are very accepting people, but when it comes to certain topics, they're not as open minded. "Seriously? I love her books. I mean ... your books. But those are ... Oh, my," Mom blushes, and leans forward to whisper, "... so steamy."

Alicia tosses her head back and laughs while I gape at my mom. I didn't know this about her. "Yes, I suppose they are."

Mom takes a drink of her wine, and Dad narrows his

eyes on Alicia. I fear the worst from him. He's never been one to talk openly about sex. Neither of my parents have. "You mean to tell us you write smut?"

Mom gasps and scolds Dad but Alicia just laughs again. "I write love stories that happen to include sex. Some call it smut, but that smut is the number one selling book genre in the world and has made me a huge success."

"Like how huge?" Dad asks.

Alicia drops her smile and meets Dad's gaze. It's intense and impressive. She's not deterred in the least by his pointed questions. "Like, I could never write and sell another book for the rest of life, and I'd still never have to worry about money."

Dad nods, seemingly satisfied with her response, but then he asks, "Aren't you embarrassed to talk about what you do for a living with strangers? I'd think it'd be so much easier to admit to writing crime thrillers than romance. Is that why you write under a pen name?"

"Not at all. I love what I write, and I'm very proud to be a part of such an important genre. Personally, I've never understood the negativity associated with romance. Let's face it, no one hopes their child grows up to commit crimes or acts of violence like we see represented in so many crime thriller novels, and yet we hope to have children or grandchildren someday. That requires sex. Sex is a natural and very normal part of life. I write under a pen name to protect my privacy, not hide. I have nothing to hide."

"Hmm." Dad nods again and picks up his drink.

And me? I'm even more amazed by the woman sitting next to me. I love her confidence and pride in what she does. It's hot and makes me want her even more.

"I see your point." Dad continues. "That's a very healthy way to look at it." He turns to Mom and takes her hand. "I'll never criticize your reading choices again."

I look between Dad and Alicia. He seems to be perfectly content with her response. The conversation shifts from careers to our plans over the next few days. There's nothing much on the agenda until Thursday's boat outing which means a couple of days of rest and relaxation without worry of a schedule.

Maybe I can use this down time to soften Alicia's resolve against dating. Because I want to date her for real even more now. I just need to find a way to prove to her a real date with me would be worth the risk.

CHAPTER TWELVE

Alicia

Watching the Rockwell brothers play beach volleyball is a sight to see. They all three have ridiculously hot bodies and can all play. It's like they're sports gods or something. Who knew?

I'd already seen Heath shirtless, more than once now that I'm sharing a bedroom with him. I always assumed Dexter and Luke were packing some seriously hard muscles under their shirts, but damn. This many abs in one place should be illegal.

Even Emily looks hot in her tiny black bikini. She finally arrived last night, the damage to her apartment much worse than they originally thought. It took longer for her to arrange for the repairs, but she's here now.

Her presence has helped me relax, but I still tense up every time Heath touches me. It's innocent and shouldn't bother me—especially since we talked about it in advance—but I can't help it. The last man to touch me like I was his girlfriend was Jeremy. That didn't end so well.

I'm supposed to be using this time to get some writing done, but I can't keep my eyes off Heath. All I've managed to do is watch him. He looks the same as he did the first day I met him, running in Central Park. Shirtless and glistening with sweat.

Those damn running shorts he wears do nothing to hide what he's packing, and he is definitely packing. Thank God I'm wearing sunglasses and have the protection of this shade umbrella to hide my ogling.

Luke jumps to spike the ball over the net and Heath dives to save the play. His long, lean body stretches as he thrusts his arm out in front of him and clasps his hands together. His forearms make contact with the ball just before he slams into the sandy ground. He grunts as he pulls his arms underneath and pushes himself up. Every muscle in his body is flexed and his skin is dark and slightly red from the sun beating down on him all afternoon.

A fluttering sensation builds in my belly and my mouth

runs dry. My eyes track the lines of sweat dripping down his back as he repositions himself to assist Emily as she bunts the ball he just saved. He's more than ready. His legs bend slightly. He jumps into the air, lifting his arm high above his head. In one swift and powerful movement, he spikes the ball back over the net. It lands just out of Dexter's reach and kicks sand into the air when it crashes into the ground.

Emily and Heath cheer, having just delivered the winning play.

I hear Elaine cheer from the deck where she's helping Henry prepare dinner. She's setting the table while Henry grills some burgers. They're all very normal activities that normal families do. It's only been a couple days since we arrived, but I'm surprised at how cool Emily's family is. They may be wealthy, but they don't act like it. It's refreshing and makes me feel kind of bad for turning Emily down all these years to spend more time with her family.

"Alicia, join us for a swim." Emily waves me toward her.

"Nah, I'm good." I watch as Dexter and Luke run into the waves, but Heath stays put. Emily says something to him before she follows her brothers. He remains planted in the middle of the volleyball court with his hands on his hips. Staring at me.

"What?" I call out.

A slow smile spreads across his face as he walks toward me. "I've been ordered to get you in the water."

"Do you always do what you're told?" I tease. This earns me a laugh. Seeing Heath in this environment gives me a very different view of him. He's relaxed, funny, playful. So unlike my Mr. Stick-Up-His-Ass.

"Nope, but you know how convincing Emily can be."

"This is true." I shut my laptop and set it on the side table next to me. "But I don't want to get all wet. I'm fine watching you guys play."

He glances at my laptop and nods in its direction. "Did you get some writing done?"

"Some." I lie. I couldn't take my eyes off him long enough to concentrate on my words.

"Enough, or do you need to get more work done?" he asks.

There's something about his tone that sends my heart aflutter. There's no judgment or frustration or annoyance. He sounds like he isn't the least bit bothered by the fact that I chose to work while he played volleyball with his siblings.

"Enough, I guess." My answer surprises me. Normally, I'd argue I never write enough, even on the days I crank out five thousand words in a single morning. I'm lucky if I wrote five hundred today.

"Good." He grins, and the dimple beneath his beard makes an appearance. It really is the cutest smile.

He reaches his hand out for mine. I hesitate. My mind is telling me don't do it, but my body betrays me. I lift my hand to his before my words of rejection exit my lips.

I let Heath distract me, and I don't mind one little bit.

We spend the next hour laughing and swimming with his siblings. It's relaxing and refreshing and just may be the most fun I've had in a really long time.

MY EYES FLICKER OPEN, and a heaviness presses down on my waist. I focus on the faint sliver of light peeking through the curtains. For the second night, Heath found his way across the invisible barrier of the bed and wrapped his body around mine.

We've only spent three nights together, and he's failed two out of three to keep to his side. With ten more nights to go, it's not looking good for him.

Although, I can't say I mind. He feels good next to me. Oddly enough, there's nothing sexual about how he spoons me. It's comfortable, secure, safe.

I keep telling myself that he's not spooning me because

he wants this. It's an unconscious action he's making in his sleep because he's an affectionate person. He doesn't really want me. I just happen to be the woman here. He made it clear, he'd likely spoon anyone who happened to get in bed with him whether he liked them or not.

Okay, so he didn't actually say it like that. In fact, he didn't say anything close to resembling that. The problem is I sense he's wanting more from this fake relationship than I do. Either that or he's a great actor.

He hasn't said as much, but his words and affection say this is real to him.

Like yesterday at the beach. After our swim, we ate dinner, then lounged on the beach for a relaxing evening. I took the opportunity to write some more, and Heath didn't mind. In fact, he sat with me under the umbrella reading a book. He listened to my ramblings while writing and even offered input on places where I got stuck. It was sweet and attentive. It was an odd form of comfort that made our relationship feel real.

I don't want real. This seemingly simple reality hops around in my brain for several minutes, and I come up conflicted.

Despite what I tell myself I want, I like this and all the PDA he's shown in the past three days. I like his arms around me. I like it when he holds my hand, hugs me close at my waist, or rests his hand on my knee. I really like it when he kisses me. So soft and gentle. It feels good. It makes me feel wanted, and that's something I've never experienced with a man before.

Needing to change positions, I roll over and face Heath. His arm tightens around my waist, and he drops his head closer to mine. But he doesn't wake up.

He looks so peaceful and unbelievably handsome. His long dark lashes curl more than the average person. It makes me a little jealous. Even with mascara and a lash curler, my lashes don't curl like that. His hard jawline is strong, and I never realized until now how much I love a bearded man. Maybe it's because it looks so good on him, but either way, I love it. I love the way it feels against my skin when he kisses me, and I love the smoothness of it under my hand when I cup his cheek. I can't help but wonder what it would feel like rubbing against other parts of my body.

Oh, God. These are thoughts I have no business thinking. But it's what I do next that really shocks me. I brush my hand down his beard, lean in, and kiss him. It's light and hardly much of a kiss at first, but then he reciprocates. I'm not sure if he's fully awake or simply reacting to my action, but either way, we are kissing, and it feels good.

His fingers dig into my waist and a low groan escapes his lips. I snap my head back and his deep green eyes stare down at me.

"Sorry. I shouldn't have done that," I whisper.

A faint smile tugs at his lips, and he shakes his head. "It's fine. I liked it."

"Regardless, it shouldn't have happened. I apologize." I slip out of his arms and out of the bed. He moans as I make my escape. I hear his arm slap against the bed, but I don't look back. I grab my clothes for the day and head to the bathroom to get ready.

I shut the door and drop against it with a sigh. *Stupid. So stupid.* What was I thinking? I wasn't thinking, that's the problem.

I don't need the complication of a man in my life. My career consumes all my time. There's no room for a man. The last time I made room for a man, he hit me when I refused to change my life for him. I'd do well to remember it.

"YOU EVER BEEN ON a boat before?" Henry, Heath's dad, asks.

"No, sir. This is a first." I look nervously at the large boat rocking against the dock. I've always loved being near the water—summer trips to the Finger Lakes or vacationing on the beach—but boats were never involved.

"Well, you look a little green. Do you get motion sickness?" He looks at me with genuine concern. I feel a little queasy, but I didn't think it showed.

"Not usually, no."

"Uh, remember the Graviton from the fair a few years ago?" Emily asks. "You puked for hours after that."

"Yeah, but that was the Graviton. That thing went round and round and round. I didn't think it'd ever stop. Nothing has made me feel like that."

"Well, either way. You better take these." Elaine hands me a packet of anti-motion sickness tablets.

"Thanks." I punch out a tablet and swallow it.

Heath takes my hand and gives it a squeeze. "We don't have to go if you think you'll get sick. We can hang around town if you prefer."

"No, I wouldn't dream of interfering with your family vacation. I'm sure I'll be fine. Besides, this outing is a family tradition. I can't take that away from you."

"What is it with you and women who get motion sickness?" Henry slaps Heath on the back and chuckles. "Lauren got sick too."

Heath tenses next to me, but he doesn't say anything. I

assume Lauren is Heath's ex, and the reason he doesn't date.

"It's okay, really. I'm just nervous. For all we know, I won't get sick. Best way to find out is to try." I force a smile, and Heath's parents laugh. Emily, Luke, and Dexter are already on the boat making themselves comfortable.

"Well, all right dear." Elaine rubs my shoulder and smiles. "If it gets too bad, you tell us. We can head back early. No need spending the day sick if it can be avoided."

"Thanks, I appreciate that." We all climb into the boat. Heath leads me to an awning in the middle where he says I'm less likely to feel sick. His parents sit behind us where the controls are located, and his siblings are scattered in the front joking and laughing.

"You don't have to sit with me. Please, don't let me keep you from enjoying your vacation."

"Nonsense. I work with those knuckleheads." He wraps his arm around me and pulls me into the nook of his side. That damn annoying flutter returns. "Besides, my time with you is limited. I'd like to enjoy *you* as much as possible."

The way he emphasized *you* makes my insides all tingly. I can't help but sink into him more. "You know, it's a shame you've sworn off women. You're good at this PDA thing. I can't say I've ever experienced this kind of treatment."

He looks down at me with a frown. "What do you

mean?"

"Just that, guys I've dated haven't been like this. Not that I've dated a lot of guys, but the ones I have dated weren't this sweet and affectionate." I lean in close and whisper in his ear. "Is it because this is fake, or are you really always like this?"

"I'm just like this." He leans down and kisses the top of my head. "And for the record, I haven't sworn off women. I just don't want to date any of the women Mom chooses for me." I glance up at him and there is so much want in his expression that I turn away. He clears his throat and continues. "My brothers love to give me shit about the PDA. I'm surprised they haven't said more to me about you. I think they respect you."

"Well, I've known them a long time. They know I'd kick their ass if they pissed me off."

That earns me a laugh, but he sobers quickly and gives me a serious look. "If the guys you've dated haven't been affectionate toward you, then what have they been?"

I turn away and look out over the water. I'm not ashamed of what happened with Jeremy, but it's also not something I like to talk about. While he hurt me, *literally*, it's the lack of trust I have in myself that pains me most.

"Hey." Heath reaches around, cups my chin, and

turns me to face him. "You don't have to tell me if you're not comfortable. I get it."

"It's not that. It's just ..." There's something in his eyes that says I can trust him. I don't want to talk about this, but at the same time, I want to tell him so he understands my hesitation with men. "It's never easy to say. It's been four—no, five years since I left him. It's still hard to say out loud."

Heath's body tenses next to me but his hand against my face remains loose and gentle. "He hurt you?"

"Once." I let out a huff. "After he hit me, I tried to leave, but he stopped me from leaving the apartment. Trent and Emily were expecting me later that night. When I didn't show, Trent came looking for me. Have you met Trent?"

He nods. "He's a good guy."

"Yes, he is." In more ways than Heath could ever understand. I can't imagine my life without Trent. "Anyway, I get so wrapped up in my writing, I lose all sense of time. It's why I'm notorious for being late, but I always show up eventually. After I didn't show, they knew something was wrong. The next morning Trent came to my apartment. When he knocked on my door, Jeremy became convinced I was having an affair with Trent. He started hitting me, telling me he'd never let me go. Trent broke down my door. And, well, let's just say he made certain Jeremy never touched me again. That was my last relationship."

Heath tightens his hold around me, his eyes scanning our surroundings without really looking at anything. I can't decipher the expression on his face. "Where is he now?"

"He served a year. Last I heard, he lives in the Bronx. Thankfully, he's never tried to contact me again."

Heath nods. He doesn't look angry like his brothers did when they found out. He looks concerned, thoughtful. "Not all men hit."

"I know. But after something like that, it's hard to trust myself again. I always thought of myself as a stronger person than that. A better judge of character. I'm not the kind of person who lets someone hit her and get away with it." The words flow out of me. I don't like talking about my doubt in myself. I don't even like thinking about it. But I'm comfortable with Heath. He puts me at ease, and I don't feel the least bit nervous about telling him.

"I don't know how I missed the signs. We fought a lot. Mostly because he hated my career. But we had our fun too. I knew he wasn't the one for me, but I never imagined him hitting me. How could I have dated someone for two years and not know he'd turn on me like that? When it happened, I felt like it was my fault, that I somehow deserved it. I didn't. I know that now. He's the one that's broken. Not me. But I can't shake my doubt in myself."

He cups my cheek and the warmth of his hand on my skin calms me. "You're strong. One asshole doesn't change that. You can't let him stop you from living your life."

"Like how whatever happened with Lauren has stopped you from living yours?" I cringe and squeeze my eyes close. "Sorry. I shouldn't have said that. I don't even know what happened."

When I open my eyes, he's watching me. "You're right to some degree. I lost Lauren a long time ago. I've lived every day since assuming I had my one chance and lost it. Maybe I was wrong."

He kisses me. But this kiss isn't like any other he's given me. Gone is the hunger and desire that has accompanied his other kisses. This kiss is full of compassion and heart.

His mouth moves slowly and deliberately over mine. Like he's trying to take away the memory of what Jeremy did to me with the caressing movement of his lips. He kisses me deeply, like we're the only two people on this boat.

"Ew, gross." Luke yells from the front of the boat. Before either of us can pull away from each other a large beach ball hits Heath in the head. "There are innocent baby eyes on this boat that don't need to see that."

I drop my face to Heath's shoulder, embarrassed that I

let my emotions get away from me. But laughter erupts from his family and more playful jabs are tossed our way.

My gaze finds Emily. She smiles and nods her approval. In fact, she looks downright smug, and I can't help but wonder if setting me up with Heath was her plan all along.

CHAPTER THIRTEEN

Heath

The first week of my family's vacation is already over, and it's time for our traditional gathering of friends. My parents spend weeks, if not months, planning for this one party. It always takes place on the Saturday that marks the midpoint of our vacation in the Hamptons. It's not a black-tie affair, but we do dress up and enjoy a gourmet catered meal with champagne. My parents go all out and skimp on nothing for this one party.

While I told Alicia about this party before we left the city, she still spent all morning fretting over which dress to wear. She brought three, and despite my reassurances that any one of them would be fine, she's been in our bedroom for hours getting ready. Emily even spent half the day with her. While she valued my opinion, she said no one would be more honest than her best friend.

But time is running out, and guests are starting to arrive.

I give a light tap on the door before I crack it open. "Are you dressed?" I ask, waiting for a response before I fully step in.

"Yes," she calls from the open door of the bathroom. "I'll be right out."

I shut the door behind me and lean against it while I wait. "My parents are excited to introduce you to a few of our closest friends. Most of the people here are for show so no need to stress over meeting a bunch of strangers. My parents can't seem to keep the guest list down."

"Still nervous," she says.

"Don't be." I shake my head. If she only knew who these people really were, she'd know she's too good for most, if not all of them. I'm about to tell her just that when she steps out of the bathroom. I push off the door and my jaw drops.

"Wow," I whisper.

She gives me a shy smile, and her cheeks blush. "Do I look all right?"

"All right?" I step forward, take her hands in mine,

and hold them out to her sides. She chose a deep blue dress that enhances her eyes. It's a one-shoulder dress with a wispy skirt that swoops down to her calves. The material hangs in asymmetrical layers with deep slits in the front that stops mid-thigh, providing a peek at her long sexy legs. The neckline is bordered with a thick band of silver sequins that wrap around the shoulder strap and down her back then around her narrow waist. "You're stunning. I won't be able to keep my eyes off you all night."

She left her hair down in big loose curls that drape down her back. Paired with silver high heels and dangling silver hoop earrings, she looks perfect. Better than perfect. She's the most beautiful woman I've ever seen.

"Heath! I'm from Brooklyn. I've never been to a party like this. I feel like I won't fit in." Her voice is shaky, and she's chewing on her bottom lip.

I rub my thumb over her lip, and she lets it go. "You'll mess up your lipstick. Although, I'm likely to do that for you since you look so damn good. I want to kiss you."

A faint smile lifts her lips and her eyes sparkle. "Save that for the party. No need to waste your affection in private."

"Maybe I'd prefer privacy. Skip the party and stay locked away with you all night." I slip my arm around her waist and hold her tight against me. I lean in close to her ear and whisper. "Every man here is going to wish you were by their side, yet I'm the lucky bastard that gets to dance with you. That's how amazing you look tonight."

Her breath catches, and she trembles in my arms. I give her a chaste kiss on the cheek and step back before I lose control. As much as I want to fist my hand in her hair and kiss her senseless, I'll wait. She's gorgeous and spent too much time getting ready. It would be really shitty of me to mess up all her hard work.

I take her hand and lace my fingers with hers. "Ready?"

She nods. We exit the bedroom hand in hand. She lets out a deep breath as we descend the stairs. The main room is packed with guests, and she tightens her grip on my hand. "Just be you, and you'll do great."

She huffs. "So you say."

"How about we start with an easy introduction? A childhood friend of Dexter's that's like a brother to the rest of us." She nods. I lead her over to Evan Brooks who already looks bored and ready to ditch the party. "Evan, where've you been hiding these past few months?"

"Hey, Heath." He leans in for a one arm hug. His smile fades when his eyes focus on Alicia's hand joined with mine.

"I'd like to introduce you to my girlfriend."

"Wait." Evan's eyes shift between us. "You're dating

Alicia? Emily's best friend?"

I chuckle. "Why am I not surprised you two know each other already?"

Alicia pats my chest with a laugh. "Heath, you really should hang out at your own bar a little more often. I see Evan there all the time."

I kiss her on the cheek. "You really should stop teasing me about that. I work all day and am tired by the time the evening crowd comes in."

Evan points his finger back and forth between us. "Does Emily know about this?"

"Of course I do." Emily walks up and loops her arm through Evan's. She presses up on her tip-toes and kisses his cheek. "Who do you think introduced them?"

"Hi, Em. Always the matchmaker." Evan kisses her cheek in return. "You look beautiful as always."

"Thanks." She smiles. "If you thought Heath was stubborn, you should try persuading Alicia sometime. It's damn near impossible to get her to try new things."

"And by new *things*, you mean your oldest brother." Evan raises his brow and stares down at my sister. "There's gotta be a story here."

"Oh, there's a story all right." Alicia laughs. "You'll have to read my next novel to hear about it."

"You're using me in your next novel?"

"Well, for inspiration, yes." She wraps her arms around my waist and giggles. She meant it as an act of playfulness, but her touch sends a rush of heat through me. "Real life experiences make for the best stories."

"But I remember how we met," I deadpan.

"Aw, is big boy Heath scared?" She looks up at me, mischief dancing in her eyes.

"Yeah, a little bit." Her smile grows, and nothing in the world can stop me from kissing her. I don't care who's around or watching. I kiss her. And not a light peck either. A full on, deep passionate kiss, tongue, and all. When I pull away, she's breathless.

When I look up, Evan and Emily are smiling at us. Evan starts to say something when a familiar voice calls my name from behind.

"Heath, there you are dear." I turn to meet Gloria's open arms. She embraces me in a hug and kisses my cheek. Her husband, George, walks up behind her.

"Hi, Gloria." I reach around her after she releases me and shake George's hand. "George." I nod. "It's good to see you both."

"So, it's true." Gloria clasps her hands together and smiles. "Elaine told us you brought a girl, but we didn't believe her. Lauren would be so pleased to see you're finally dating again."

"Yes, it's true. This is Alicia. Alicia, allow me to introduce you to Lauren's parents. Gloria and George."

"Lauren, your ex-girlfriend?" She looks confused.

"Not just girlfriend, dear." Gloria patted Alicia's arm. "Heath and Lauren were engaged."

Alicia glances at me before turning back to Gloria. "I hadn't realized."

"That doesn't surprise me. Heath hates talking about Lauren. Even after all these years. Our Lauren died just a few short months before they were to be married. Lord knows, we all understood his decision not to date again, especially us. Losing Lauren, well, that nearly killed us too. But we found a way to continue. It's so good to see Heath finally has, too. He deserves to be happy."

"I can't even begin to imagine." Alicia leans into me and tightens her hold on my hand. The gesture makes me smile. Not just because I love how she feels next to me, but because she understands my pain and struggle over losing Lauren.

"Come on, darling." George wraps his arm around Gloria and tugs her along. "Let these two get back to enjoying their evening. It was nice meeting you, Alicia."

George leads his wife away, leaving me alone with Alicia. When I glance down at her, she's smiling at me.

"Care to dance?" she asks and points toward the ballroom where soft music is playing. "I can't believe your parent's house has a ballroom. You know this isn't normal, right?"

"Yes, I know." I chuckle. "And yes. I'd love nothing more than to dance with you."

I lead her onto the dance floor. With one hand in hers, I slip my other around her waist. She places her free hand on my shoulder and leans into me.

She looks up at me, her eyes glistening. "Sorry about Lauren. I wouldn't have said anything had I known."

"No need to apologize. It was ten years ago. It actually feels like another lifetime."

"Still, that couldn't have been easy." She looks nervous, her eyes shifting toward the floor. "May I ask how she died?"

"Cancer. We found out six months before our wedding. It had progressed too far by the time we found out. There wasn't anything the doctors could do to save her. She died three months later."

"And you haven't ..." Her voice cracks and she pauses, taking a deep breath. "You haven't dated anyone since?"

"No, but not for the reason you may think." I squeeze

her hand close to my chest and hold her tight. "I loved Lauren very much. We had a once in a lifetime kind of love, but I no longer feel broken without her. Despite what my family thinks, I'm not still heartbroken. I've moved past the loss. She's not why I haven't dated anyone."

Alicia's face is close to mine. She leans in until we're cheek to cheek. "Then why?"

"I haven't met anyone since her that made me think it was possible to love like that again. I mean, why date when I already know the person isn't the *one* because I already had the *one* and lost her? I had my chance at love, and she died."

Alicia stiffens in my arms, and she lifts her face from mine so she can look into my eyes. The words I spoke were clipped and therefore too harsh. There's so much more I want to say to her right now. But if I tell her what I really think before she's ready to hear it, I could push her away. Hell, for all I know, she'll never be ready. So, I don't say what I'm thinking.

Instead, I add, "But maybe I was wrong. Maybe there isn't just *one* love out there for each of us. Maybe we can have a second chance at love as long as we open our hearts to the possibility."

"Maybe." Her shoulders relax slightly, and her smile is soft, but there's a sadness in her eyes that I don't like. Then she surprises me and kisses me. It's sweet and sensual, and it's the first time she's kissed me besides that morning she thought I was sleeping. I've initiated and taken every kiss up to this point, and the level of excitement I feel from her lead overwhelms me.

When she breaks the kiss, she rests her cheek against my chest. I rest my head on hers and hold her tight. It's a touch and closeness that feels so much more intimate than a simple dance.

In this moment, Alicia is *mine*, and mine alone. There may be several other couples dancing around the room with us, but I only feel us. I'm very quickly moving past the wanting her stage, and squarely landing in the middle of need. Reminding myself that this woman is not for me is becoming more and more of a challenge. No matter how much I might want or need her to be mine, she isn't.

What would she do if I told her how I really feel? Would she run? Stay? Tell me she feels this *thing* building between us too? Because I want to tell her that I haven't met anyone that made me think it was possible to love like that again. *Until you.*

CHAPTER FOURTEEN

Alicia

By midnight, most of the guests have left, but there's still a surprising number hanging around drinking late into the night—including Heath's parents. I don't know how they still have so much energy. I've been fighting off the yawns for over an hour and trying my best to hide it, but Heath eyes me and smiles.

"Are you ready to call it a night?" he asks.

"I am." I cover my yawn with my hand. "I don't know why I'm so tired."

"It's been a long day." He takes the drink I'd been nursing the latter half the evening and sits it on a side table. "Come on, let's get you tucked in bed."

"You don't have to go. Stay. Enjoy the remaining guests."

"Not a chance." He plants a chaste kiss on my lips. "Plus, we have appearances to uphold. What would my parents think if I sent my girlfriend to bed alone?"

"Are you using me as an excuse to leave the party early?" I tease.

"Maybe." He kisses me again with a grin. "Let's go."

Heath nods his goodbyes to a few of the guests as I let him lead me away from the party and up the stairs. When we reach his bedroom, he holds the door open for me. I head straight for the chair to rid myself of these heels.

I can't remember the last time I wore heels this long, and my feet are screaming at me. I don't think we sat in one place for longer than thirty minutes all night. We danced, we talked, Heath introduced me to more people than I'll ever remember, and he never left my side once.

"Do you mind if I take the bathroom first?" I stand, my feet feeling so much better, and head to the bathroom.

I don't make it two feet before Heath grabs hold of my arm, twirls me around, and tugs me close to him. His arm is around my waist and his other hand cups my cheek. Before I can catch my breath, his lips crash into mine. Hot, hard, passionate. His mouth covers mine hungrily and when his teeth nibble at my bottom lip, I melt into him.

His kiss consumes me. My head spins, and a spark ignites inside me that burns every inch of my body. As quickly as his mouth claims me, he's gone. I open my eyes to find he's staring at me with a fierce, burning desire.

"What was that for?" The words barely come out. My heart is pounding, and my lungs struggle for air.

"I like kissing you." His voice is deep, husky, and full of need. "And it just felt ... right."

"Okay." I suck my bottom lip between my teeth. He growls before he kisses me again. This time with a hunger and desire so intense I feel it in my bones.

His large hands slip around my neck and the warmth of his touch sends a delicious shudder through me. A hot ache grows between my legs as his lips trail around my chin and down my neck. The way his beard brushes against my tender skin is electrifying. It's prickly and yet somehow soft as silk as his lips glide down my bare shoulder to the neckline of my dress.

His hands drift down my arms then slip around my ribcage before pressing up on my breasts. When his thumbs swirl around my nipples, I gasp.

"Heath, please," I manage to say between breaths.

He pulls back. A rush of cold air engulfs me at the loss

of his body. He runs his hands through his hair with a pained look on his face. "I'm sorry. Tell me to stop, and I will."

I shake my head and reach for him. My fingers loop into the waistband of his pants, and I pull him back to me. "Don't stop. I need more of you."

"Good," he shudders, "because I need all of you." His mouth is hot and demanding against mine, and I can't get enough. I pull at his tie and loosen it from his neck. Once it's out of the way, I fumble with his shirt buttons. He releases me long enough to strip off his shirt. Then his hands and mouth are on me again. And damn, does he know what to do with both.

His fingers find the zipper to my dress. He pulls it down then pauses again. "You sure about this?"

"Yes," I say a little too eagerly. I can't remember the last time I wanted someone this much. Hell, I don't think I ever wanted someone as much as I want Heath right now. "Fuck me. Please."

He smiles against my lips. "Like one of your book boyfriends?"

"Oh, God." I moan at the thought.

His smile turns to a chuckle. "So, that's three orgasms then."

I laugh. "If you think you've got it in you, yes."

"I'm certainly willing to try." He backs me up against the wall and drops to his knees. His hands slip up the skirt of my dress, brushing lightly against my skin, and I shiver. The lightness of his touch is tantalizing and arousing. He loops his fingers around my panties and pulls them down slowly. His hands move back up my legs, his mouth trailing close behind. I tremble as his mouth gets closer to my center. I brace myself by resting my hands on his shoulders. The anticipation building inside me is intense as his lips and tongue tease me by kissing, licking, and nipping me everywhere except where I want it most.

His hands inch further up my body, taking my dress with them. When his hands reach my breasts, he cups them with a hard squeeze and pushes to his feet. He strips my dress over my head, leaving me completely bare before him.

I squirm and gasp as his mouth, his tongue, and his breath marks every inch of me as he works his way back down my body, claiming me in the most delicious way. His fingers slip between my legs, and he groans. "Fuck, you're wet. And you taste and smell so sweet. I can't get enough of you."

His mouth clamps down on my breast, and he bites my beaded nipple, eliciting a moan.

"You like?" he asks as he slides a finger inside me and

swirls his tongue around my tender skin.

"Yes. More." He alternates between sucking and tugging my nipples with his teeth, and it feels so damn good. It's intense and erotic and the best kind of pain I've ever felt. His thumb finds my clit. He presses and swirls around the bundle of nerves while pumping his fingers inside me. My legs tremble as my excitement builds and I begin to lose control. He just started touching me, and I'm so close to coming undone for him.

"Come for me, beautiful. Let me feel you squeeze around my fingers."

And I do. My body comes at his command like I'm programmed to obey.

He drops to his knees again, lifts one of my legs over his shoulder. His mouth is on me before my body has a chance to come down from my orgasm. He licks me and sucks on my clit, making me cry out.

"So sweet and beautiful," he whispers against me before he slides his tongue inside me. I tremble and struggle to keep myself upright as he works me over again and again. I'm so sensitive from my first release that his tongue, lips, and beard are almost too much. It's sensory overload, and I'm about to lose complete control.

I buckle over and clench my fingers in his hair for

support. He must sense my weakness because he wraps his arms around me and braces my body between him and the wall. But he doesn't slow his attack on me. If anything, he comes at me harder and faster and with such fervor, it's like he's been starving for days, and I'm the only sustenance that can satiate his hunger.

Oh. My. Fucking. God. I'm coming again!

I'm delirious and dizzy and completely lost in this man. He stays with me—licking and sucking—until I still. He slowly slides my leg off his shoulder and kisses his way up my body until he's standing and staring down at me. He lifts me into his arms and carries me to the bed.

I've never been more satisfied by a man.

And we're just getting started.

CHAPTER FIFTEEN

Heath

There has never been a more sensual woman in my bed. I slowly lay Alicia down before me and step back to admire her naked form. Soft curves, perfect creamy skin, plump breasts, and sexy long legs that I can't wait to feel wrapped tight around me.

I kick off my shoes and strip off my pants, releasing my aching cock. I've walked around all evening half-hard for this woman. Now that she's naked in my bed, my cock is rock hard for her.

Lifting her leg, I kiss a trail of open mouth, wet kisses up her leg and to her flat stomach. She sucks in a breath as I lick circles around her navel.

The graceful lines of her feminine curves draw me up, and I take a breast into my mouth. My cock thickens as I settle between her thighs, and her nipple pebbles in my mouth like a ripe raspberry, sweet and luscious.

"Heath, please." I pop her breast from my mouth and tip her face toward mine and kiss her, slowly increasing the pressure until she parts her lips and lets me in. She tastes like champagne and chocolate and sin.

She moans as the hardness of my arousal presses against her. She arches her back and her breasts flatten against my chest. Her pebbled nipples tangle with my chest hair, and I struggle to restrain from slamming inside her. I fight the need to feel her come around me, trying to make this last. She's like a sorceress who's lured me in with her seductive body and sweet fragrance.

She's exquisite and mesmerizing and intoxicating.

I find the sensitive spot below her ear, kissing and nibbling, taking little morsels of her skin into my mouth as I lightly suck. She smells like lavender and vanilla. She tastes sweeter than any dessert I've ever eaten.

When she makes little humming noises, I can't resist sucking on her neck until she squirms beneath me. Her moans and gasps of pleasure propel me with each suck and bite I take. It's beautiful and alluring and hot the way her body answers mine.

"I need you inside me. *Now*." She grasps at my shoulders and digs her nails into my skin.

"Soon, beautiful. Soon." I exhale forcefully, trying to rain in the rampant hunger threatening to overtake me. I need to take this slow, or else this won't last long. I owe her at least one more orgasm.

I reach for the bedside table and fish a condom out of the drawer, grateful I brought them with me at the last minute. She watches me with a heated gaze as I grasp my cock and give it a pull. I'm so hard for her, it hurts. If I don't calm down and give myself a little relief, I'll come as soon as I enter her.

I push up on my knees and tower over her. She watches me as I stroke my cock before I slide on the condom.

Summoning the willpower to pace myself, I lower my body over hers and brace myself with my elbows. Her body is so soft and pliant beneath me. The mere anticipation of what I'm about to do makes me harder. I cradle her face with my hands, and she lifts her lips to kiss me. It's soft and sensual, and in this moment, she makes me believe she's mine.

My jaw clenches as my tip nudges into her. I still as emotion and strife wash over me. It's been too long since

I've been with a woman like this. I focus on the moment, the pleasure, and how fucking amazing she feels as I slide inside her.

She lifts her hips and takes me deep. I feel every one of her muscles contract around me as her body adjusts to my presence and then accepts all of me. Our fit is so perfect, that when our bodies lock into place, it's like we're two puzzle pieces joining together.

"So good," she breathes, her voice raspy. "More. I need more."

I move, slow and languid at first. As her body awakens, I pick up the pace. Her breath quickens and comes in fast, furious gasps as she clings to me. As her body writhes and twists, I can tell she's getting close to another release. This woman is so responsive to me, book boyfriend be damned, I'm making this woman come again or else die trying.

We devour each other in a frenzied heat of passion and desire. She rocks her pelvis and grinds her hips against me as I quicken the pace. She tightens around me and squeezes her eyes closed. "Look at me, beautiful. I want to watch you come this time."

She obeys. Her eyes lock with mine, and I'm lost to her heat. One more deep thrust is all it takes, and she falls apart, squeezing me and pulling me over the edge with her. Her heat coils tighter and tighter around me until nothing could stop me from coming with her.

I kiss her hard, swallowing our cries of pleasure. Like a man possessed, I drive into her, wringing out every last drop of our release. Her arms and legs tighten around me, and our bodies fuse together. We never break eye contact, and a sexual experience has never felt so personal in all my life.

I lift my body off her and roll onto my back. We're both struggling to catch our breath as we come down from this euphoric moment.

I slip out of bed and into the bathroom to dispose of the condom. When I return, she's laying in the middle of the bed with a sated grin.

She glances at me and shakes her head. "Oh, my God. What was that?"

I chuckle as I slip into the bed next to her and pull the covers over our naked bodies. "I believe that was the third orgasm you demanded."

She huffs. "I didn't demand it."

I raise my brows. "Challenged?"

"Yeah, maybe." She laughs and curls into my side. She drapes an arm over my chest with a wide smile. "And you certainly delivered."

"I aim to please." I kiss the top of her head and hug her

tight. This feels good. Too good. Like home and everything I've ever wanted with a woman. *I am so screwed.*

"I want to do it again," she says as she kisses my neck.

"Fuck, woman. I thought you were tired?"

"I was, but someone woke me up. Now I want more." She rolls over on top me and wraps her soft hands around my cock, and fuck if I don't get hard again. "But this time I want to ride you until we're both so worked up, we're about to explode, and then I want you to fuck me from behind."

"Whatever you want, beautiful." And that's exactly what we do. Only this time it's slower, and I last for what feels like an eternity. An eternity with my cock buried inside her is a wonderful place to be. Even more amazing is watching her come undone for a fourth time while she takes control of her pleasure riding me. The look on her face when she comes around my cock is a beautiful sight. It's one I hope to see again before this arrangement of ours is over.

WHEN I WAKE, ALICIA'S nuzzled up next to me with her arm sprawled over my chest and her legs tangled with mine. It's heaven.

I've woken up with her in my arms for the past few mornings, but this morning is different. This time she came to me. She's wrapped around me by choice, and my heart squeezes.

Her soft breath brushes across my chest as I shift my body out from under her. She lets out a low hum, but she doesn't wake.

I stare at her for a moment, in awe that she gave so much to me last night. I never expected this to happen between us. Not when we struck the deal to pretend to date each other, nor when I kissed her last night. The kiss was inevitable. The entire week had been leading up to it, but what came after surprised me. Even with our undeniable chemistry, I didn't expect her to give all of herself to me. Not yet at least. I just hope last night leads to more than one night of intense passion.

I grab a change of clothes and head to the bathroom. She looks so peaceful. I decide to let her sleep as long as she needs. We had a late night together. I should probably stay in bed too, but I'm already up, and sleep will not return with all the memories from last night running through my mind.

Fifteen minutes later, I exit the bathroom freshly showered and dressed for the day. Alicia is still sleeping, so I quietly leave and head downstairs.

Mom is in the kitchen with a pot of coffee brewing and breakfast underway. I kiss her on the cheek, and she smiles.

"Morning, Mom."

"Good morning. You're up early." She hands me two mugs. "Coffee should be ready. Pour me one too?"

I take the mugs and nod. "You know me. I never sleep in late."

"I know. But I thought maybe after last night you'd find a reason to sleep in." Mom doesn't look up at me as she speaks. She keeps her eyes focused on the bowl of batter in front of her.

"What's that supposed to mean?" I know exactly what she means, but I want to hear how far she takes her meddling.

"Everyone loved Alicia." Mom cracks an egg and adds it to the bowl. "And it looked like you two were getting along so well."

"We were." I keep my voice low and even.

I hand her a filled mug, and she takes it from me with a smile. Mom is always all smiles. "Thank you, dear."

She takes a sip and gets back to mixing the batter.

"Is there more you want to say?" I ask.

"No. Well ..." She looks at me with a knowing gaze. Like she knows some big secret that I'm not privy to and for a moment I think she knows my relationship with Alicia is fake. But then she continues. "It's just, we really like Alicia. We think she's good for you. She's different from Lauren.

Don't get me wrong, we loved Lauren, but Alicia challenges you in a way Lauren didn't. I can tell you really like her, but if you're not attentive to her needs, she might not stick around."

I raise my brows and frown. "Attentive to her needs?"

"You know what I mean." Mom huffs and glares at me. "You should still be in bed with that girl making her feel special, not down here drinking coffee with your mother."

I drop my head into my hand and rub my eyes. I can't believe I'm having this conversation with my mom. Is she insinuating I don't know how to take care of a woman? If she only knew.

I reach for Mom and pull her into a hug. "I don't know what you're trying to say, Mom. But I can assure you, everything with Alicia is fine. I'm letting her sleep in because she needs the rest."

I kiss the top of her head and swallow the lie like the rock that it is. It scratches and burns as it tumbles down my throat and settles in my stomach with a thump. Things are far from fine with Alicia. They're more complicated than they've ever been, and I have no idea how I'm going to say goodbye to her when our arrangement ends. Not only are my feelings at stake, but so are those of my family.

CHAPTER SIXTEEN

Alicia

The house is quiet as I make my way downstairs. I slept later than I would've liked. I don't know what time Heath got up, but I was more than a little disappointed when I rolled over and found his side of the bed cold. I would've rather woken up to a repeat of last night than an empty bed and a lonely shower.

It's almost 10:00 am when I walk into the kitchen. Elaine is the only person around and she's stacking a few waffles on a plate. "Did I miss breakfast?"

"Well, good morning, dear." She turns to me with a huge smile. "Not at all. We haven't eaten yet. I just started a few of these for Henry and Heath. They should be back in a moment, and everyone else is still asleep."

"Oh, good. I was afraid I slept the morning away and missed breakfast. I don't usually sleep this late." Which is true. Being an early morning riser is one of the few things Heath and I seem to have in common. That and the amazing chemistry we have between the sheets.

"Not in this house." Elaine chuckles. "Henry and Heath are my only early risers. And you, of course. Emily might be up soon, but I wouldn't expect to see Luke or Dexter for another couple hours. I think they were the last ones standing at the end of the party."

"What's that about me?" Dexter comes scooting into the kitchen still in his pajamas and house slippers. He leans down and kisses his mom on the cheek before he grabs a mug from the cabinet. "Morning, Alicia, Mom."

"Well, if this isn't a shock. You're never up this early." Elaine huffs with her hands on her hips.

"Gotta keep you on your toes, Mom." He pours a cup of coffee then turns and hands it to me with a neutral expression. "Here, I think you might need this more than me considering how late my brother kept you up last night."

He winks as my mouth drops open and my face heats. I take the coffee and drop my head to hide the deep shade of red that has to have taken over my face. "Thanks."

"No problem." I glance up to see a huge, knowing—and might I add atypical—grin on his face. Heath and I were so absorbed in the moment last night that neither of us considered how loud we were. When I look over at Elaine, she's busy pulling plates out of the cabinet. If she heard what Dexter said, she's not letting on.

Dexter grabs another mug and pours himself a cup of coffee. "How long until breakfast is ready?"

"Give me ten or fifteen minutes." Elaine grabs a bowl of batter out of the refrigerator and reheats the waffle iron. "I would have prepared more had I known you'd be up so early."

"Where's Dad and Heath? 'Cause I know they're up," Dexter says.

"In the garage. Your dad wanted to show him the old car he bought. Heath hasn't seen it yet."

Dexter nods as if that's the most natural answer. He picks up the coffee pot and asks, "Do you want any more coffee, Mom? We're gonna need another pot."

"No, I've had more than enough," she says.

"I'll take more," Heath says from the doorway. He sits his mug on the island counter then slides his arm around my waist and kisses me on the cheek. "Morning, beautiful."

"Morning." I see Dexter grin out of the corner of my

eye and feel my cheeks blush even more.

Heath leans in close to my ear and whispers, "You looked so peaceful sleeping in my arms this morning. I couldn't bring myself to wake you, even though I desperately wanted to."

I turn to look at him and his lips are there waiting for mine. He kisses me. Tender and deep. There's something different about this kiss. It takes me a few moments before I realize what that is.

This one isn't fake.

It means something, and that scares the hell out of me. My insides tingle and my heart rate kicks up several notches. I feel foggy. Yet at the same time a million thoughts are swirling around in my brain, and I can't seem to focus on any one of them. This has gone too far. I need to stop it before one of us gets hurt, but I can't stop kissing him. He feels too good, and my traitorous body melts into him.

"Hey, lover boy!" Emily slaps Heath on the shoulder, and I jerk back in surprise. She leans on the counter next to me and tosses us a teasing grin. "Do you think you can stop kissing my best friend for one day so I can steal her?"

"Oh, I think I can manage," Heath says without taking his eyes off me. "We haven't made any plans for the day."

"Good. 'Cause I'm in desperate need of some girl time."

She loops her arm through mine and tugs me close. "Let's go shopping, then grab a late lunch."

"Sure, I'd love to. It feels like ages since we've done anything like that."

"Yay!" Emily claps like a little girl who's been given a treat for good behavior.

"All right, everyone." Elaine interrupts. "Head to the dining room. Breakfast is served."

WE'RE AT A LITTLE dress boutique not far from Emily's parents' house looking for something fun to wear for the bar crawl on Wednesday night. Every year toward the end of the vacation, the adult children of her parents' friends all gather for a bar crawl. Emily goes out with the girls, and her brothers go out with the guys. They move from bar to bar until they eventually meet up.

"Is there ever a year where you guys don't find each other?" I ask.

"Not yet. There are only six bars, so it doesn't take long for us to reunite. It usually happens by bar three. There was one year we didn't meet up until bar five, but that's unusual."

I nod and continue flipping through the racks. I can feel Emily's eyes on me from the next rack over, but I avoid looking her way. It's been over an hour since we left, and she hasn't said anything to me about Heath, but I know she wants to. I always tell her about the guys I go out with but talking to her about Heath doesn't feel right. Besides, I'm not really dating him. We're fake dating.

"All right, spill," Emily says from right next to me. I'm so focused on ignoring her that I jump when she finally speaks.

I turn my back to her and flip past the dresses in front of me, but I don't really see any of them. "Spill what?"

She grabs hold of my shoulders and spins me around. "Don't act dumb with me. I'm at a distinct advantage here. I know you better than anyone, and I know my brother. You two have progressed so far beyond fake dating. Tell me everything."

I shrug her off and look away. "I'm not talking to you about your brother. It's too weird."

"Oh, my God." Emily clasps her hands over her mouth. "I knew it! You had sex with him."

"No... I... I can't... Ugh." I drop my head into my hands and groan. Emily knows about every guy I've ever been with, but I can't talk to her about Heath. I just can't.

She gasps. When I look up at her, a slow smile forms on her face. "You like him. Like, really like him."

"No. It's not like that."

"Then how is it?"

"You know." I step away from her, anxious to put some distance between us. "You're the one who set this whole thing up."

She follows me around the rack and leans in close to me. "Yeah, I know what I set you two up to do, but something tells me that's changed."

"Nothing has changed. We're just making it look real for your parents."

"You don't have to have sex with him to make your relationship look real."

"I didn't say I had sex with him."

"You don't have to say it. You had sex with Heath."

"Em, stop!" I stomp my foot, and she flinches. I'm not ready to talk about this, and it has little to do with the fact that Heath is her brother. I don't know how I feel about what happened last night. It was so real and fantastic, and if I walk away from him after that, it might hurt everyone involved.

Emily reaches for my arm and gives it a gentle rub. Either she senses my internal struggle, or she simply decides on a softer approach. "Alicia, it's okay. To be honest, I hoped that you two would like each other. And maybe even decide to date for real."

"I'm not going to date Heath." The words fly out so fast, they're out before I can stop myself from speaking. Now that I've said the words, I feel sick to my stomach. They feel like the biggest lie I've ever told.

"Why does it have to end? No one said you weren't allowed to like him."

I bury my face in my hands to muffle my groan. I want to scream and cry but I don't. Instead I look at Emily and take a deep breath. "It's not that. Heath is a very nice guy. But we're too different. He's a family man and wants a normal schedule. He works normal hours. My career is unconventional and doesn't lend itself to that kind of lifestyle. In the long run, it would never work out."

Emily gives me a sad look and pulls me into a hug. "Heath is not Jeremy."

I sag into her hug and sigh. "I'm not trying to suggest that he is, but it wouldn't work between us. We're too different."

"But you'd like it to work, wouldn't you?"

I pull out of her hug and cross my arms over my chest. "Will you stop? I'm sure Heath will make some woman really happy someday, but that woman is not me."

"Why not?"

"Ugh. Why won't anyone listen to me? I've told you I

just want to focus on my career. I don't need or want a man in my life right now. There's time for a man later." The words spill out of me like vomit and with every word I feel worse. Because she's right. I do like Heath, way more than I should. But there's no way a man like him would be okay with my career schedule. My fans have come to expect a new book from me at least every two months. I can't let them down. This would drive a wedge between us and destroy whatever good we share now.

Emily wags her finger at me and chuckles. "Sorry to inform you, but you can't control the timing of love."

"Love?" My jaw drops. "Have you lost your mind? There's no love going on between Heath and me."

"Whatever you say, Alicia."

Emily spins around and browses the racks in the next aisle over. She's humming to the background music and looks like she doesn't have a care in this world. Apparently, nothing I said phased her. I grab a couple dresses off the rack next me and head to the fitting room. I need a distraction. While trying on dresses won't be enough, it's all I've got.

One more week, then I go home. All I have to do between now and then is make sure we stick to the plan.

CHAPTER
SEVENTEEN

Heath

The annual bar crawl is the one night I'm guaranteed quality time with my brothers. With working different shifts at the bar, it's hard for us to find the time to just hang out.

This is also the only night during our family vacation that it's just us guys. Evan always joins us too. He's practically like a brother anyway, and I can't remember a family vacation without him around.

Others do the bar crawl as well, but they don't stick with us and usually end up doing their own things. It's more about the annual tradition than it is about staying together the whole night. At least until the guys meet up with the girls.

We've been out for about an hour, and we're at our second bar. I'm still waiting for my brothers to give me a hard time about Alicia, but so far, they haven't said a word. I'm ninety-nine percent positive they suspect Alicia and I slept together. The other morning at breakfast, Dexter certainly acted as if he knew something happened between us.

When they ask me if I've slept with her—and they will undoubtedly ask—I don't know what I'll say. I've never been one to talk about the women I date but I've also never dated someone my brothers knew better than I did. I get the sense they'd step in and protect her, even from me, if they had to.

Alicia and I have had sex every night since Saturday. I wasn't sure what to expect from her when we went to bed on Sunday. We were both nervous when we stood on opposite ends of the bed from each other. Neither of us knew what the other was thinking after the night we shared. But then she stripped, baring herself to me. We didn't need words to know what was happening next.

We've fucked like our lives depended upon it every night, but we haven't talked about what happens when we get back to the city. I want to keep seeing her, but I'm not convinced she feels the same way. I don't want to scare her, but at some point, this conversation has to happen.

I've been out of the dating scene for so long that I have no clue how to start that conversation. It's been weighing on my mind for days. Every time I think I know what to say to her, I freeze up. At least hanging with my brothers for a night is a good distraction.

Like how Dexter is harassing Luke about his latest conquest. Luke was never one to date anyone seriously. He's the player of the three of us. He's more outgoing, charming, and flirtatious than Dexter and me. We're the quiet, brooding type until we get to know someone. Luke sees women in the moment and never thinks of them as long-term girlfriends or marriage material. If there's one of us that never gets married, it'll be Luke. I'll be shocked if a woman ever manages to tie him down.

"Are you really going to do that dance competition?" Dexter asks.

"Did Stephanie or Kate tell you about that?" Luke practically snarls. Stephanie and Kate are two regulars at the bar. Ever since they found love, they've been determined to set Luke up.

Dexter snorts. "Stephanie was in the other night and said you agreed to enter. How did she get you to agree to that?"

"I never agreed to it. They're just trying to sucker me

into dating their friend."

"Wait, what did I miss?" Evan slides back in his stool. "I go to the bathroom for five minutes, and Luke's got a date."

Luke glares at the three of us over the rim of his mug. "I don't have a date."

"Whatever." Dexter finishes his beer and waves at the waitress for another round. "If she's not a date, then what is she?"

"I don't know." Luke sighs. "Apparently, one of Stephanie's former co-workers needs a dance partner. I haven't met her yet. They want to bring her in sometime in the next month so we can meet. They seem to think we'll hit it off. Whatever that means."

We're all struggling to keep from laughing. Luke always gets grouchy when he thinks he's being set up. I'd say it's a safe bet Stephanie and Kate are setting him up.

"Or maybe they just want to see their favorite bartender settle down with a nice girl." Dexter jokes.

"Ain't ever gonna happen." Luke shakes his head. His knuckles are turning white from how tightly he's clenching his mug.

I slap him on the back as I lean back in my chair. "One of these days, a nice girl is going to come along and teach you a lesson."

He narrows his eyes on me and smirks. "Like Alicia's teaching you a lesson."

"Hey, we're talking about you, not me."

"Not anymore." Luke's frown is gone, and his face is all smiles. "So, tell us, big brother, what's it like shagging a romance author?"

And just like that, the table turns. I'm surprised it took this long for one of them to say something. "I wouldn't know."

Luke points at me with a determined look. "You've been sleeping with her for the past week. There's no way you've managed that long without banging each other."

I shake my head and avoid looking at any of their faces. I've never been good at lying. "Just because we're sleeping in the same bedroom doesn't mean I've actually had sex with her."

Dexter snorts. "You seem to forget you two were pretty loud the night of the party. And you haven't exactly been quiet since then either."

"I don't know what you think you heard, but you've apparently let your imagination run wild."

"We share a bedroom wall," Dexter deadpans. I glance up at him, and there's no doubt he knows the truth.

"I'm not talking to you guys about this. Let it go." I tilt

my head down and glare at Dexter through raised lids. He knows not to push these topics with me. I'm surprised he's said as much as he has.

"Fine," Dexter says. The waitress arrives with our next round and Dexter helps her pass them around the table. Once she's gone, and we all have a new beer, Dexter pins me with a stare. "We'll let the sex go. But we're not done talking about you and Alicia. We like her. She's cool, and you two seem to be getting along."

I rub my eyes, already exhausted with this conversation. If I knew what Alicia was thinking, I'd be more comfortable talking about this. But for all I know, my feelings are one-sided. "Yeah, she's funny, kind, and has a great personality. It makes *pretending* to date her so much easier."

"Wait." Evan's head shoots up, and he stares at me. "You're pretending to date her?"

"Yeah, it's not a real relationship." Saying the words leaves a sour taste in my mouth and a sick feeling in my gut. "We both needed dates to get our moms off our backs."

"That explains why Emily's okay with this," Evan says.

"It was Emily's idea." Luke adds.

"Don't say anything. We're doing this for Mom's benefit. If she finds out this isn't real, she'll never forgive me."

Luke drops his hand to the table with a thud, his eyes

wide. "Mom's benefit, my ass. We're doing this for you."

I raise my hands in defeat. "Whatever saves me from having to go out with Tiffany."

"No, man. You don't get it." Luke leans across the table, his gaze hard and determined. "The second Emily brought it up, we knew it was the right move for you. You and Alicia are perfect for each other. We can all see how much you like her."

I take a deep breath and let it out slowly. There's no use trying to deny the truth to my brothers. They can see through my lies better than I can see through them myself sometimes. Even Evan can recognize my bullshit from a mile away. "I do like her. But it's complicated."

Evan shrugs. "What's so complicated about liking someone? When you like a girl, you tell her."

"Oh, yeah. And how's your love life?" I ask. Evan's dated a few women over the years, but he's never had a long-term girlfriend. And I'm pretty sure I know the reason why.

"Just because I haven't found the girl for me, doesn't mean I'm not right. When I do find her, I sure as hell hope I'm not a chicken shit like you. Just tell her how you feel."

I hold my gaze on Evan's, wanting to challenge him. I'm pretty sure he's been secretly in love with the same woman for years and hasn't said a thing. But that doesn't change the truth behind his words. If I don't tell Alicia how I feel, then I'll lose any chance I could have to win her heart. She'll never make the first move. Hell, she may freak out when I tell her. "Even if it were that simple, she's not looking for a boyfriend right now."

Evan huffs and raises his beer. "Sounds to me like you need to work harder to change her mind."

Luke and Dexter raise their mugs to Evan's and they all cheer to his declaration. He's not wrong, but this is new territory for me, and I've no clue how to proceed. I haven't even considered dating anyone in ten years.

My phone pings, saving me from responding. I pull it out of my pocket, and my distraction is enough to make them move on to another topic of conversation. Alicia's name pops up on the screen and I smile.

Alicia: How in the hell do you put up with these women?

Me: Thought you and Emily were best friends?

Alicia: {Rolling eye emoji} Not talking about Emily. These other women are crazy.

Me: I take it you've met the reason I needed a fake girlfriend.

Alicia: No wonder you came looking for me.

Me: {Smiley face emoji} Quoting Pretty Woman?
Alicia: It's very fitting for this situation. {Kissing face emoji}

I laugh because she's right. That's exactly why I went looking for her. Well, not exactly looking. But it is why I agreed to this charade. The women Mom wants to set me up with are horrible, stuck-up women who I can't stand to be around. All any of them want is to marry a wealthy man, so they can continue to live a life of luxury. A good-looking, wealthy man is a bonus, but good looks are not required.

Tiffany is the worst. She's had her sights on me since she was in high school. She's the same age as Luke, and I tried to pawn her off on him, but she wanted the eldest son. She thinks it's more prestigious to marry the eldest. Little does she know, age in my family means nothing. My parents treat us all equally, and I won't inherit more than my siblings just because I'm the first born.

Thoughts of Tiffany talking down to Alicia fill my mind and I'm suddenly angry and anxious to find her.

Me: Where are you?
Alicia: Rusty Nail, I think.
Me: We left there about 30 minutes ago.

Alicia: Must have just missed you. {Frowning face emoji} We arrived about 20 minutes ago. With this crowd, I'm ready to go home and call it a night.

Me: You can't call it a night. We haven't found you yet.

Alicia: Well, I guess you better hurry up and find me soon. {Heart eyes emoji} Maybe you'll get lucky.

I laugh, and my dick twitches at the idea of sneaking off with Alicia and doing naughty things in some dark corner. I'm about to text her back when Dexter nudges my arm. "What are you laughing at?" he asks.

I look up at my brother and smile. "Alicia's met some of the girls Mom wanted me to date. She's not enjoying their company. Says she's ready to go home and call it a night."

"Oh, God," Luke whines. "Please tell me Tiffany's not there."

We all laugh because none of us can stand Tiffany. "I'm sure she is, but Alicia didn't give me any names."

Evan sits up straight and takes a sip of his beer. "Ask her which bar they're going to next. We'll meet them."

Me: Evan wants to know what bar you're going to next.

Alicia: Emily says yay. Meet us at High Tops.
Me: We'll head there next.
Alicia: Looking forward to it. {Winking smile emoji}

"Well what'd she say?" Luke asks, his question a little too eager.

I raise my brow. "High Tops."

"Cool. Maybe there'll be somebody new in the group that I can stand to be around for one night."

Evan gives Luke a light punch in his upper arm. "Stop thinking with your dick."

"But I like thinking with my dick." He waggles his brows and downs the rest of his beer. "Drink up, boys. We've got girls waiting for us."

"You're such a pig." Dexter shakes his head and takes a slow drink of his beer just to irritate Luke.

"Yep. Now drink that beer before I make you wear it."

Luke reaches across the table and swats at Dexter's arm. His beer slashes over the rim and down his hand. Dexter sets his mug on the table and flicks his wet hand at Luke. They go back and forth with this playful banter several times. Watching them relax and pick on each is refreshing.

I'm getting a taste of what I'm missing by not hanging

out at The Rock Room after my shift. Maybe it's time I change that for more than one reason.

CHAPTER EIGHTEEN

Alicia

"It's rude to text when you're in the company of others." Tiffany's high pitched voice grates on my nerves. I've spent about an hour with this woman, and I'm losing my mind. I don't know how Emily and her brothers have survived years with this woman around. And to think, Heath's mom likes her enough to set him up on a date with her.

I meant what I said—no wonder he came looking for me.

I slip my phone back into my purse and toss Tiffany a fake smile. "I'm not trying to be rude, just answering a text from my boyfriend."

"Boyfriend." Bridget snorts like it's impossible to imagine me with a boyfriend. "Where is he?" Her tone is condescending, and it pisses me off.

"Her boyfriend, my brother Heath, is with the guys," Emily says, matching Bridget's tone. Emily has spent most of the evening defending me. She might be more pissed than I am at their behavior.

"My Heath!" Tiffany slaps her hand to her chest and drags out that statement with a dramatic *I don't believe you* sigh.

"Heath has never been and will never be yours," Emily says.

"That's not true. He was supposed to be going out with me tomorrow night, but Elaine said those plans have been canceled. She assured me they'd be rescheduled later this summer."

"Those plans were canceled because I'm here." I wave and look at her like she's dense because let's face it, she is. "Remember me, his girlfriend?"

"No matter what Mom said or didn't say, there will be no date with my brother. Not now, not ever." Emily lets out a low huff in frustration.

Tiffany ignores Emily's declaration and stares at me with disdain. "Heath would never date somebody like you."

She looks down at my clothes with a wrinkled nose like I smell bad or something. "You're not his type. You don't even look like you're from the Hamptons."

"I'm not." I shrug like her words and actions mean nothing to me. She's bugging the hell out of me, but I refuse to let her know that. "I'm from Brooklyn."

"Brooklyn?" She says it like it leaves a bad taste in her mouth. "He would never date someone from Brooklyn."

Emily slaps her hand on the table and glares at Tiffany. "Shows how little you know my brother. He doesn't care if Alicia's from the Hamptons or Brooklyn. It doesn't matter. He doesn't date people because of what family they come from or how much money they have."

Tiffany gasps and her jaw drops like she's offended. "That's not why he dates me."

"That's because he doesn't date you. Never has." Emily grabs my arm and drags me from the table. "Come on, Alicia. Let's get out of here. I can't believe I ever hung out with those women."

I can't help but laugh at Emily's disgust. From the way she's acting, I would've thought they insulted her and not me. "They really are obnoxious, aren't they? Do you hang out with them every year on vacation?"

"Yeah, but typically she's not that bad. Maybe it's

because you're here, and she feels threatened."

"I doubt it, but I appreciate your loyalty." I wrap my arm around Emily's shoulder and hug her close. "Something tells me Tiffany and Bridget are always bitches."

"Maybe and I just never noticed." She rests her head on my shoulder and sighs. "Sorry, they've been so nasty to you."

I shrug it off with a smile. "Don't sweat it. Let's sneak out of here. I told Heath to meet us at High Tops."

"Maybe if we sneak over there now, we'll get some time alone with guys before the rest of the girls show up."

"Sounds good to me." My smile grows at the thought of seeing Heath. "Whatever it takes to get away from these women."

EMILY AND I GRAB our drinks and find a table toward the back of the bar. We're far enough back that it won't be easy for the girls to see us when they show up, but we can see if they walk in.

"I hope the guys show up before the girls," Emily says. "I'm tired of dealing with Tiffany."

"She's determined to put me in my place."

"She's just jealous. She's been trying to get Heath

ever since Lauren died. Actually, she started her shit before Lauren died. I swear, one of these days she'll catch on and leave Heath alone."

"Well, I don't care what happens between those two after this week. I just wish she would leave me out of it."

"What?" Emily looks at me like I've lost my mind. "I thought you liked Heath."

"I do like him."

"Then why would you say such a thing?"

"Em, this isn't real. After this week, he's free to do whatever he pleases. Whoever he decides to date after this arrangement ends is none of my business. Although, I hope he has better taste than Tiffany."

Emily gives me a wide eye gaze. I can't tell if she's going to cry or yell at me. "Heath really likes you. Whether he said it or not doesn't matter. He does."

"I said I like him too." I have to focus on keeping my expression neutral. I actually like Heath a lot, but I don't want to tell Emily that. If she knew how much I liked him, she'd never stop trying to keep us together.

I'm at the prime of my career and have four more book deadlines to meet this year alone. A guy would be too much of a distraction. To appease her, I toss her a small bone. "I imagine we'll become friends and stay in touch when this is over."

"No." The word is clipped and harsh. The bone I tossed did nothing to calm her down. "He *really* likes you, Alicia. Not as a friend. But more. Trust me."

"Em, I—"

"Girls, I can't believe you left without us." Emily looks over her shoulder and her body visibly slacks at the sight of Tiffany, Brittany, and the rest of the women we ditched.

Tiffany plops in the chair next to me, and I swallow a groan.

"We assumed you'd figure it out." Emily's stare is cold and hard. "And look, you did."

Emily and Tiffany are in a death stare match. I wouldn't be surprised if claws come out next. The last thing I want is a fight, so I do my best to diffuse the tension. "We just needed some fresh air and ended up here. We should've come back for you guys first."

Tiffany shrugs Emily off and cuts her eyes to me. "What I want to know is why you think you're dating Heath."

"Oh, jeez. This again? I know who I'm dating." I meet her stare. She's trying to intimidate me, but it's not working.

She breaks her eyes away and starts down another rant. "Well, I can believe that you *think* he's dating you, but there's no way he really is. I mean, He—" Tiffany squeals and waves her hand in the air. I follow her eyes and immediately understand her excitement. Heath and the rest of the guys just walked through the door.

She's waving frantically to get his attention, but his eyes are on me. He tosses me a big smile before he stops by the bar and orders a drink.

Emily smirks at me from across the table like she knows my secret desires. She leans in close and whispers, "Yeah, that look on your face definitely says you don't care who he dates after next week."

I push her away. "Oh, shut it."

Tiffany squeals even louder, and I think my eardrum bursts. She leans in close to me and says, "I'm just going to go say hi." She hops up and runs to the bar. I think she's trying to make me jealous, but it's not gonna work. Even if Heath and I were really dating, I wouldn't be bothered by her behavior. I'm not a jealous person.

She tries to put her arm around Heath, but he shrugs her off and ignores her. He continues talking to Dexter. I laugh at the desperation in Tiffany's attempts to get his attention.

A moment later, Luke wraps his arm around Tiffany and slowly steers her away.

I lean over closer to Emily. "He really can't stand her."

"Oh, my God. He *hates* her," Emily says. "And she's clueless to how much he dislikes her when it's so obvious to everyone else."

The hotness level in this place increased tenfold when the guys entered the bar. The Rockwell men really are a good-looking group of guys, and their friends, especially Evan, are equally as hot.

Luke leads Tiffany back to our table and helps her into the seat next to me. "Hey, ladies. Fancy meeting you here."

Emily shakes her head and rolls her eyes. "Whatever, bro. You knew we were here."

He gives me a wide grin and winks. "Well, Alicia and Heath have been planning their meetup all night long."

I reach over and give his arm a playful slap. "Hey, I haven't planned anything."

Heath comes up behind me and wraps his arm around my waist. "What haven't you planned, beautiful?"

Hearing him call me beautiful puts a huge smile on my face. I turned to look at him. The second our eyes meet, his lips are on mine. It's a quick, yet hot, passionate kiss.

"Meeting up with you boys," I say a little breathless.

Tiffany gasps and Bridget curses.

When he pulls back, I smile. "Did you miss me?"

"I did." He gives me a chaste kiss before he whispers in

my ear. "One evening away from you is too long."

A loud harrumph sounds next to me as Tiffany slides out of her chair. She knocks into my arm as she grabs her drink and says, "Let's go, Bridget. This conversation is tiring." We all smile and Luke hoots as they walk away.

"Thank God," I sigh. "If that's all it took for them to go away, we should've started the evening with that kiss."

Heath laughs and his dimple catches my eyes. I want to reach out and touch it, but I don't. "Sorry, beautiful. I needed that downtime with my brothers."

"I get it. Just please tell me I'll never have to endure that woman again."

"I wish, but unfortunately, she'll be at the picnic at the clubhouse on Saturday with her parents."

"And then I'll never have to see her again?"

"Yes, never again." He leans over and kisses me on the cheek. "I promise."

"Good." I pat him on the back and slide out of my seat with a wink. "Now, if you'll excuse me."

I make my way across the bar and down a side hallway leading to the bathrooms. Like so many of the other businesses I've been to on this trip, High Tops is upscale and a little on the fancy side. Instead of a community restroom with multiple stalls, each side of the long hallway is lined with private restrooms—one side for the men and one side for women.

I slip into the first unoccupied restroom to relieve myself and freshen up. The interior of the restroom is nicer than any public restroom I've ever been in. I expected a room no bigger than a half-bath or powder room, but it's very spacious with a private stall and a small sofa along one wall. The room has a classic black and white decor with shiny white tiled floors, white marble countertops over a black vanity, and black and white striped walls.

After washing up and checking my makeup, I open the door to leave but Heath is leaning on the door frame waiting for me.

"Can I come in?" His voice is gravelly and sends a tremor down my spine.

I give him a broad smile, but I don't move to let him through. Instead, I stand in the doorway with one hand on the door and the other on the frame blocking his path. "Is there something you need?"

His eyes darken, and his nostrils flare. He leans toward me, his lips mere inches from mine. "You. I need you."

"Me, huh?" I run my finger along the neckline on his shirt. His chest rises and falls quickly as my finger brushes across his skin. I haven't been able to stop thinking about him all night and my insides are tied in knots over the same need pulsing through me.

"Alicia." His voice cracks and his jaw trembles.

I fist my fingers in his shirt and pull him in. He reaches behind him and locks the door. The second I hear the lock click, I pull his mouth to mine. Fuck, he tastes good. Like man, and beer, and something salty. I let loose of my control, and he envelops me. I'm a rag doll under the strength of his hands and the hardness of his body against mine.

He cups his hands around my face and takes over the kiss. His tongue sweeps across my lips, asking for access. When I grant his silent request, he deepens the kiss. There's so much hunger and intensity in the way his mouth ravishes mine that I don't even notice our bodies move until my back is against the wall and he's pressed against me.

My hands roam down the tight muscles of his back and tug at his waist. Even with his body crushed against mine, he's not close enough. I ache to have him inside me. Needing him closer, I wrap a leg around his waist, so his hardness presses against my center. I roll my hips, and he lets out a low growl.

He pulls back and drops his forehead against mine. "Alicia." He struggles to catch his breath. "I want you so badly." His eyes are dark with need, and he presses his hips into mine, his excitement evident.

"Then take me."

With our eyes locked, his lips find mine again. There's no gentleness to this kiss. It's hard and passionate. Every swipe of his tongue and movement of his lips says I'm his. And in the heat of this moment, I am his. Only his. I'll worry about the reality of our relationship status tomorrow.

I tug at his shirt, needing to feel skin against skin. We're on the same page because he rips his shirt over his head before he grabs the hem of mine and does the same thing. His mouth is on my breast, nipping and sucking on me through my bra. I fumble for the button on his jeans, but when he pulls my bra down and sucks hard on my breast, I lose focus on what I'm doing and fall limp in his arms.

He presses me further into the wall, giving me the support I need to continue undoing his jeans. As soon as I unzip them, I slip my hand around his hardened cock and squeeze. He sucks in a breath and clamps his lips around my nipple again.

"Fuck, that feels good." He says between licks and nips on my beaded nipple.

I pump and pull him toward me. "I need you inside me, now."

He lets me go and steps back. The loss of his warmth

makes me gasp.

"Strip." There's no hesitation in his command as he pulls his wallet out of his back packet to retrieve a condom.

We both move quickly, removing our pants. I snatch the condom from his hand and tear it open. The heat in his eyes intensifies when I roll it on him and give him a gentle squeeze.

He lets out a raspy moan, lifts me onto his body, and wraps his arms around my ass. With my back pressed against the wall, he sinks into me, filling me completely in one quick thrust.

There's nothing slow or gentle about this encounter. He thrusts into me hard and fast. It's urgent, needy, and demanding. And so fucking hot. He pushes me to climax faster than I ever imagined possible. And when I scream out his name, his mouth covers mine and consumes my cries. My release crashes through me like a tidal wave, and his chases after me.

When our bodies still, he cradles the back of my neck and drops his forehead to mine. We're both gasping for air. I struggle to regain a coherent thought.

"Fuck, Alicia," He breathes against my neck. "What are you doing to me?"

"Nothing you're not doing to me, too." As soon as the

words are out, my heart rate kicks up, and I tense in his arms. This is getting too real. This has moved way past *just having fun* and has landed smack in the middle of *relationship zone*. I can't have a relationship with Heath. Relationships mean there are real feelings involved. Feelings are dangerous and lead to pain.

Shit. How did I let this happen? I've been so caught up in the moment. I let my guard down, and Heath worked his way past all my defenses.

If I'm not careful I'll get hurt again. When that happens, I'll lose one of the most important people in my life—Emily. There's no way I can sacrifice my career for a relationship with Heath but sacrificing Emily would be the end of me.

Heath and I are too different. He'll never understand my choices. My need to write at all hours of the day will be too much. Eventually, I'll disappoint him, and he'll hurt me.

I have to get this under control before it's too late.

CHAPTER NINETEEN

Heath

It's the last event of our family vacation, and true to tradition, we're gathered at the clubhouse with all the other area families. Many of them meet early in the morning, including my parents, for a round of golf. By mid-afternoon, every hand has a drink, and we're back to talk of business and life in the city.

I leave Alicia with Emily while I make my rounds and get a drink. I grab a beer from the bar, and before I turn to leave, Dad squeezes my shoulders. "Hey, son. Where's that pretty girl of yours?"

"She's with Emily." I look around the patio and don't see either of them. Maybe they snuck off for some private girl time. "Not sure where they're at though."

"I'm sure they'll show up soon." Dad smiles with a gleam in his eyes. "I really like Alicia. Your mom does, too."

A smile creeps across my face. "I'm glad to hear it. Although, I'm not convinced Mom likes her. I've no doubt she'd set me up with any one of these women if Alicia was out of the picture."

"Oh, trust me. She does."

There's something in Dad's eyes that says he's being truthful. He's never supported Mom's meddling, but he's never stepped in to stop her either. I get the sense that if she continued to push me after this, he would. "I hope you're right. And I hope this means Mom will stop trying to set me up with Tiffany. With or without Alicia in my life, that's never going to happen."

"And thank goodness for that." Dad chuckles. "Tiffany is all wrong for you."

"I'm glad at least *you* recognize that."

Dad wraps his arm around my shoulder for a side hug. "Your mom just wants you to be happy, as do I."

"I am happy, Dad. Even before Alicia, I was happy." I look up at Dad. He's taller than me by about two inches, and his shoulders are broader. He's a big guy, and as a kid, his size intimidated me.

"Maybe." He releases me to order a beer from the bar. We stand in silence while we wait for his drink. I scan the patio again, and I still don't see Alicia or Emily. I start for my phone, but Dad takes his beer and continues before I get it out of my pocket. "You're certainly happier now, though. That woman has had such a positive influence on you."

There's more truth to his words than he realizes. I thought I was happy before I met Alicia, but now I don't know if I ever really knew happiness. "We just started dating. It's way too soon to put my happiness in Alicia's hands. This relationship may not last."

Dad's smile grows, and he nudges my arm. "Oh, I wouldn't be too sure about that. I know a good match when I see it."

"Dad," I sigh.

"I know, no pressure." He grasps my shoulder and snickers. Leading me away from the bar, he stops when we're out of earshot of others. "Dexter tells me you're considering expanding the business."

Grateful for the change in subject, I nod. "Nothing's been decided, but we've discussed options."

"Business must be better than I thought if you're considering opening another location."

"Not a second location—at least not for quite some

time—but expanding our current footprint may be an option."

"A bigger bar rather than another one?" Dad asks.

"Not exactly." I love how interested Dad is in our business. He's been supportive of this venture since day one. "We'd like to be able to host more events and host them without losing the main bar area for our regular patrons. Emily was right when she said there was a lot to be made in event planning and hosting. Our events calendar is booked solid for the next year."

Dad beams with pride. "My baby girl may have a gentle heart, but she's ruthless when it comes to business. Just like you."

"Are you talking about me again, Daddy?" Emily walks up with Evan on her arm.

"We're just talking about your event planning successes." Dad towers over Emily. He kisses the top of her head with a wide grin.

"Well, I can't take all the credit." With a playful grin, she lightly kicks my leg. "My brothers carry more than their fair share of the burden. Without them, there would be no success."

"You're much too modest, sis." I poke her in the side right where I know she's ticklish. She jumps back into

Evan, and he wraps his arm around her to keep her from falling over. The look of longing on his face further feeds my suspicions about his feelings for my sister.

"Hey, no tickling!" She kicks at me again, but this time she misses.

"I forgot how ticklish you are," Evan says before he lets her go. "If I recall, your worst spot is behind your knees."

Evan starts for her legs, but she jumps back. "Don't you dare!" Laughter erupts and she scowls. Evan holds his hands up and nods as a peace offering. Emily relaxes and our moment of fun is over.

"Where did you leave Alicia?" I ask.

"She left shortly after Evan and I started talking business. I thought she'd be with you."

"I haven't seen her since I left her with you." I glance around the patio, and I don't see Alicia anywhere, but my eyes quickly find Tiffany. She's laughing with some of her friends, acting like she doesn't have a care in the world. "I wonder where she's at?"

"Maybe she went to the restroom." Emily shrugs. "I'll go check."

"Thanks." I pull my phone out of my back pocket. I have a missed text. My phone has been silenced all afternoon, so it didn't ding.

Alicia: I wasn't feeling well. Luke offered to take me back to the house.

Shit. The time stamped on the message is from an hour ago. Why didn't she come and get me? I would've taken her back. Hell, I would have welcomed a good reason to leave myself.

"Emily," I call after my sister. "No need to check for her. She texted me that she wasn't feeling well, and Luke took her home."

"What do you mean she wasn't feeling well?" Emily steps up to me with her hands on her hips. "She was fine earlier."

"I don't know. That's all she says." My eyes lock with Emily and her gaze softens. I'm worried, and she must see the concern in my eyes.

"You better go to her." Dad pats my back. "Don't upset that girl and lose her. Your mom will start pushing Tiffany again."

"Not funny, Dad." I start to type out a response to Alicia. "Tell Mom I'm sorry to leave without saying goodbye. I'll see you all at home."

Me: Are you already home?

Alicia: Yes, Luke headed back to the clubhouse about fifteen minutes ago.

Me: Okay, I'll be there soon.

Alicia: No, you should stay. I need to rest.

Me: I'm coming home.

I head out through the lobby just as Luke is heading back in. "Hey, did Alicia text you?" His long blond hair falls over his eyes. His shoulders are stiff.

"Yeah. Why didn't she come and get me?" I ask.

Luke looks pissed. He runs his hands through his hair and gathers it into a ponytail at the base of his neck before he lets it go. "I don't know, man. She seemed upset. Did you say something to her?"

"No." I glare at Luke for even suggesting such a thing. "Last I saw her, she was fine. I just got this text from her saying she was sick."

Luke crosses his arms over his chest and pins me with a stare. "She kept saying that, but I don't believe her. Something happened."

I huff at the accusatory sound of his voice. I hate that he sounds like I did something wrong, but I love how protective he is of Alicia. It's like she's already a part of my family. "She hung out with Emily while I mingled with Dad's friends. Then she disappeared."

Luke drops his arms and relaxes. The anger in his eyes softens and is replaced with concern. "She can claim she's sick all she wants, but I'm telling you, something happened to upset her."

"Okay. I'm gonna head to the house and check on her. Thanks for taking care of her."

"No problem." Luke pats my arm as I walk past. "And Heath." He calls after me. I turn to face him. His expression is one of protection and love, similar to how he looks when he's watching out for Emily. "I like Alicia. We all do. Don't fuck it up."

"I don't plan to." I say before I head out the door.

CHAPTER TWENTY

Alicia

I stare at myself in the mirror—my face now washed, and my hair pulled back in a ponytail. It's a little after five, and I'm in my pajamas. I feel ugly and a little bit like a silly girl who thought she could fit in with the cool kids only to find out she was wrong.

I've never let the opinions of others get to me. Not even in high school when the popular girls went out of their way to make unpopular girls like me feel bad about themselves. I never put much weight on the unfounded opinions of others. I was from a poor family and was considered a nerd because I got good grades. I never cared what the other kids thought because what they thought didn't matter. There were more important things in life than being popular or following all the jocks around school.

But today I fell into a spiral of self-doubt and inferiority.

Tiffany's mother cornered me after Emily left to talk to Evan. I was headed toward Heath when she crossed in front of me and started asking me questions. I didn't realize she was Tiffany's mother until her words had already gotten to me. I'm mad at myself for not making the connection sooner. And even angrier at myself for letting her words make me feel like shit.

But I can't stop playing the conversation over and over again in my mind.

"YOU'RE ALICIA, RIGHT? HEATH'S new summer fling," she says.

"I'm Alicia, yes," I answer with my head held high.

She looks me up and down with a sneer on her face. I can't say I've ever actually seen someone sneer before, but this woman did. "Well, I can see why Elaine is so upset about you. You're not Rockwell material at all. Where are you from?"

I swallow hard and try not to let my anger show. This woman doesn't know me. Plus, Elaine has been great. If Elaine doesn't like me, she's a great actress because she's treated like a member of the family from the moment I arrived last week.

"Brooklyn," I say with a hint of annoyance.

"Oh." The woman tsks and shakes her head. "That will not do. Not for our Heath."

"Our Heath?" Why does this woman think of Heath as hers?

"We're a very close community. We all look out for each other, including everyone's children. I'm afraid a girl from Brooklyn will never be good enough for a nice man like Heath. You don't deserve him."

My face drops, and I feel like Jeremy slapped me across the face all over again. There's something in her tone and word choice that are reminiscent of Jeremy. Repeatedly on that horrid night, he told me how I didn't deserve to be treated like a nice girl. He said I deserved to be controlled by a man like him. Hearing those similar words from this woman is like a punch in the gut.

"Who are you again?" I ask, hating how shaky my voice sounds. She grins, knowing full well she's gotten to me.

"Cheryl Jones." She reaches out and offers me her hand, but I don't take it.

Now I see it. The same upturned nose, bleach blond hair, and dark blue eyes. "You're Tiffany's mother," I say.

"Yes, and while we understand Heath still likes to have

fun with his girls, don't get comfortable. He's intended for Tiffany."

AN HOUR, MAYBE MORE, has passed, and I still can't get her words out of my head.

I turn off the bathroom light and crawl in bed. I just want to hide under the covers, forget this afternoon ever happened, and wake up when it's a new day. But it's early, and there's no way I'll be able to avoid everyone tonight.

I'm not sure how long I lay there before the bedroom door opens, and I hear footsteps cross the room. I figured Heath would come even though I told him not to. I'm not ready to tell him what really happened. I'm not sure if I'll ever tell him how Tiffany's mom made me feel today. Tomorrow we go home. After the date with Mom next Friday, we go our separate ways. There's no need to dwell on the insults from people I'll never see again.

A few seconds later, Heath climbs under the covers. His warm hand slips around my waist, and it feels so good to have him next to me. He nuzzles his face into the back of my neck and breathes in.

"Hey, beautiful," he whispers. "You okay?"

I nod, unable to speak. I love his term of endearment

for me. *Beautiful*. It's sweet, and I've heard him say it enough times now that I believe it.

He plants a soft kiss on my neck, and I suck in a breath. "What can I do to make you feel better?"

I roll over to face him and the look in his eyes catches me off guard. There's genuine concern in the way he looks at me and something much more intimate than I'm expecting to see.

I kiss him. Soft. Slow. Sweet. This simple kiss means so much more to me than anything else we've shared. And we've shared a lot.

I break the kiss before it turns into something more. As much as I'd love to be closer to him right now, it wouldn't be right. I won't use Heath just to make myself feel better, wanted, or good enough.

On a sigh, I bury my face in his chest. "Just hold me."

His arms wrap tighter around me, and he pulls me into the curve of his body. He engulfs me like I'm made to fit next to him. "That, I can do."

THE NEXT DAY IS uneventful. No one, not even Emily, asks me anything beyond if I'm feeling better. Heath and Luke keep looking at me like they know something happened, but they don't ask. Emily acts like she wanted to pull me aside, but she doesn't. Everyone is giving me space, and I'm grateful.

We finish a late lunch, pack our bags, and load them into the car. Emily left earlier in the day to get back to her apartment and make sure everything was cleaned up. But she made me promise to meet her for lunch this week to talk.

Luke and Dexter aren't in a rush since neither of them need to be at work until later in the afternoon tomorrow. But Heath and I both need to get our workdays started early. I rarely take vacations and haven't written much in two weeks. I've jotted down a few notes and scene ideas, but it's been years since I've gone this long without writing, and now I'm behind schedule. I can't wait to get back in front of my desk and get back to my normal routine. Hopefully, I'll be able to make up for lost time.

"We're so glad you joined us this summer." Elaine pulls me in for a hug. The tightness of her arms around me are a reminder of how silly I was to let Cheryl's words get to me yesterday. "We have Sunday dinner every week as a family. Please, join Heath when you can. We'd love to see you."

"I have dinner with my mom on Sundays. It'll be hard since I'm all she's got." At least this is the truth. Now that I've gotten to know his parents, I hate that we've lied to them.

"I understand, but it'd be lovely if you could make it sometime. Maybe we can plan dinner on another night, so we don't interrupt your time with your mother."

"I'd like that." She hugs me again before releasing me.

Henry steps ups to me with a huge grin. "You take care of my son, okay?" Henry hugs me too. It's an embrace I'm not familiar with—a father's embrace. My father died when I was little, and I don't remember much about him. If hugging Henry is what it's like to hug a dad, I missed out on a lot. "I like seeing Heath happy, and this is the happiest he's been in a long time. Whatever you're doing, please keep doing it."

"I'm just being me." Henry hugs me tighter, and I feel Elaine's hand squeeze my arm. I swallow the lump forming in the back of my throat, and it hurts like hell going down. *Could these two make me feel any worse about our betrayal?*

"Come on, Dad. Let her go." Heath chuckles as he takes my hand. "It's a long drive back to the city. We better get on the road."

I glance up at Heath, and he looks completely unaffected by what we've done. He smiles at his parents like this is all normal, and I really will see them again at a Sunday dinner sometime soon. But I won't because none of this is real. I shouldn't be freaking out about this, but I am. This was the plan all along. All I have to do is stick to the plan.

Heath hugs his parents, and they say their goodbyes. Within five minutes, we're in the car and heading back to the city.

Same as the drive over, he holds my hand, but this time, it feels right. Like he belongs to me.

I've been staring out the passenger side window for a while when Heath squeezes my hand and asks, "You okay over there?"

I turn to face him. His brows are furrowed, and his expression is filled with worry. "I'm fine."

"You sure? It's not like you to be this quiet." It's then that I realize we're almost home. I'd zoned out for most of the drive.

"Just thinking." I smile hoping that will ease his concern. "I really like your parents. They were very welcoming. Thanks for trusting me to do this for you."

"It's me who should be thanking you. For everything. I enjoyed these past two weeks with you."

"Me, too." Too much, in fact. It's time I stop lying to myself. Somewhere along the way, we'd stopped pretending and this thing between us became real. Backpedaling is going to be hard, but it has to be done. "You surprised me. A lot."

A slow smile spreads across his face. "How so?"

"Well, my first impression of you was somewhat skewed due to the way we met. I walked away from our park run-in with an entirely different opinion of you."

His smile grows, and his dimples show through his beard. "I'm glad. That day wasn't exactly my finest moment. Then again, you threw me for a loop."

"Sorry about that." I squint my eyes and wrinkle my nose at the memory of the things I said and did that morning. He must've thought I was some type of crazed sex fiend. "I didn't expect to ever see you again. I tend to do crazy things when I'm starting a new book."

"Well, those crazy things were quite memorable. It's not a meeting I'll ever forget." He lifts my hand and kisses the back of it—an action I've gotten used to on this trip. I'll miss it.

"I guess all we have left is a dinner date with my mom," I say.

He sighs and a sadness passes over his face. "Has a date and time been scheduled?"

My heart drops knowing this is almost over. After next Friday, I won't see him again even though that's what I want. "Yeah. Friday at seven, if that works for you."

"Yep, that works. Should I pick you up or meet you there?" He pulls into a parking space just outside my apartment building and throws the car into park.

"You can pick me up. It'll look better if we arrive together. Mom is easily suspicious when it comes to me and men." I take my seatbelt off and grab my purse. "Well, I guess this is goodbye."

"I'll walk you up." He squeezes my hand one last time before releasing me.

"You don't have to do that. I can handle my bags."

"I know you can handle it, but I'm still walking you up." He pops the trunk and gets out of the car. I want to argue with him, but I know it won't do any good. Heath is a gentleman above all else.

We walk up the steps and into the elevator side-by-side. There are so many things I want to say to him right now, but I can't seem to find the words. I sense he wants to say more too, but he doesn't speak.

We reach my apartment door. I start to say goodbye but stop myself. Instead, I unlock the door and walk in, leaving the door open for him to follow. I'm not ready to say goodbye. Not yet.

I hear the door shut behind him followed by the flip of the lock. A smile covers my face. He's not ready to say goodbye either.

"Where would you like your bags?" he asks.

I point toward the hallway. "Last door on the right is my bedroom. If you don't mind."

He nods and takes it to my room while I head into the kitchen for a glass of water. My mouth is suddenly very dry. I down a glass, then pour myself another. I hear his footsteps behind me, and my heart starts beating faster.

"Would you like something to drink?" I ask.

"No, thank you." I feel him right behind me. He doesn't touch me, but I know he's close. I take another sip of my water before I sit the glass down and spin around. He's so close we almost touch. He steps closer—his chest brushes against mine—and slides his hands around my waist.

"Alicia?" My name leaves his lips as a question.

"Yes?"

He leans into me. His lips don't touch my skin, but his breath brushes across my cheek as he speaks. "May I kiss you goodbye?"

"Yes," I breathe.

Our eyes lock, and I'm frozen in place by the intensity of his gaze. His large hands cup my cheeks, and he tilts my head to the side as his mouth covers mine in a gentle caress that sets my body aflame. The kiss is slow and thoughtful. Like he's committing every inch of me to memory through this kiss.

He breaks away and drops his forehead to mine. Despite the gentleness of the kiss, we're both breathing heavily.

"Stay," I say.

His eyes darken and his hands tense around my face. "What are you saying?"

"I don't want you to leave. Stay the night with me." I instantly feel betrayed by my own words, but I mean it. I don't want him to leave. Not yet.

"There's no place else I'd rather be." This time his mouth claims mine in a hungry kiss that's both demanding and sensual. It's the kind of kiss I've always dreamed of receiving—firm, rough, erotic. I feel wanted, desired, and needed. He's not kissing me right now out of obligation or simply as a lead-in to sex. His mouth is on mine because he wants to taste me, become one with me.

He lifts me up and sets me on the counter. I spread my legs and pull him into me. His hands slide up my thighs and squeeze my hips. God, how I wish I wore a dress today. My pants are so restricting, and I want his hands on my bare skin.

Fumbling with the buttons on his shirt, I slowly undo them until they're completely undone. When I spread my hands across his chest, he groans.

His hands slide up my sides. He grabs the hem of my

shirt and strips it over my head. His mouth is on my neck, my collarbone, then my cleavage. When he nibbles at the edge of my breast, I gasp.

"Heath. Please."

He looks up at me and kisses me. "Tell me what you want."

"Take me to bed, now."

He doesn't hesitate. He wraps his arms under me and lifts me into him. When we reach my bedroom, he tosses me onto my bed and steps back. His eyes rake down my body, his desire undeniable. No words are needed between us. Simultaneously, we kick off our shoes and strip off our pants.

He takes a condom out of his pocket and strokes his cock before he rips open the wrapper. Now it's my turn to take in his body as he sheaths himself. Fit, tall, and lean. Every muscle on his body is well defined. He doesn't quite have six pack abs, but the definition is there and sexy as hell.

He crawls up my body, kissing my stomach, chest, and neck until he reaches my mouth. His tip easily finds my entrance, and he slowly nudges inside me. He spreads me open inch by inch until he's given me every bit of him.

He stills, leans down on his elbows, and cups my face. "You feel so damn good."

"So do you." With our eyes held together, he slowly

moves inside me. I'm not sure if anything has ever felt this good. It's too good, and I know I'm screwed. Saying goodbye to him at the end of the week is going to be painful.

But I will let him go. I can't keep him. Not now. Not ever.

I have to focus on my career and there's no time for a relationship with Heath. It's best for everyone involved if I push my feelings aside and stick to the plan.

One more date. Then we say goodbye.

CHAPTER
TWENTY-ONE

Heath

The sun shines through the bedroom window and hits my face. It takes a minute for my eyes to adjust but when they do, I smile. Alicia is tucked in next to me with her arm and leg draped across me.

I didn't know what to expect last night when I dropped her off. My heart soared when she granted me permission to kiss her goodbye, and it flipped a few times in my chest when she asked me to stay.

Alicia is the first woman since Lauren to make me think I could have the things I lost—like a home and a family with kids. This woman makes me feel alive and hopeful.

And yet she leaves me with a sense of dread, too.

She's been equally affectionate, and there's no doubt she feels this connection between us when we make love, but she's given me no indication she wants more from me than this fake arrangement.

Alicia is different from me in so many ways. Her outgoing and vibrant personality draws me out of my shell. I'm normally irritated with people who share her habits and personality quirks, but with her they don't bother me. I find myself laughing at her and exercising a level of patience I didn't know I possessed.

Maybe I'm being too much of a romantic, and I'm letting this intimacy get to my head. For all I know, our differences could become too much, and we'd end up hating each other after a few short weeks. But it has been a few weeks, and I can't get enough of her.

Hell, I think I'm falling in love with her. I've been falling ever since that mouth of hers kept my attention at the park the first day we met. Our differences are one of the things I love the most about her. They're the making of a long-lasting relationship and provide the perfect balance between us.

She's everything I need. She grounds me, and I can't let her go.

Alicia stirs. I squeeze her closer, and she welcomes my

embrace. She lets out a soft moan before her eyes open, and she looks up at me. She's smiling at first, but then she jumps up and looks surprised I'm here.

"What time is it?" she asks.

"Not sure. I haven't checked. Late enough that the sun is up." I reach for her to pull her back to me, but she resists. "Come, let's stay in bed a little longer."

She bunches the sheet up around her naked body and stiffens. "I can't. I have to get to work."

"A few more minutes won't hurt." I brush her hair out of her face. The pained look in her eyes gut me. I can't tell if it's regret, fear, or worry. Maybe all three and more. "Are you okay?"

"Of course," she blurts out quickly. "It's just—I've hardly written in two weeks, my book tour starts this week, and I'm anxious to get back to my next project. I'm behind schedule."

"I guess this much time away is unusual for you." I keep my voice calm, even though her reaction this morning is anything but calm.

She forces a smile. "I never take time off."

"I understand." I do, and I don't. I'm committed to my career. I'm ready to get back to it too, but life is too short to work all the time. I know all too well how quickly the good things in our lives can vanish. I want to argue that point, but I don't want to risk upsetting her more. "Maybe we can meet up for coffee later?"

"Maybe." Her voice sounds empty, and a weight presses down on my chest. "I need to check my schedule."

I take her hand in mine. She starts to pull it away, but I give it a gentle squeeze. She's acting like I'm a one-night stand she regrets and wishes would take the hint and leave. She stares at our joined hands like she's debating on how best to get away from me. "Everyone needs to take breaks. Surely you can fit one in?"

She turns away, but not before I see the regret in her eyes. That look is all it takes to make my chest hurt. Does she regret the time we spent together or what she's about to do next? She's pulling away from me, and I hate it. "I'm way behind. And I have a book reading Wednesday evening that I haven't prepared for. I really need to focus."

I sigh and try to hide my frustration. "It's just coffee, Alicia."

"I know. Text me later. Maybe I can break away." She leans down and gives me a quick kiss, but it lacks the heart and desire all her other kisses have had. This one feels distant.

I want to ask her what changed between last night and

this morning. Why is she skittish and closed off? She was more affectionate with me when all this between us was fake.

But that's the problem. It hasn't been fake since the night of the party. At least not for me.

Instead, I nod and tighten my lips to keep from saying anything I might regret later.

Shit. Maybe I've been wrong this entire time. I swear she feels this connection between us. Why else would she have given so much to me in private? Maybe none of that means anything to her, and I'm the only one that feels this way.

"Okay." I climb out of bed and slip on my boxers. I cup my hand under her chin and turn her eyes to mine. "Thanks for everything these past two weeks. It meant so much more to me than the original plan." I want to say more, but I'm afraid of pushing her further away.

She sits on the bed and watches me get dressed. I have everything on but my shirt. If memory serves, it's in the kitchen. I pause in the doorway and toss her a smile and a wave before leaving.

Her silence is crushing.

A million emotions rush through me as I make my way to the kitchen. I don't know how to process any of them.

Maybe I'm overreacting, but my gut tells me I'm not.

Fuck. How did my heart get so attached to this woman so quickly? I should've told her how I felt—that this wasn't fake for me—before I went and fell in love with her.

I grab my shirt and slip it on. I'm about to open the front door when she calls my name. I turn around, and she's leaning on the wall at the end of the hallway with nothing but a sheet wrapped around her body. She looks like a temptress with her long legs peeking out between the edge of the sheet and her blond hair hanging in messy waves around her shoulders. I want to run to her and show her again what she'll be missing if she pushes me away.

"What is it, Alicia?" My words are harsh and clipped as I struggle to hold myself back.

She sucks her bottom lip between her teeth, something I've learned she does when she's nervous. "I'm sorry. I'm not good at this sort of thing."

Her admission kicks my heart rate up a few notches. She's trying, and I'll take it. "Don't worry about it. I don't want to pressure you if you're not interested."

"It's not that, it's just … I don't … ugh." She lets out a long breath and looks up at the ceiling. "I'll try to make time for coffee. No promises though. When I get into my writing zone, I forget about everything else. Just ask Emily.

It irritates the hell out of her."

Her words are sincere, and I can tell she's trying to fix this awkward morning. "How about I text you later? If you can make it, great. If not, we'll try for another time."

Her smile grows. "That sounds perfect."

"Have a great day, beautiful." I want to pull her into my arms for a kiss. I want to peel that sheet from her body and devour her again and again like I did last night. But I don't. Instead, I toss her a smile and leave.

AS EXPECTED, ALICIA DECLINED my offer for late morning coffee or lunch. I'd hoped after she apologized and tried to soften the blow of her mini freak out—because she was definitely freaking out on me this morning—she'd meet me for one or the other. But she declined with three-word answers and left no opening for me to continue the conversation.

Me: Can I persuade you to take a coffee break? I'll come to you.

Alicia: No time, sorry.

Me: Maybe a late lunch?

Alicia: Can't, really busy.

I read over this brief conversation so many times today, trying to decipher what she's thinking, and I've got nothing. I want to text her again and ask her to dinner tonight, but that will make me look eager and needy. The last thing I want to do is make this worse than it already is, and eager and needy would probably scare her off for good.

I toss my phone on my desk behind me and run my hands down my face and over my beard. I've been sitting here staring out the window behind my desk for hours, getting nothing done. I let out a low growl, frustrated I let this get out of hand.

"What's got you all worked up?" I jerk my head around, and Mom is standing in the doorway of my office. "After such an exciting vacation, I'd think you'd be happy, but you look miserable."

"Thanks, Mom." I spin my chair around to face her. "What are you doing here? I thought you and Dad were staying another week."

"Your dad got called into the office. A client emergency they needed him to deal with, but I didn't come here to talk about that."

"Then why are you here?" I say a little too gruff. I see her flinch slightly, and I cringe.

She narrows her eyes on me like she's going to scold me. "I wanted to make sure everything was okay with Alicia. She seemed ... how do I put this ... anxious, maybe even distraught, as you two were leaving."

"She's fine, Mom. She was still tired from feeling ill." I know that's bullshit. Alicia was never ill. I still don't know what upset her, but something did. I wanted to push her to tell me, but I let it go.

Was that my mistake? Maybe she's upset with me for not asking. I'd love to know what really happened, but how can I ask now?

"Heath." Mom pins me with her *don't give me that* stare. "She was *not* fine, and I know your little secret. Or should I say, lie?"

My eyes widen, and I stop breathing for a moment. "What are you talking about?"

"Don't treat me like I'm stupid. It's insulting."

"I don't think you're stupid, Mom."

She crosses her arms over her chest and looks down her nose at me. "Then why did you lie to me about being in a relationship with Alicia?"

I shake my head a little too quickly. "Mom, I—"

She holds her hand up and stops me. "Before you go off and try to make up some excuse or deepen the lie, I know you and Alicia faked this relationship for my benefit. I knew what you were up to the second I saw you two together that night in the bar. While a part of me is really pissed at both of you for lying, another part of me understands why you did it. I just want to apologize for making you feel like you had to pretend to date some poor girl just to appease me."

"Mom." I drop my head into my hand and rub my eyes. I knew better than to try to pull one over on Mom. "I'm sorry. If you're going to be mad at anyone, be mad at me. Alicia didn't want to lie to you. It's not her fault."

"I figured as much." Mom crosses her arms over her chest and leans against the door frame. "She's a sweet girl. Your dad and I really like her. We'd like to see more of her."

I would, too. But I'm afraid that's not what Alicia is looking for. "Well, since she's Emily's best friend, I'm sure something can be arranged."

Mom rolls her eyes. "Are you really that dense?"

"Huh?"

"Heath." Mom steps forward and leans down on my desk so her eyes are level with mine. "Wake up. This girl is perfect for you."

"I know," I bark back quickly. Saying it out loud makes Alicia's rejection that much harder to accept. But I'm done lying to Mom. I was never good at lying anyway. "It doesn't matter. She doesn't want me."

"The hell she doesn't. I know a girl in love when I see one. That girl is so taken with you, it's a wonder she let you leave."

Love? One of us is in love, but it's not Alicia. "She doesn't love me, Mom."

"Maybe she doesn't realize it yet. But the foundation for it has already been laid. Soon enough, she'll open her eyes. Trust me on that. And you better be ready for her."

"I wish you were right. I want you to be right, but I don't know if Alicia will open up to me like that." Last night I thought there might be a chance, but after this morning I don't think she's going to give me a chance beyond our short-term arrangement.

Her shoulders sag, and she lets out a long exhale. "Heath, you have to try. Don't let this girl go without a fight. She's wonderful for you. And it makes me ..."

Mom wipes away a tear that escapes her eye.

"Mom, please don't cry."

"It just makes me so happy to see you happy. I've waited so long to see you smile and laugh like that again. I've missed seeing you with a woman on your arm. Alicia did so much more for you than get me off your case about dating. She taught you that you can love again."

Everything Mom says is true. A part of me knew it the day I met Alicia in the park. Her free-spirited and jovial personality lured me in immediately. She seduced me with the sexy words she spoke and the lustful gaze in her eyes.

"Heath." Mom's soft tone draws my eyes to her. "I saw the way you looked at her and touched her. I see it in your eyes now. She could be the one."

"You don't think I know that?" Mom flinches at my tone. I take a breath to calm down. "Yes, Alicia *is* the one. Is that what you want to hear? I'd love to figure out if there could be more between us, but none of that matters if she doesn't give me a chance. She's had a rough time with men. She doesn't trust easily. I can't make her do something she's not comfortable doing. And I won't hurt her by pushing her too hard."

"She'll give you a chance. Trust me. She may resist at first. I don't know her well, but I know she looks at you the same way you look at her. You have to find a way to prove to her that you're worth it."

"Oh, that's all, huh?" I sigh and drop my head back on my chair. If I'm going to get her to agree to date me, I've got a hell of a lot more to overcome than her past pain. I've got to prove to her that I support her career. Her writing is important to her. She gave up a lot to go with me to the

Hamptons, and I'm so grateful for that.

Oh, hell. That's it. Her career is her life. She gave up two weeks of her precious schedule to help me out. I'm such an idiot for not seeing it sooner. All she sees from me is an uptight, rigid businessman who works nine-to-five, shuts off at the end of the day and goes home. I didn't work once while we were on vacation, and she whipped her laptop out to write several times. I don't even hang out at my own bar after work hours in order to create a separation from work and personal time. That's not how she operates, nor is it the career she chose for herself. Why would she think we're compatible?

If I'm going to fully earn her trust and heart, I need to show her that I support her, that I'd never expect her to sacrifice her writing time for me. I need to show her I respect her career as much as I respect her.

With a little give and take, we could be together without it impacting her career and needs. And I know just where to start showing her my support.

CHAPTER TWENTY-TWO

Alicia

For the past two days, I've been in a constant state of confusion, nervousness, and longing.

Even now, sitting in the break room of the bookstore, waiting for my event to start, I can't concentrate. This has never happened to me before. Nothing—not even Jeremy—broke my concentration.

I'm not equipped to process these feelings, nor do I have the time to deal with them. That sounds awful, even in my own head, but it's true. I don't know what I was thinking when I asked Heath to stay Sunday night. He was supposed to drop me off then leave. But he lingered. Then asked to kiss me goodbye. That was all it took for me to admit to both myself and him that I wasn't ready to say goodbye.

I'm still not sure I'm ready to say goodbye, but I have to. Goodbye is inevitable. If I don't say it now, it'll only get harder down the road.

He's all I've thought about, and I need to push him out of my mind. I need to focus on the book signing that starts any minute now. I've got two weeks of events planned, and if I don't get it together, I won't survive. My fans expect to see a confident, sassy author with spunk, not some weak, nervous sap who can't speak a coherent sentence.

I pick up my phone again to check for messages. The only message all day was from Emily telling me she can't make it to my signing tonight because she has to manage an event at the bar. I've received nothing from Heath. I've checked my phone every ten to fifteen minutes looking for a text from him and am met with disappointment. Every. Time.

True to his word, he texted me late Monday morning to meet for coffee. Even though I told him I'd try to make time, I lied. I knew I would tell him no, and I knew I would make up some excuse as to why I was too busy to take a break.

Same thing happened on Tuesday. I wanted to say yes. I wanted to see him, I really did, but I couldn't. I expected him to text me again this morning to invite me to coffee or lunch. But he didn't. The crushing disappointment I felt both surprised and scared me.

I told myself I would stop being so damn stubborn and say yes this time. Heath has proven to me that he's nothing like any other man I've met. He's kind, considerate, and affectionate. He has such a big heart, and I'm pretty sure he genuinely cares about me. He's in this just as deep as I am.

But he didn't text, he didn't call, and he didn't invite me for coffee or lunch today. My regret is overwhelming. I need it to go away. I hate feeling like this. Thoughts like this are exactly why I don't date. It's a distraction I can't afford.

A light knock on the break room door causes me to jump in my seat. I really need to get a grip.

"Hey, babe." Trent's smiling face beams at me as he walks in. "You ready?"

"As ready as I'm gonna get." I paste on a smile and hope he can't see how uneasy I am. I look behind him and frown when Emily doesn't follow him in. "I hate that Emily isn't here."

He sighs and rubs the back of his neck. "I know. She told me to apologize to you a million times."

Emily and Trent have attended every one of my local book signings, and I've come to rely on their presence. Knowing I have friends in the audience that support me has always kept me calm and boosted my confidence. "It sucks."

"I know, babe. She feels really bad." He squeezes my hand and smiles. "I'm still here, and you're an old hat at these now. What is this, your hundredth signing?"

I huff and shake my head. "I don't know how many I've done now. But I still need my friends."

"And you have us. Even if one of us isn't physically present. We still support you." He pulls me up out of the chair and hugs me. I feel marginally better and am grateful for the distraction.

"I know. I just like knowing you're both here."

The bookstore owner, Lisa, cracks open the door and peeks in. "I think we're ready for you. You've drawn a huge crowd, and I think we've sold every copy of your book for the signing."

"Every copy! Wow, that's amazing." My signings always do well, but this is a first. My first thought is to call Heath, and I immediately feel nauseous. I shouldn't be thinking like this. I celebrate these accomplishments with Trent and Emily. Not some guy I fake dated.

But he's not just some guy. I meant what I told Emily when I said I liked Heath and could see us as friends. The problem is, I see us as more than friends. I can't go there.

"Yep. We would've sold more if we had them. It's

packed out there." Lisa's voice drags me out of my thoughts.

"Well, then. Let's not make them wait another minute." I check my reflection in the mirror one last time, adjust my hair, and shove all thoughts of Heath out of my mind. I need to be present tonight.

"Come on, beautiful. You look fabulous."

I spin around, and stare at Trent with wide eyes. "What did you say?"

"I said you look fabulous." He narrows his eyes in confusion. "Come on. Let's not keep your fans waiting."

I nod and let out a deep breath. This is ridiculous, and I've got to get a grip. Trent has called me and Emily beautiful countless times. I'm sure he'll do it again. I can't let one word screw with my concentration just because Heath called me that. I crack my neck and shake my arms to my side before I smile and follow Trent out to the main floor.

It's showtime.

I CLOSE MY NOTES on the excerpt I read. Normally, I read something from the recent release, but today I decided to share something from my current project. The project Heath—my imperfect book boyfriend—inspired. This project is unlike anything I've written to date. The characters are more raw, real, and personal. I write highly flawed heroines and pair them with the perfect—and *mostly* flawless—book boyfriends.

I don't typically write heavy dramas or stories weighed down with angst. I write light-hearted comedies full of steamy romance with the perfect man to save the day. It's the furthest characterization from reality I can get without writing pure fantasy. Although sometimes I think my books are pretty damn close.

In just a few short weeks, Heath inspired me to do something different, something real. To be honest, I didn't even know I was doing this. I've been writing romance novels for so long that I developed a style and a formula to my writing. I typically stick to it religiously. As much as I hate to admit it, Jeremy played a huge role in my writing style choices. I've denied Jeremy's long-term impact on my emotional state, but I think it's time to accept the truth. He's influenced me more than I ever imagined possible, and my writing has become a coping mechanism.

I didn't recognize the driver behind the pattern in my writing because I didn't want to. I still don't want to. It's so much easier to pretend that night didn't happen.

And now that I see the impact one bad man had on me, I feel weak and foolish. I know that's dumb. What he did was serious and would traumatize anyone, but I thought I was stronger than that.

"Alicia." Lisa's hand reaches over and taps my shoulder.

I shake my head and look around at all the expecting eyes staring at me. I'd zoned out. "I'm sorry, what was that?"

Lisa points toward the woman standing at the front of the crowd. "Go ahead and repeat your question."

The woman nods with a smile. "It's so nice to meet you. I love all your books."

"Thank you." I give her a warm smile.

"The excerpt you read seems different from all your other books. What inspired this new hero? A new man in your life, maybe?"

Fans always want to know about my love life. With every new release, they never fail to ask. But I don't answer those questions. Instead, I give a variation of my stock answer. "I meet new people all the time, and while I do draw on personal experiences to create new characters, I don't use specific people to inspire my characters. Instead, I keep a running list of traits and actions I've observed in others and build characters from there."

A woman a few rows behind raises her hand. I nod for her to speak. "I personally love your perfect book boyfriends. They make for a great escape. Are you at all concerned about losing loyal fans with such a flawed male lead?"

I laugh. "Oh, I worry about losing fans with every new book I release." I hear a few other chuckles from the crowd but am mostly met with silence. Suddenly, my palms are sweaty, and my breath catches in the back of the throat. Did I miss the mark on this one? Maybe it was too risky to step outside my norm.

I scan the room, searching the faces of my fans for signs that everything is okay. Fans rejecting a book is my worst nightmare, and I really want them to love this new one. I'm about to continue when my eyes land on the familiar green eyes I've looked into so many times these past two weeks. Heath smiles and nods in encouragement. It's exactly what I need to find my strength and answer my fan.

"We're all imperfect," I say. "While I love my perfect book boyfriends, too, it was time for me to branch out. I was compelled to write a story where both the hero and the heroine are flawed. This novel will still contain all the other elements you love—steam, humor, and a happily-ever-after. But instead of the hero showing the heroine the way to happiness, they work toward that ending together. Both showing the other that they deserve another chance at love."

As soon as the words are out of my mouth, I freeze. I shift my eyes to Heath, and he smiles when our eyes meet.

There's heat and desire and want behind his smile. But there's something else there, too. Something deeper and more meaningful. It's something I don't want to admit I see or maybe feel.

I divert my eyes and avoid looking in his direction. The rest of the signing goes smoothly, and my fans accept all my answers with excitement and enthusiasm. I even read a second excerpt—which I never do—after several fans begged for me to read my favorite passage from my recent release.

An hour and a half and countless signatures later, my hand is numb, and my mouth is dry. The store has mostly cleared out except for a few stragglers, Trent, and Heath. Heath is still leaning against the back wall in the same spot I first saw him.

Lisa returns with a water bottle, and we say our goodbyes. Another successful book signing party under our belt. I've held signing events at her bookstore for years and each one is more successful than the last.

Trent stands next to me reading his phone. "Emily wants us to swing by the bar to celebrate. You up for it?"

"Sure. As long as we don't stay out too late." I take a drink of water and see Heath push off the wall. I turn my back toward him. I'm not ready to face him. If he looks into my eyes at close range, he'll know how I feel. He'll know I want more from him than what we agreed to, and I can't let that happen. I can't let myself try for something more no matter how much I want to. It's too great a risk.

"When was the last time a guy came to one of your book events?" Trent asks.

I look up at him and frown. "You're here. You've come to all of them."

"I don't count." He snorts. "I'm more like the annoying brother you always wanted."

"Trust me." I playfully punch him in the arm. "I never wanted a brother."

Trent drops his smile and leans in close to my ear. "He hasn't taken his eyes off you all night," he whispers. Before I can respond, Trent leaves.

I feel Heath's closeness before he speaks. If I turn around, I know he'll be close enough for me to touch, hold, and kiss. That's what his presence does to me.

"Alicia." My name rolls off his tongue like a promise.

I turn to face his bright green eyes, and I shiver. That same promise is written all over his face. A promise to care for me and protect me. A promise that he's not Jeremy and would never hurt me like he did. It warms my insides and terrifies me all at the same time.

"Hi, Heath." My voice is breathless as I struggle to

regain my composure. "I didn't know you were coming tonight."

His lips turn up, and his dimple peeks through his beard. *God, I love that dimple.* "I wanted to surprise you. Hope you don't mind."

"Not at all. Thanks for coming. Now you've gotten a taste of the public life of being an author." I spread my arms out to the side and shrug.

"It was interesting. I had no idea so many woman were comfortable talking about love and sex in an open forum like this. I'm enlightened."

I can't help but laugh. "Maybe now my actions on our first meeting make a little more sense."

"A little." He nods and hands me a small box. "I got something for you. A congratulatory gift."

My eyes widen, and my smile grows. No one has ever given me a gift for one of my book launches before. It's a sweet gesture that renders me speechless. My fingers brush against his when I reach for the box and a jolt of electricity runs through my body. It's a feeling I get often around him, and one I don't think I'll ever get used to.

"Thanks. You shouldn't have." I pull at the ribbon tied around it. He places his hand on mine, stopping me from continuing.

"Don't." My eyes shoot up to his. I'm confused. "Open it after I'm gone. It's not much, but when I saw it, I had to get it for you."

"Okay." He leans in and kisses my cheek. He lingers for a moment longer than I'd expect for a cheek kiss. His beard scratches me and his breath tickles my ear as he steps into my space. My heart rate kicks up, and the world around me fades away into a cloud of haze.

"You're an amazing woman, Alicia," he whispers in my ear. "Don't ever let anyone convince you otherwise."

With one final kiss just below my ear, he turns and walks out of the store without another glance in my direction.

I want to run after him–to beg him to stay. But I don't. Instead, I focus on the small box and pull the ribbon the rest of the way off. When I lift the lid, I gasp. Inside is a silver paperweight in the shape of an open book. It's beautiful and elegant. The words engraved on the pages are simple and powerful.

Real life is better than fiction.

I lift the small piece of metal out of the box and turn it in my hand. An inscription on the bottom catches my eye.

You're better than fiction.
Always, Heath

I'm left breathless, confused, and wanting him more than I ever did before. A part of me wants to run after him and tell him how I feel, but the sensible side of me convinces me to stay put. This is uncharted territory for me. Despite not having the time for a boyfriend in my life, I want him.

"What's that?" Trent walks up behind me. I quickly place the paperweight back in the box.

"Nothing. Just a small congratulatory gift." I grab my purse from under the table and stuff the present inside. "You ready? Let's go give Emily a hard time for missing the signing."

I half expect Trent to probe more about the gift and the fact that Heath came. But he doesn't. Instead, he tells me about the date he had last week and how the woman wouldn't stop talking about her dog. I laugh and poke fun at his experience and am very grateful for the distraction.

CHAPTER TWENTY-THREE

Heath

My nerves eat away at my stomach as I step out of a cab outside Alicia's apartment. The only communication with Alicia since our brief exchange at her book signing on Wednesday were the few texts planning tonight. I had hoped to hear from her yesterday about the present I gave her, but she's been silent. I didn't expect the gift to cause her to run into my arms and profess her love for me, but I at least thought she'd message me to say thanks.

Seeing her at the signing only confused me more. As soon as her eyes found mine in the crowd, the air in the room changed. I know she felt the shift, too. I saw it in her reaction and in the words she used. That entire speech she gave about imperfect book boyfriends was in part meant for me. I know it.

When did dating someone become so hard? I don't remember it being this challenging when I was younger, but then again, I haven't dated anyone in years. Sure, I've gone out with a few women here and there, but nothing serious.

I'm serious about Alicia.

I want to be with her. Always.

All I need to do is figure out how to win her heart.

I step out of the elevator at exactly 6:30 pm as agreed. Normally, I'd arrive ten or fifteen minutes early, but I didn't want to stress Alicia out tonight. We're meeting her mother at the restaurant at 7:00 pm, and thirty minutes should give us plenty of time to get there since it's only a couple blocks from Alicia's apartment.

When she opens her door, I'm struck by her beauty. I don't know how it's possible, but she's more beautiful than ever. Her long blond hair hangs in loose curls around her shoulders just the way I like it best. She's wearing black dress pants and a light blue blouse almost the exact same color as her eyes.

She's breathtaking, and I'm speechless. She gives me a gentle smile and waves me in. "I'm almost ready. I just need two more minutes."

I shut the door behind me, as she walks down the hall to her bedroom. I wanted to bring her flowers. Now that I'm here, I wish I had. But I was afraid flowers would be too much and make this look like a real date and not our last date. Fuck our last date. I hate the sound of that.

She comes back out, grabs her purse, and smiles. "Ready?"

"Whenever you are." My heart is beating fast, and I hope she can't tell how nervous I am. She, of course, looks as calm and collected as she did the day I met her in the park. In a way, her calmness makes me even more nervous. If she wanted more with me, she'd be nervous, too. Right?

"Do you want to walk to the restaurant?" she asks. "It shouldn't take us more than fifteen or twenty minutes."

"Sure. A walk would be nice." We ride down the elevator in silence. It's awkward for me, but she still looks unaffected. It's driving me crazy. I rack my brain for something to say to ease this tension inside me, but I come up blank. Conversation with her came so easy to me while we were in the Hamptons, but now that we're home, and I know with certainty that I want her, I'm mute.

We step outside and the warm evening air hits my face. We walk for about a half a block when she finally breaks the silence. "Thanks for the gift. I love it."

"You're welcome." She brushes her hair behind her ear, and her hand shakes. It's the first sign of nervousness I've seen in her since I arrived. In an odd sort of way, it makes me feel better.

"Is there anything I should know about your mom?" I ask. "You haven't told me much about her."

"Not really. I already told her that we'd only been dating a few weeks, the same as what we told your mom. I told her I went on vacation with you and your family. She knows you're Emily's brother, and she'll probably spend the evening criticizing me."

I laugh at her honesty and resignation of how her mom was going to behave without even giving her mom a chance. She must be exaggerating. I can't imagine anyone finding fault with Alicia, and not enough that they could criticize her all night. "Criticizing you, huh?"

Her chuckle turns into a snort. "Yes, Mom can't seem to help herself. Nothing I do is good enough for her."

"Why?" I'm confused by the idea that she wouldn't be good enough for her own mother. My parents may meddle in my life and drive me crazy sometimes, but they've never made me feel inadequate.

"I'm an only child. It was just the two of us after my

dad died. She's always wanted more for me, especially when it comes to marriage and kids. That's where we always end up butting heads."

"You don't want to get married and have kids?" I probably shouldn't have asked this question, but I need to know her answer. I want her, and one day I also want a family of my own. I'd like to know that's an option with her.

"Someday, yes. I just don't know when I'll be ready for something like that. I don't know, it's just—marriage and kids are scary." She diverts her eyes away from me and her uneasiness is evident. "How about you? Do you want kids someday?"

"That was my dream at one point. I thought I'd have a couple by now, but that didn't work out. Sometimes I feel like I missed my chance already." She looks up at me and our eyes connect. We hold each other's gaze, and I can't help but add, "But if the right person came into my life, definitely."

She quickly looks away, but not before I see the fear in her eyes. My heart drops. I don't know how I expected her to react, but that wasn't it.

The silence between us doesn't last long before she sighs and says, "I have no doubt Mom will love you. You have a nice guy quality about you that Mom will eat up."

"Nice guy?" I raise a brow.

"Yup. You're nice, respectful, and polite. The fact that you come from a prominent family, have a good job, and would be a good caretaker is a major bonus. She'll love you. And knowing Mom, she'll be planning our wedding before dessert is served."

"Well, let's start with an introduction. I'm not sure I'm ready to plan a wedding just yet."

That earned me a laugh—a beautiful and intoxicating laugh that lights me on fire. I want to make her laugh like that more often. If she would let me, I'd spend the rest of my life trying to make her laugh.

WE ARRIVE AT THE restaurant at the same time as Alicia's mom. She immediately pulls Alicia in for a hug. "Alicia, dear. I see you so infrequently, I hardly recognize you."

"Mom, don't start."

"Well, it's true. You never come to see me. It took this lovely man to get you to even consider having dinner with me."

"That's not true. We have dinner together every Sunday."

"And you missed the last two." Her mom turns to me

and smiles. "Well, aren't you a sight for sore eyes?" She surprises me when she pulls me in for a hug. "I'm Susan, and I must say, it's very nice to finally meet you."

I give her a kiss on the cheek before she releases me. Her smile grows, and the delight in her eyes is unmistakable. I hear Alicia beside me doing her best to hide her laughter. "It's nice to meet you too, Susan. I'm Heath. I've no doubt we would've met sooner had it not been for my family vacation. I hope you'll forgive me for that."

"There's nothing to forgive." She swats at my arm like I'm being silly. "You're here now, and I'm delighted to meet you." Susan tosses Alicia a smile, but even I can tell it's forced. In one glance, Susan is telling her daughter to not screw this up.

"Shall we take our table?" I point to the hostess behind us who's ready to seat us. Susan nods and turns to follow. Alicia takes my arm and leans into my shoulder.

"I hope you know what you're getting into. Mom can be relentless."

"I've got this." I lean down and kiss her on the top of her head at the same time her mom turns to look at us. It was an unintentional moment of affection, but one that earns a huge smile and a gleam in Susan's eyes.

We settle into small talk through ordering our drinks

and dinner. The appetizer is delivered just as Susan asks, "Tell me again, how did you two meet?"

"Emily," Alicia says. "Remember, I told you he's Emily's older brother."

Susan nods. "That's right. Now Emily is a darling. So sweet and kind. Alicia, why can't you be more like that girl?"

"Mom, not this again."

"I'm just saying it would be nice if you put yourself out there more like Emily does. At least she dates and tries to meet a nice man."

Alicia's jaw drops, and with a dramatic swoosh of her hand, she points at me. "And who's this?"

Susan waves at the air like she's swatting away a fly. "You know what I mean. If you were more like Emily, maybe you would've met Heath years ago."

Alicia drops her head into her hand and sighs. "I don't know why you always compare me to Emily. She hasn't dated anyone in a while, Mom."

"More recently than you, though," her mom snaps back.

I wrap my arm around Alicia's shoulder and hug her close. "It wouldn't have worked years ago. Sometimes timing is everything in relationships."

"Yes, I suppose," Susan says. "But being more like

Emily couldn't hurt."

I look across the table at Susan and give her my most charming smile. "I'm afraid I'm gonna have to disagree with you on this one." Susan tilts her head to the side and narrows her eyes. I feel Alicia tense next to me. I give her shoulder a squeeze to let her know I've got this. "If Alicia were more like Emily, that might be a bit weird for me, being she's my sister and all." I can see the smile spread across Alicia's face out of the corner of my eye. Susan nods in understanding. "Besides, Alicia is perfect the way she is. I wouldn't change a thing."

Susan shakes her head at my last comment and lets out a low harrumph. "Oh, come now. Surely you would prefer she stop writing."

"Why would I want that? She loves writing."

"You're a successful man. I'd imagine owning your own business affords the luxury of living off a single income. She doesn't need to write with you in her life."

I toss my head back and laugh even though I don't think her comment is funny. I now understand what Alicia meant when she said her mom would criticize her. The woman doesn't even support her daughter's career. I can't fathom what that must be like for Alicia. "That might be moving a bit fast for us since we've only been dating a little over a month. However, even if we were at that point in our relationship, I'd never dream of encouraging Alicia to quit her job. It's a huge part of who she is."

"I can appreciate you wanting to support her, but her schedule is unacceptable. The hours she works are outlandish. At a minimum, you need to get that under control."

"Mom!" Alicia balls her hands into fists in her lap. I slip my hand under the table and rest it on hers. She's tense, and I can feel her heavy breathing. I rub my thumb against the back of her hand, trying to relax her.

"I wouldn't dream of asking her to change her work schedule for me." I kiss her cheek, hoping this and my words help calm her down. She's getting too worked up over this. I'd much rather enjoy this evening than have her pissed the entire time. "I accept her as she is—career choice and work schedule included."

Alicia lifts her hand to my cheek and tugs me to her. She kisses me softly. It's sweet, endearing, and lingers even after she pulls away.

"Thank you," she whispers.

Either Susan said all she wanted to say, or the level of affection Alicia and I shared was enough to appease her, because she didn't say anything else critical the rest of the night. When Susan isn't focused on her dissatisfaction over Alicia's life choices, she's a very pleasant woman to be around.

We eat, we drink, and we laugh. We enjoy each other's company, and all thoughts of our time together ending, leave my mind. For the rest of dinner, Alicia is mine, and I'm happy.

CHAPTER
TWENTY-FOUR

Alicia

Aside from the expected criticism, dinner with Mom was perfect. Heath was perfect. Everything he said, every action, and every moment of affection he showed me was exactly what I needed Mom to see and hear. As fake boyfriends go, Heath is the best.

When he defended my career with such conviction and sincerity, I almost cried. No one has ever defended my career and my work schedule like that. Not even Emily or Trent.

He played the part beautifully. So well, in fact, he had me believing we were really in a loving relationship. He made me feel appreciated in a way no one has ever made me feel before. I'll always be grateful to him for that. If I were any other woman, I'd have a hard time convincing my heart that this ends tonight.

We walk hand-in-hand back to my apartment. Neither of us say much. It's like we're old friends who don't need words to know what the other is thinking or feeling. We're content, and equally satisfied with how well this arrangement worked out for both of us.

We stop outside my apartment, and he hesitates after he opens the door to my building to let me in. When I turn around, his familiar green eyes are conflicted and lack the brightness I'm used to seeing. I don't understand where the look is coming from, but it makes me want to hug him. The urge to spend more time with him is strong. I'm not sure what to do with that urge, but it is what it is. I can't walk away without him.

"Do you want to come up?" I ask. I didn't plan on inviting him up tonight. This was just supposed to be dinner with Mom, but I want him one last time before we say goodbye.

He nods, and my stomach does flips. He wants me one last time, too.

I take his hand and lead him to the elevator. My heart is pounding in my chest like a bass drum, and I don't know why I feel so nervous. My insides are churning like this is the first time we're going to have sex. I feel flushed, and my palm is sweaty in his hand. If he notices, he doesn't react. Maybe his palm is sweating, too.

I'm more aware of his closeness than I've been since I met him. His body is angled to my side, and his chest rubs against my arm. I feel every breath he takes. The rise and fall of his chest excites me. I want him more than I've ever wanted him, or anyone for that matter.

Scratch that. I don't just want him. I *need* him tonight. I've never needed a man like this before, and that need terrifies me. Needing someone this much challenges my independence and risks everything I worked so hard to protect—my career and my heart.

But I don't have time to process that fear. I let go of his hand long enough to unlock my door. As soon as we step inside, his arm snakes around my waist, and he pulls me into him. I moan at how good his chest feels pressed against my back. He's hard and warm and comforting. And I forget about everything else but him.

His free hand brushes my hair from my neck, and his lips gently nip just below my ear. It sends a shiver through me that causes me to visibly shake in his arms. The need inside me intensifies.

He spins me in his arms. His mouth is on mine before I can catch my breath. His kiss is hungry and demanding. He kisses me like he owns me, and I can't get enough of it.

Every emotion we've shared over the past three weeks comes out through this kiss. The way our tongues tangle and tease and taste each other is a full exploration of those emotions.

As kisses go, I'll never forget this one.

"Alicia." The gentle way in which he whispers my name doesn't match the force with which he's kissing me. It's a promise that while he may be taking what he wants, it's all for my pleasure.

His hand cradles my neck before sliding around to the back and into my hair. His fingers fist around my hair, and he tugs my head back. I feel vulnerable and exposed and so very turned on. His mouth crushes into my neck. He feasts on me like I'm the best thing he's ever tasted.

He unbuttons my blouse and pulls down my bra. I'm at his mercy and fall limp in his arms when his mouth closes around my exposed nipple. Everything about this man feels so damn good. I don't want him to stop.

I regain enough of my senses to undo his pants and slip my hand around his hard cock. When I squeeze him from the base and pull, he clamps down on my nipple, and I cry out. It's pain and pleasure and pure ecstasy.

He backs me up to the wall and presses his body against mine. I reach for his cock again, but he stops me. He grabs my hands and holds them above my head with one hand while his mouth and other hand roam down my body.

"I want you. All of you." His words brush across my skin.

"Then take me."

I gasp when he bites my nipple. His tongue swirls around it, soothing the bite, and I think he could make me come from this action alone. He does it again. It's the best form of pain I ever felt.

"More," I moan.

His lips trail up my chest and around my neck. He has me so worked up that his beard brushing across my sensitive skin sends tremors throughout my body. His kisses are fierce and sensual. He licks and nips and sucks at my body, and I'm about to come completely unglued. "Heath, please."

He pulls back and pins me with his deep green eyes. His stare is full of longing, desire, and need. A need so deep, he looks like he'd break if I refused him. We're both breathing heavily, and his hesitation worries me. "Heath?"

He shakes his head before he drops it to my shoulder. He releases my hands which he'd held above my head and pulls me into him. I run my fingers through his hair. The low groan that escapes his lips makes me ache for him in a way I can't quite interpret.

"Heath, what's wrong?"

He lifts his head and gently kisses my lips. "I need more, Alicia."

"I don't understand." And I really don't. I'm half naked, wedged between his body and the wall. It couldn't get any clearer that I'm okay with this. "I'm offering you all of me."

He swallows and pulls back just enough so our bodies are no longer touching. A chill runs through me and a sense of dread consumes me. "But for how long? Tonight? A week? A month?"

"I ... I ... What are you saying?" My head spins, and my vision blurs. I know what he's asking but the question spills out anyway.

"I can't do this without knowing you'll still be mine tomorrow."

My fear comes crashing to a halt and lands right between us. He wants more—a relationship—and I can't give him that. "But our agreement was only through tonight. This is it."

"We never agreed to this." He points between us and steps back into my space. His face is inches from mine. For a moment I think he's going to kiss me again, but he doesn't. "This level of intimacy is so much more, and I don't want to let you go."

"But you have to." I push him away, and he stumbles back. I can't breathe, and his closeness suffocates me. I need space to think and formulate my thoughts, so I can make him understand that this can't happen. "I can't give you more."

"Alicia, please." He reaches for my hand, but I step around him. The panic that fills me is unexpected. "I'm asking you to try. Give us a chance."

"Us?" I cry out. Hot tears fill my eyes, and I turn away. I can't look at him. Every raw emotion and feeling he has for me is written all over his face. I feel like shit for the words I'm about to say, but I have to make him understand. "There is no us, Heath. This was never meant to last."

"Regardless, it still happened." His voice strengthens. He steps around me and lifts my face, forcing me to look in his eyes. "You feel this, too. I know it."

"No. No, you're wrong." The tears I'd been fighting break free and run down my cheek. He wipes them away before he drops his forehead to mine.

"Please, don't push me away. I know you're scared. I'm scared, too. I never thought I'd meet someone that made me feel like this again. I can't lose you."

I can't take his closeness. It confuses me and clouds my thoughts. I push him away and regain my resolve. "How can you lose something you never had?"

The pain in his eyes nearly breaks me. I never wanted to hurt him, but with that one sentence, I did. But I can't give him what he wants. Not now. Maybe not ever.

"I think you should leave," I say, the words clipped and harsh.

His eyes gloss over before he turns around and runs his fingers through his hair. He stands with his back to me for what feels like an eternity before he adjusts his clothing. He takes a deep breath. I think he's going to speak, but he doesn't. A moment later, he walks out the door.

He's gone.

I collapse on the floor and cry. Why? I don't know. This is what I want. I can't date him. It'll only result in pain. His leaving is the best thing that he could've done for both of us. He may not see it now, but one day he'll thank me for pushing him away. I'm all wrong for him.

I'd rather have him upset with me now because if this continued it would destroy me to see the feelings he has for me turn to hate. I remind my broken heart that it's better this way.

I just hope I don't end up regretting what I've done.

CHAPTER
TWENTY-FIVE

Heath

It's been six days since Alicia shattered my heart. Yep, shattered.

Completely.

Devastated.

Destroyed.

I wasn't prepared to experience feelings of love again. Although, I never expected to find someone like Alicia, either.

Before meeting Alicia, I believed I had my one chance at love. I'd convinced myself that I was okay with spending the rest of my life alone, never getting to experience how it felt to have the woman I love next to me again. It almost hurt more because I knew enough to not take those feelings for granted as I had the first time.

Joke's on me. I found love again, but it didn't find me.

I'm still going to spend the rest of my life alone. Only now, my life is filled with more pain and heartache than it was pre-Alicia.

Losing one love is bad enough. Losing a woman I never really had, well, that fucking sucks.

She broke me in two when she said I couldn't lose something I never had. It was a mean, low blow. It was also true.

I have no one to blame but myself for my current state of despair. I willingly let myself get too deep. I opened myself up to her, foolishly thinking she felt the same intense connection to me that I feel for her.

I was wrong.

I'll pay for this mistake for years to come.

Losing Lauren was hard. It took years for me to pick up the pieces of my soul and put them back together after she died. Lauren and I had known each other since we were kids. We started dating in college and had been together for five years when I proposed. We had a lifetime of friendship and love holding us together. I haven't known Alicia long enough for her to hurt me this deeply. It doesn't make sense, but it's true.

Then again, Lauren didn't leave me by choice. The knife stabs so much deeper when a person chooses to cut your heart out. Alicia didn't set out to hurt me, I know that, but she's still responsible for her actions. She chose to leave me.

There's a soft knock on my office door before it cracks open. Dexter's head pokes through. "You okay, bro?" He asks as he steps inside and shuts the door behind him. "You haven't spoken to any of us in days."

I keep my eyes trained on my desk. If I look up at my brother, I'll lose it. I've never been very good at hiding my emotions, and the knowing eyes of my siblings will cause me to crumble. I've avoided them for this reason even though I could use their support and advice. I was a no-show for our Monday morning meeting, which is something I've never done. I've worked from home most of this week. I expected one or all of them to show up at my apartment and demand an answer as to why. To my surprise, they left me alone. I was both grateful and disappointed they didn't come to me.

I snuck in early this morning and have been holed up in my office with the door shut all day. Until now, no one has bothered me.

I'm not ready to talk about what happened with Alicia.

Plus, they're all friends with her. I don't want to give them a reason to be upset with her. It's not her fault I didn't keep my heart out of our fake relationship. That's all on me.

"Do you want to talk about it?" Dexter asks.

"No," I growl.

"I think maybe you should. Talking might help."

"I said no!" I raise my voice to a near yell. Dexter doesn't flinch. He stands stock still with his arms across his chest and stares at me with sympathetic eyes.

"Damn." A slow smile spreads across his face. "You really do love her."

A deep rumble builds in my chest as I fix to yell at Dexter again. Apparently, he finds my anger amusing because he laughs. This just makes me even angrier. "It doesn't matter what I feel."

"That's where you're wrong. How you feel means everything. We left you alone when Lauren died. Mostly because there wasn't a damn thing any of us could do to make it better. But that's not the case this time around. Come on. It's time for an intervention."

Dexter opens the door and leaves my office without giving me a chance to argue. It's almost five o'clock, and I'm past ready to go home. It doesn't sound like that's happening anytime soon. When I walk out this door, my siblings are going to block my exit and force me to talk.

As much as I don't want to do this now, I suck it up and head out to the bar. Once my siblings get an idea in their heads, there's no changing their minds anyway. If they want an intervention, I'll give it to them. It's not like additional damage can be done. Alicia took care of that all on her own.

The bar is oddly quiet for a Thursday. It's still early, but it's typically one of our busiest days. Dexter's walking a few feet in front of me, Luke is behind the bar, and Emily is sitting at a bar stool next to her friend Trent. I'm surprised to see him here. I've met him several times over the years, but we're not friends. He certainly doesn't know much about me.

"You look like hell," Luke says as he rests his elbows on the bar. He's wearing his typical devilish grin, and it pisses me off.

"Shut the hell up. I'm aware of how I look," I bark back, in no mood for his antics. "I didn't get much sleep last night."

"Girlfriend keeping you up too late?" Luke waggles his brows. Despite my angry tone, his grin grows.

Dexter sits in the stool next to Emily. I stop a few feet in front of them. I feel like I'm standing in front of a firing squad with the way they're all staring at me. Emily sits on her hands with a sad, concerned look in her eyes. Dexter and Trent are on either side of her with their arms crossed over their chests. Their expressions are a mix of concern and determination. Then there's Luke. He leans in behind them with that damn grin. The urge to beat it out of him is strong.

I sigh, drop my head in my hand, and rub my eyes. "I don't have a girlfriend."

Luke chuckles. "What did you do, ditch Alicia already?"

Emily turns and hits Luke upside the head. "Shut up."

"Ouch." Luke frowns and rubs the side of his head. "What did you do that for?"

"All right." Dexter pins Luke with a glare. "That's enough."

"What? I'm just getting answers." Luke shrugs like he has no clue why anyone would be upset with what he's said.

Dexter clears his throat before he speaks again. "Want to tell us what happened?"

"There's nothing to tell. We fake dated. Now it's over. End of story."

Dexter shakes his head before I even finish speaking. "If it's the end of the story, why are you so upset?"

I cross my arms over my chest and match his stare. "Who says I'm upset?"

"Look in the mirror, bro. You're upset."

Hell yeah, I'm upset. I've no clue why I'd even try to deny it. I couldn't convince my siblings I'm fine if my life depended on it.

But I don't want to have this conversation right now. I want to be left alone to deal with this loss in my own way, and I certainly don't need my siblings telling me the obvious. Anyone in my position would be upset. An amazing, funny, kind, and generous woman won over my heart. Then crushed it.

Trent straightens in his seat as he watches me through narrow eyes. "Why don't we all take a step back? Maybe if you tell us what happened, we can help."

"Why exactly are you here?" I know he's friends with Alicia, but I don't need another person telling me how to feel about this or how to handle this situation. I'm sure my siblings will take care of that without his help.

"Consider me a neutral party." Trent's expression shifts from a look of concern to one of understanding. "If you tell us what happened, maybe I can offer some insight into Alicia and why she did what she did."

"What makes you think she did anything?" I snap. Even though she's the reason I feel like shit, I still feel the urge to protect her. This is all my fault for letting myself get too close. Alicia may have acted like she felt more for me, but she never once said she wanted more. I made that assumption all on my own.

"Oh, let me take a guess here." Trent starts. "You two were getting along great—you liked her, she seemed to like you. Then you asked for more, and she pushed you away. Am I close?"

Damn. Trent seems to have Alicia pegged. "Maybe."

He nods with a sigh. "There are things about Alicia's past you don't know. She's been hurt badly before."

I drop my arms to my side. My shoulders sag as the memory of our conversation on the boat floods back to me. I can't imagine the scars that she's living with. As much as I hated to do it, it's the main reason I walked away without pushing her. The last thing I want to do is add to her pain. "She told me about Jeremy."

"She what?" Trent's jaw drops.

"She told me about what he did to her. How you showed up and saved her."

Trent stiffens, and his eyes widen. "Well, fuck me."

"What's that supposed to mean?"

He shakes his head and chuckles. "It means that if she told you about him, she's in deep."

I snort. "If she's in deep, she has a hell of a way of expressing herself."

Emily jumps out of her seat and grabs hold of my arms. She looks up at me with tears in her eyes. "I'll go talk to her. Maybe I can talk some sense into her."

"Oh, no you don't," Trent says. "You'll do no such thing."

She spins around, tears now flowing down her cheeks. I want to pull her into my arms and hug those tears away. I hate seeing any woman cry, especially my sister. "She's my best friend. She'll talk to me."

"Under normal circumstances, yes. But you're also Heath's sister. Let me go."

Emily's face hardens as she wipes away her tears. She looks like she's going to argue with Trent, but then she sighs. "You're right."

Trent steps up to Emily, gives her a hug and kisses the top of her head. "I'll let her know you're concerned, and that you'll call in a few days."

He stops next to me and squeezes my shoulder. "You're a good man, Heath. Don't give up on her."

I nod and watch him as he leaves the bar. When I turn back to my siblings, Dexter pats the stool next to him and Luke sets down a glass of whiskey on the rocks. That's their cue that the conversation is over and now it's time to sit, drink, and bullshit about nothing.

We don't do this often, but tonight, I need this. I may be in a sour mood, but spending this time with my siblings helps. We talk about nothing significant and laugh often. By the time I leave the bar and head home, I feel better. With my siblings by my side, I'll be fine no matter what Alicia decides. By the time I get home, I've almost convinced myself of that.

CHAPTER
TWENTY-SIX

Alicia

I'm an asshole.

Full on, I-should-be-ashamed-of-myself, asshole.

It's been a week since I rejected Heath. I still can't get the image of his broken expression out of my mind. The sadness and tears that welled up in his eyes wreck me. I didn't mean to hurt him. Heath is a great guy, and I never wanted to cause him pain.

But I did anyway.

I never should have given into my desire for him. That's where I made my mistake. Sex always leads to feelings. And feelings always lead to heartache. I know that.

I'd be lying if I said I didn't feel anything for Heath. I

do. I feel way more than I should.

My career has always been first in my life. That was the root of all of my issues with Jeremy. It didn't matter what I did to please him, it was never enough. If I got up early to work, he got mad. If I worked late in the evening, he got mad. He got mad when I worked during a normal eight-hour workday. No matter what I did to please him, he hated it. Because at the root of it all, he didn't want me to work.

We fought about it often. I made sacrifices for him. When it became too much for him, look where that got me—beaten and held hostage in my own apartment.

I'll never make that kind of sacrifice for a man again. Not even for a good man like Heath. I don't care what he said or how great a guy he is, my career will eventually become a problem. People say all kinds of things when they're trying to win someone over, but they don't truly mean it. Jeremy fed me the same line of bullshit, and it was all a lie.

Despite these truths, I miss Heath. I miss his smile and his adorable dimple that broke through his beard when he gave me a huge grin. God, I miss that beard and the way it felt when he kissed my neck. I miss the way he held my hand or lightly touched the small of my back to let me know he was near. I miss his bright green eyes and how they'd light up when he looked at me. And I miss how he made me feel wanted and special.

Fuck, I miss him way too much. Now my chest hurts again. I don't know what this pain means, and I can't seem to get it to stop. Every time I think about Heath, which is always, I hurt. He invades my every thought.

Even my apartment is a constant reminder of him. He's in my kitchen, pressed up against me with his lips on the back of my neck. He's by my front door, pinning me against the wall with his mouth roaming down my body. And he's in my bed with his body wrapped around me, spooning me close to him.

There's no escaping these memories, so I grab my laptop and head out. Maybe getting out will help clear my mind.

I head toward Coffee Stop in need of a coffee and chocolate croissant. Chocolate always makes me feel better. I'm halfway there when I stop. The memory of my last visit floods through my mind. I can't go back there either. Every time I visit Coffee Stop, I'll be reminded of my second chance meeting with Heath when I only knew him as Mr. Sexy-As-Hell-Stick-Up-His-Ass.

"Fuck," I mumble to myself and drop against the building next me. I don't want to go home because I see Heath at every turn. I can't go to my favorite coffee shop because he's there, too. I can't even go to my favorite bar and have a drink because Heath co-owns that damn place.

I've really made a mess of my life this time.

To make this mess even worse, I can't call my best friend for support because she won't support me. She'll support her brother.

With no other options coming to mind, I resolve to head home. I'll open a bottle of wine and drink my memories away. Maybe if I get drunk, I'll stop thinking about Heath for one night.

I push off the wall and turn back toward my apartment when I hear someone call my name. I turn toward the voice and break down in tears. Within seconds, Trent is by my side, hugging me tight.

"Hey, now. None of this." Trent's voice is soothing, the same as it was that day he rescued me from Jeremy.

"I don't know what's wrong with me." I manage between sobs. "I hurt all over."

"Come on." Trent wraps his arm around my shoulder and leads me down the sidewalk. "Let's get you home."

I stop, causing him to stumble. "I don't want to go home."

"Why not?"

"Because I see him everywhere."

Trent nods and looks around before he takes my hand. We cross the street, and he leads me into a nearby bar. It's early afternoon, and the place is mostly empty. I only see one other person sitting at the opposite end of the bar from where we sit down. He orders us each a drink, then stares at me.

"You want to tell me what's really going on?" he asks.

I dry my eyes and take a drink of the wine he ordered me. If anyone can help me understand how I'm feeling, it's Trent. But I still don't want to talk about it. It hurts too much.

"Babe." He squeezes my hand. "Tell me what you're thinking. That's the only way I can help you."

"I'm thinking I'm an idiot." I toss the rest of my wine back and wave at the bartender for another glass. "I should've known better than to get close to Heath. He wants more. I can't give that to him. He'll end up trying to control my life just like you know who did."

Trent's shoulders sag. He looks at me with pain in his eyes. "Heath is not Jeremy."

"I never said he was."

"You kinda just did." He doesn't take his eyes off me as he sips his beer. "What makes you think Heath would ever try to control your life?"

"I don't know. Maybe because I'm scared. Every part

of me hurts. I can't help but feel the need to run. This can't be a good sign."

"Listen, babe." Trent shifts his body so he's facing me. "Don't screw this up. At some po—"

"I'm not screwing anything up!" I know he's trying to help but I don't like how he said that. "I'm protecting myself."

"I believe you think that's what you're doing, but you're not. You know I love you, and please understand that this is coming from a good place." He pauses and places his hand on his heart before he tilts his head down to look me in the eye. "You're screwing this up. Heath is a good man."

I huff, feeling way too defensive. "I know he's a good man."

"Then why are you letting Jeremy win?" he says in a matter-of-fact tone.

"What's that supposed to mean?" I'm no longer upset. I'm irritated with how he's talking to me. He's making me feel like I've done something awful to Heath when I didn't. All I did was stick to the plan.

"By walking away from Heath—a man I suspect you're falling in love with—you're letting Jeremy win."

"Love?" I almost drop my glass of wine. Why the hell is he talking about love? I can't possibly love Heath. Sure, I like him. He's a great guy. I had a lot of fun with him these past few weeks. But love? I don't even know what that looks like.

"Yes. That's why this hurts so much." Trent pauses and waves at the bartender. He puts in an order of wings and fries before he turns his attention back to me. "And trust me. Heath loves you, too. He actually looks worse than you, and you look like shit."

All I can do is stare at him in disbelief. A few minutes ago, I was crying and could barely contain my emotions, and now I'm pissed. I'm not sure what point he's trying to make, but I know he's got one. "What are you talking about?"

"Love, babe." He leans forward and squeezes my shoulder. "You two are falling in love with each other, but you're letting what Jeremy did to you screw it up. I know Jeremy hurt you, but you gotta let that shit go before you lose what may very well be the best thing that ever happened to you."

"But how do I know I can trust myself?"

"I think the question you really should be asking yourself is, do you trust Heath?"

"I do." I answer Trent without even thinking about it. I didn't have to think about it because it's true. I trust Heath without question. I'd trust him with my life and never give it a second thought. Realization washes over me, and I sink.

"Oh, my God, what have I done?"

I drop my head onto the bar and groan. I've been so fixated on my lack of trust in myself, I never even considered how much I trust Heath. I have no doubt whatsoever that he'd never hurt me like Jeremy did and that's all I need to know.

I turn my head to Trent and he's watching me with a gentle smile. "It's okay, babe. Let's eat some wings and make a plan to win him back."

And we do. By the time he walks me home I feel better and confident that I'm ready to take this next step in my life. I'm still scared, mostly because this is new territory for me, but I'm also excited. For the first time since Jeremy, I'm opening my heart up to the possibility of love.

CHAPTER
TWENTY-SEVEN

Heath

It's been two weeks since I last saw Alicia, and I'm finally starting to feel like myself again. I still miss her, but at least I'm getting back to my normal schedule. I'm sleeping again thanks to my running. When she first broke it off with me, I couldn't sleep. I also stopped all my other routines.

While I'm still running for the simple act of moving forward, now it's also softening the edges of my pain. Losing Alicia hurt, but I'm better equipped to deal with the pain than I was when I lost Lauren. Maybe it's because I'm older and a little wiser. Or maybe it's because there's a small part of me that's still hanging onto hope.

Whatever the reason, I feel better when I run.

Central Park is quiet for a Saturday morning. Summer is nearing its end. It's the time of year when families are taking last minute vacations before school starts back up or enjoying the last of the warm weather on the water.

It rained last night, and the moisture in the air is heavy. I take a deep breath and smile as the musty, decaying scent of wet soil and dying vegetation fills my nostrils. I don't know what it is about this smell, but it always makes me feel alive. Which is weird since it's the smell of dead plants and earth. Come spring, we'll welcome the fresh scent of budding leaves, green grass, and blooming flowers all thanks to these dying plants. It all goes hand-in-hand. Without one, we wouldn't have the other.

Kind of like the transition of my broken heart to a healed heart. I would've loved Lauren with all my heart for the rest of my life, but that wasn't in the cards for us. I didn't realize it until now, but she primed my heart and made it possible for me to love. If I had gone thirty-six years of life without love, I wouldn't have recognized my feelings for Alicia. It took that one love and loss for me to know what it felt like and to know that I could have it again.

Just like the cycle of life. You love. You lose. You love again.

My feet pound on the pavement as I near the last turn in my morning run. This stretch takes me past a small pond where, no matter the weather, people are gathered around the edge feeding the ducks, standing on the footbridge watching the fish, sitting on the benches drinking coffee, or catching up with friends. It's the place I always imagined I'd bring my kids if I had any. It's picturesque and made for families and love.

Maybe one day that dream of mine will come true.

I pass the pond to take the final trail that will lead me to my apartment. That's when I see her. In slow motion, I come to a stop.

Alicia is standing in the middle of the trail wearing the same leggings and sports bra she wore the first day we met. Her hair is even pulled back into the same tantalizing ponytail that became the object of my fantasies before I knew how that hair felt between my fingers. My cock wakes up at the memory of her silky hair in my hands and her naked body next to mine. I swallow the groan that builds in my chest and tamp down my desire for her.

She's not mine.

She never will be.

She made that very clear.

She gives me a tentative smile but doesn't move toward

me. We're both frozen in place. The urge to go to her and take her into my arms is strong, but I don't. The pain from her rejection is still strong. If she pushed me away now, I might not recover.

She steps toward me and stops when she's only a couple feet away. She's as beautiful as ever, but she looks tired. Her eyes are a little bloodshot and maybe even puffy, like she's been crying.

Shit. I don't care how much she hurt me. I don't want her to cry.

"Hi." Her voice is low and breathy, and the sweet sound hits me in the chest like an arrow. A heaviness presses down on me and every nerve ending aches.

"What are you doing here?" I ask, my voice gravelly and hoarse. There's no way she's here by accident. By the way she shifts on her feet, she has something to say.

She opens her mouth then stops herself. Her eyes meet mine then quickly shift to the ground. Her nervousness makes it even harder to not wrap my arms around her. I want to comfort her and tell her it will be all right, but that would be a lie. Nothing about what's going on between us is all right.

"Alicia?" She looks up at me with glassy eyes. My stomach drops. If the sadness in her gaze is any indication, she's doing just as bad as me. "Why are you here?"

She squeezes her eyes closed and covers her face with her hands. "You look so mad. I don't know what I expected, but seeing you mad wasn't it."

"Sorry. I didn't realize ... I mean ... I'm not happy, but I'm not mad at you, if that's what you're worried about." At least that much is true. I'm not mad at her. I'm mad at myself and the situation. I hate the decision she made, but I understand why she made it.

"I don't want you to be unhappy."

"I'll get over it."

"Heath," she huffs and shakes her head. She reaches for my hand, but I jerk it away.

"What do you *want* from me?"

She flinches at my harsh tone, and I take a step back. I didn't mean to snap, but seeing her has thrown me off. This is supposed to be my safe place. The one thing I do for myself to reduce stress and cope with all the bullshit in my life. I can't do that when she's part of the bullshit.

She reaches for me again, but I pull back. If she touches me, I won't be able to control my urge to hold her.

"I'm sorry." She wraps her arms around her midsection. The strong, sassy woman that grabbed hold of my heart is gone. The woman before me is small and fragile. "This is so much harder than I thought it'd be."

"What's so hard?"

She takes a deep breath and closes her eyes. A few seconds pass before she opens them and looks at me. "Inviting you to an event of mine tonight."

What the hell? That isn't what I expected her to say. This woman crushed me. Now she wants my support by attending one of her events. There's no way I can do that. Thankfully, I have an out. "I have plans with my brothers tonight."

"I know. They promised to make sure you came if I personally invited you. They refused to blindside you by dragging you there without knowing I'd be there."

I roll my eyes up to the sky and swallow my curse. And here I thought she came to see me on her own accord. "I don't think that's such a good idea."

"Please, Heath." She shifts on her feet and nibbles on her bottom lip. "It's my final interview for my latest book tour. I have some things to say that I'd like you to hear."

"Why not tell me now?"

"I've never said some of these things, and I need the security of a safe platform. I'm comfortable with interviews. I'm not comfortable with this." She points back and forth between us with a look of desperation in her eyes. "I don't know how to do this. Not yet." She pauses and swallows hard. "Will you come?"

The strong, vibrant woman I fell in love looks like she's about to break. I hate it. All I want to do is be that strength for her. Maybe that's why I agree, or maybe it's the hope that swells inside me. "Okay. I'll come."

She sighs deeply and meets my stare. "You will?"

"If you can take the time to invite me personally, I can take the time to be there."

"Thank you." She bounces on her heels and fidgets with the end of her ponytail. "I can't tell you how much this means to me. I ... Thanks, really. I'll let you get back to your run."

She turns to walk away.

"Hey, Alicia."

She spins around so quickly she stumbles but catches herself before she falls. "Yeah?"

I smile. "It's good to see you."

She nods and smiles before she heads across the footbridge. I keep my eyes on her until she disappears. Only then do I begin running again, heading in the opposite direction.

I was dreading my night out with my brothers. But now that I know I'll see Alicia, I'm looking forward to it. She didn't give me any indication what she planned to say, but I hope it means she's giving us a chance.

CHAPTER TWENTY-EIGHT

Alicia

This is a really bad idea.

I don't know why I thought it'd be easier to pour my heart out to Heath via an interview. I wasn't nervous when I came up with this bright idea. But now that it's time to walk on stage, I can't stop shaking.

It was an easy sell to my agent. My fans have wanted to know more about my love life for years, but I've refused to answer those questions. I also haven't had anything good worth sharing until now.

At least, I hope this ends up being good.

When it's all said and done, Heath could reject me. His rejection will hurt, but it can't hurt any worse than I've already hurt myself.

There are so many things I need to say to Heath, but I don't know how to say them. I've never been in this position before, and I have no clue how to talk to a guy I like about my feelings. I would've thought I'd be better at this being a romance writer, but no. I'm more comfortable talking to my friends, and that's all this is. It's just a friendly discussion with the girls. This, I can do.

The side curtain leading to the stage opens indicating they're getting ready to announce me. Someone checks the microphone clipped to my collar and gives me the thumbs up.

My agent said this venue held about five hundred guests, and it's a sold-out event. I can't believe I agreed to do this in front of five hundred strangers. It's not for them though. It's for the one person who's not a stranger.

I hope he came.

The stage lights brighten signaling the final seconds before my name is called. This is no different than any other event. A series of standard questions with a couple tacked on at the end about my love life. My answers are prepared. If all goes well, I'll win Heath back tonight.

I take one last breath as Ruth, my interviewer, introduces me to the crowd as contemporary romance author, Alexis Stone.

I walk out, and the crowd cheers. It's a sound I never tire of hearing. I love my job, and I love that it makes so many people happy. Having my fans come out to listen to me talk about my work and my life makes every sacrifice I've made worth it.

But tonight, I plan on making a few other sacrifices.

In the center of the stage is a small end table with plush chairs on either side. Ruth stands to hug me before I take the seat opposite her. I adjust the skirt of my dress. It's lavender, the color Heath said he loved on me.

"I'm so excited to have you with us tonight. Your success is unparalleled. I feel like we've done this so many times now." Ruth laughs, and it puts me at ease.

"Thank you." I smile. It feels natural for the first time in days. "It does seem like we've done this a lot. Does that mean I write too many books?"

The crowd laughs along with Ruth. "Never. I think it's safe to say we all love your books and would be sad if you stopped."

I fake a sigh of relief and run the back of my hand over my forehead to exaggerate the action. "Good, because I have no intention of stopping."

The crowd claps and hoots in excitement. I settle into

the interview and all my worries fade away.

Ruth asks me a series of questions about my recent release and current work in progress. All standard questions that I've come to expect over the years as an author. I know each question and the order in which to expect them. As she nears the end of the standard questions and gets closer to the personal ones I approved, my palms sweat and every nerve ending in my body tingles.

So much for being relaxed. I can't remember the last time I've been this nervous. Why I thought this would be easier than just talking to Heath is beyond me.

"We have a special treat for your fans today." Ruth smiles and waggles her brows to the crowd "For the first time, Alexis has agreed to talk about her love life."

A collective gasp sounds through the theater followed by claps. Ruth turns to me, her smile warm and comforting. "Your fans have been dying to know about your love life for years, and you've remained closed-lipped. But tonight I understand you've got something to share."

"Yes." I paste on a smile and scan the crowd. The theater is packed. I can't make out the faces, but I hope Heath is out there listening. "There's not a lot to tell, but my fans have been curious about the woman behind the stories. I'm finally ready to answer their questions."

"Okay, if you're ready, let's get started."

"Fire away." I clasp my hands in my lap to keep my arms from shaking. I'm not new to talking about love. I've done it for years about my characters. I keep telling myself this is no different.

"This may seem like an odd question to your fans considering your talent at writing such emotional love stories, but have you ever been in love?" Ruth asks.

"Well, I'm twenty-seven years old, and I think I'm in love for the first time in my life. I've only ever had one serious boyfriend, and what we shared was not love."

"How do you know you weren't in love with him?"

"I think when you love someone, you should be willing to put them first. Or at least make some sacrifices for the relationship. I've put my career above everything else in my life. I was unwilling to change to create any form of work-life balance to make a relationship successful. While both people should willingly accept the other for who they are, there should also be some give and take. If that can't happen, how can it be love?"

Ruth smiles and nods. She knows I'm nervous about this. I'm grateful she's trying to make this easy on me. "Does that mean you've met someone who you're willing to put first in your life?"

"Yes." Despite how nervous I am, I don't hesitate with my answer. "I've never been in love, so I have nothing to compare my feelings to, but I do know this person means more to me than my career. I by no means want to give up my career. But I also know he'd never ask me to do that. For the first time in my life, I've met someone I'm willing to make sacrifices for."

"So the skilled romance writer finally gets her own happily-ever-after." Ruth's voice rises in excitement and the audience cheers.

I wave my hands to the side and shake my head. The crowd quiets at my reaction. "I haven't earned my happily-ever-after just yet." I cringe and cover my face. "I screwed it up and pushed him away." A mixture of gasps and sighs moves across the audience as my words sink in. "But I'd love a second chance to change what I said to him and rewrite that ending."

"We all love a second chance romance, don't we?" Ruth smiles. "If you could say anything to this man, what would you say?"

"That's the hard part." I take a deep breath and rub my hands down the arm rests of the chair. "I'd say I'm sorry and beg him for forgiveness, but that doesn't feel like enough. If he'll give me the chance, I'll spend the rest of my life trying to make it up to him."

Instead of being met with gasps and cheers, silence fills the theater. It's almost more than I can bear. I bite my bottom lip and twist my hands in my lap. I squeeze my eyes closed and fight back the tears I feel coming on. I've cried enough this week, and I refuse to cry in front of my fans.

The murmur of voices in the crowd draws my eyes open. I scan the crowd but it's impossible to make out the faces. Heath said he'd come, but maybe he changed his mind. Or maybe I wanted it so badly I fooled myself into thinking he'd be here.

The murmur grows louder, and a few gasps fill the air. I look to Ruth for guidance.

A huge smile spreads across her face. "Maybe you'll get an opportunity to rewrite that ending tonight." She tilts her head to look around me and points. "Is that by any chance the man who's earned your love?"

I turn around in my chair and jump up. Heath is standing near the edge of the stage behind me. I'd hoped he'd be here to hear my confession and make himself known to me. But I never expected him to come to me like this. "You came."

"Of course, I came." Heath's familiar baritone voice filled the room. Someone must've given him a microphone.

I hear the muffled sound of the microphone dropping to the ground as Heath leaps onto the stage. In three large strides, he's in front of me. He wraps an arm around my waist and his other hand around my neck. His lips are on mine before I have a chance to breathe. It's sensual, deep, and claiming. This kiss says I'm his, and for the first time in my life I want to be owned by a man—this man.

"Heath."

His lips ghosts across mine. "Mmhmm." He doesn't stop kissing me as he acknowledges I spoke.

Everything around us fades into the background and it's only the two of us remaining. My nerves are in knots with the next words I need to say. I need to tell him how I feel and how utterly terrified I am of these feelings. "I've never been in love before."

His lips freeze against mine and his eyes are wide as he stares down at me. I swallow and force myself to continue. "I'm terrified. I've never been this terrified in my life. I feel like I'm gonna be sick when you're not around, and when you are near, I can't stop shaking. I'm anxious and nauseous until you touch me. Your touch grounds me and calms me. No one's ever done that to me before. It scares me."

He kisses me gently before he pulls me into a close hug. His lips are next to my ear and he whispers. "I'm not gonna lie to you, beautiful. Love is scary, and it can be painful at times. But it's worth the risk for the right person."

I pull back and look into his bright green eyes. I see every emotion I've ever dreamed of seeing in a man as he looks at me—love, and compassion, and desire. "Am I worth the risk?"

"Yes." He blurts out, and I suck in a breath. He's so confident in his response and that it makes me even more nervous. And it's not just his confidence that has me unnerved, it's the next question I need to ask him.

"Do I scare you?" I hold my breath as I wait for his answer. He silently watches me with a careful gaze like he's thinking about his words. His confidence is still visible but he's holding back for a different reason. "Tell me."

He sighs and squeezes me tighter. "I've been scared and sick to my stomach ever since we had dinner with your mom. You pulled away from me and that was painful. I was scared I'd never see you again."

"I'm sorry. I never meant to hurt you."

"I know. It only hurt because I love you. I was afraid you didn't love me back."

Tears well up in my eyes and a knot forms in the back of my throat. "No one has ever said those words to me before."

"That's a shame." He lightly kisses me. "Because no

matter how scary love can be, it's a wonderful feeling. It hurts like hell to lose, but every minute you have it is a minute worth living. I can't promise you things will be perfect. I can't promise we won't argue and fight. But I can promise you that I'll protect you, care for you, and love you for as long as you'll have me. So, what do you say?"

There's so much happiness and longing in the way he looks at me. It calms me and the nerves that were eating me alive a few moments ago have settled. "I think ... I mean ... Yes. I love you, too."

A wide smile covers his face and that dimple I love so much pops out. He wraps his arms around me, lifts me off the ground and spins me. The crowd cheers, and I'm suddenly reminded we're not alone. We're on stage and the microphone attached to my shirt likely picked up our entire conversation and broadcasted it throughout the theater.

"Shit, I think we just said all that to the entire crowd." A few people whoop, whistle, and yell out words of encouragement.

Heath just smiles and holds me tight. "Well, it makes a damn good ending if you ask me."

"It's perfect. And from the most perfect book boyfriend a girl could want."

He raises a brow. "I thought I was an imperfect book

boyfriend."

"Never. You're better than fiction and exactly what I always dreamed of finding. That's perfect in my book."

EPILOGUE

Alicia

Four Months Later

The End!

Two of my favorite words.

Finishing a novel will never get old. This is my forty-eighth novel and every time I get to type those two three letter words beside each other I get excited like it's the first time. There's something remarkably satisfying about completing a novel. Especially one with two people's love story wrapped up in a beautiful happy ending.

This novel holds a special significance that no other novel possesses. It's the first novel I've written in completion while in a relationship and living my own happily-ever-after.

Writing this book took longer than normal. I usually

write a completed first draft in less than a month, not four. I've made sacrifices for my relationship. And I'm completely okay with that.

Life with Heath couldn't be any better. In fact, these past few months with him have been the best months of my life.

Things have moved fast between us. We've been inseparable since the night we got back together. At first, I was afraid we were moving too fast. Especially with this being my first good relationship. But neither of us want to be apart.

Every concern or worry I had vanished when he moved in with me two months ago. It just made sense. He spent most of his nights with me anyway. When we were apart, we were both miserable.

Speaking of being apart. I'm anxious to tell him I finished my novel.

Checking the time, my shoulders sag when I see it's 3:00 am. He's probably been asleep for hours.

I was so sure my late-night writing habits would bother him. But he's been so supportive and understanding. He's never complained, nor has he expected me to change my schedule for him. I did in the beginning, but I quickly fell into my old habits, and he didn't mind.

Shutting down my laptop, I head to the kitchen to get something to drink before I slip into bed. To my surprise, Heath is still up and sitting on the couch. I lean against the wall and watch him. He's staring at something in front of him, but I can't tell what it is.

"What are you doing up?"

He jumps in his seat and snaps his head around to face me.

He slaps a hand to his chest and lets out a long breath. "Jeez, you scared me. I didn't hear you walk out."

I laugh at the startled look on his face. "Sorry. I was being extra quiet because I assumed you were asleep."

His shoulders relax and he yawns. "I've been going over the proposal for the expansion. What time is it?"

"After three." I push off the wall and head toward him. He scrambles around, digging into the couch next to him. "Did you lose something?"

"No, I got it." His voice sounds panicked, and I pause. His hand clenches into a fist next to his leg. I glance from his hand to his face and his eyes are wide.

With my hands on my hips, I smile. "Whatcha you got there?"

"Nothing." A sheepish grin covers his face. He shifts on the couch and discretely slips his hand under his leg before he pats the couch next to him, inviting me to sit.

With a sideways glance, I sit down next to him. "I don't believe you. You're up to something."

"Nope, I'm not doing anything." He smiles as he leans over and kisses me. I can't be sure, but I think he just stuffed whatever he's hiding under his leg. He's trying to distract me with a kiss, and I let him. When his shoulders relax, I slide over onto him and straddle his lap.

He groans when I slide my tongue over his bottom lip. I'm not playing fair, but I don't care. I want to know what he's hiding. I'll figure it out one way or another.

"I finished my novel." I say against his mouth.

"Congratulations." He smiles and parts his lips so we can explore each other's mouths. "We need to celebrate."

I take this moment to enjoy him. I almost lose focus when his hand slips under my shirt and squeezes my breast. Maybe he's trying to distract me too.

I rock my hips forward and grind into his thickening cock. I just about have him right where I need him in order to take control.

His hand works its way around my back and unclasps my bra. At the same time, I run my hands down his chest and tug his shirt up. When his mouth makes its way down my neck, I make my move. While his mouth and hands are distracted, I slide my hand down to his waist and then under his leg. As soon as I reach my prize, he growls.

"Dammit, Alicia." He drops his head back on the couch, struggling to hold back a laugh.

"What's this?" I stare at the small robin egg blue box in my hand. My heart rate kicks up like someone turned up a dial to high speed. I look from the box to him. He's smiling with confidence. I want to open it, but I can't make my hands move. I'm excited and terrified. I'm worried that I just ruined something special and now it won't happen.

Heath takes the box from me and kisses my cheek. "So much for my plans. I guess I'm doing this now."

My breathing quickens, and I feel lightheaded. "What are you doing now?"

He opens the box and holds his eyes on mine. "Asking you to marry me."

Tears well up in my eyes. "You want to marry me?"

He leans forward and kisses each of my eyelids, then my cheeks, and finally my lips. "More than anything."

I melt into him, cupping my hands around his face. I kiss him deep and hard before I break away. I want to say yes with all my heart, but I hesitate. "You don't think this is too fast?"

"No way." He wipes away the tear that falls down my

cheek. "You're my everything, and I want to marry you. What do you say?"

"I say yes. A hundred times over. Yes. Yes. Yes." I kiss him between each answer until our bodies are so close that every molecule of air has been pushed away.

My happily-ever-after is complete.

EXTENDED
EPILOGUE

Heath

Two Weeks after the Engagement

Alicia made me the happiest man in the world when she agreed to marry me. She made me even happier when she agreed to elope.

Even though I didn't actually get married before, having already gone through a long engagement and the wedding planning process before, I wasn't excited about doing it again. I would've done it for Alicia if that's what she wanted, but I'm glad she didn't.

Two days after she said yes, we applied for our marriage license. Turns out in the State of New York, a couple only has to wait twenty-four hours before they can exchange vows. The next day we arrived at the courthouse and scheduled our civil union in front of a judge and a court appointed witness.

Maybe it wasn't the most romantic of ceremonies, but she's mine and I'm hers. We're married and that's all that matters.

This morning we returned from our honeymoon at a secluded cabin in the Smoky Mountains. Now we're standing on the sidewalk outside The Rock Room where our friends and family are waiting for our arrival under the disguise of a Christmas party planning meeting.

"You're nervous." I pull Alicia into my arms and kiss her. We didn't tell anyone we were getting married, and our families think we took a vacation, not a honeymoon.

"Very." She buries her face in my neck. "My mom and Emily are going to be so upset with me."

I kiss her cheek. "Probably. And my mom may try to ground me." I laugh. "But they'll also get over it and be happy for us in the end. Our marriage is about us and no one else."

"You're right." She smiles as she kisses me. "We're here to celebrate, so let's go before we freeze to death in the weather."

She takes my hand and starts for the door, but I pull her back to me. I cup her cheeks and kiss her deeply. I will never tire of this woman or the feel of her mouth on mine. When I pull away, she's panting.

"Keep kissing me like that and we won't make it inside."

Her playful threat makes me groan. I'd like nothing more than to take her home and make love to her all night. Even spending a week locked up in a secluded cabin with her wasn't enough. There will never be too much Alicia in my life.

I wrap my arm around her waist and tuck her into my side. My favorite place for her to be. "I love you."

Her smile grows, and she kisses my cheek. "I love you, too. Now let's go."

With our arms wrapped around each other, we walk into the bar. After discarding our coats behind the bar, we find our family and friends gathered around a large table along the back wall.

"Finally," my mom says when she sees us walking up. "It's about time you showed up."

"Mom." I shake my head. "We're not that late."

"Maybe not, but you're still late." She leans up and kisses my cheek. "And you're never late."

"People change." I chuckle.

"Yes, but you don't." Mom pats my chest and winks at Alicia. "Now that you two are here, we can begin."

"Before that, Alicia and I have an announcement." I scan the table and everyone is watching us with either suspicion or excitement. Alicia's mom, Susan, looks worried. My dad has a huge smile on his face and my siblings, Evan, and Trent look suspicious. They all exchange glances like they share some secret and are waiting for the right time to spill it.

Alicia and I share a loving glance before I turn back to our family. "Alicia and I got married."

"Married!" Both our moms yelled at the same time. My dad's smile grows and lifts his beer to us with a nod.

Dexter slaps the table and holds his hand out to Evan. "Hand it over."

Evan pulls several bills out of his pocket and gives it to Dexter, who's grinning from ear to ear. The rest of my siblings and friends are staring at us in disbelief.

"Did you all make a bet on us?" I ask.

"Yep." Dexter laughs. "These fools all thought you were going to announce your engagement. But not me. I knew something was up the second you called in and said you were taking Alicia on an *impromptu* vacation. Neither of you have ever taken—"

"You're married?" Susan yells, cutting Dexter short. "But you can't be. I wasn't there. You can't get married without your mother. You're my only daughter and I have to—" Susan clasps her hand over her mouth and her eyes widen. "Oh my, you're pregnant."

"Mom!" Alicia gasps. "I'm not pregnant."

"But you have to be pregnant. Why else would you elope?" Tears stream down Susan's face. Alicia lets go of me and rushes to her mom.

"Mom, don't be upset." Alicia hugs her mom and kisses her cheek. "We eloped because we didn't want to wait. We got married because it felt right."

Susan smiles through her tears. "I'm happy for you dear, I really am. But you're my only child. I wanted to celebrate that moment with you."

"And that's what we're here to do now. Celebrate." Alicia tightens her arms around her mother, and my heart swells. I'm truly the luckiest man alive.

"Well, I say drinks are on the house." Luke holds up his mug. "Cheers to the newlyweds."

I squeeze Luke's shoulders and laugh. "Drinks better be on the house since I'm part owner of this house."

Everyone laughs. We share a few more tears but mostly it's an evening of celebration and joy.

All-in-all, we have a great night. Watching Alicia with my family tonight made me realize that she was a part of my family long before we even met. My siblings loved her before I loved her. And now that she's my wife, my life is complete.

I TURN OFF THE bathroom light and find Alicia sitting cross-legged on the bed wearing my favorite satin nightgown. She's staring at her wedding ring and the look on her face is not sad or happy. She's deep in thought about something serious, I'm sure of it.

I sit next to her on the bed and take her hand in mine. "Hey, you okay."

She sinks into my side and rests her head on my bare chest. "Yeah. Tonight just made me realize there are some things we never talked about before we got married."

I stiffen and tighten my grip on her hand. "You're not having second thoughts are you?"

"No!" She jerks up and cups my cheek. "Never. I will never have second thoughts where you're concerned."

"Good. Don't scare me like that." I pull her into me and kiss her. "Then what things haven't we talked about that you want to talk about?"

Her eyes shift to her lap. I follow her gaze. She picks up her pack of birth control pills and hands it to me. "Kids for one. I know you said you thought you'd have kids by now, but we never talked about it before we got married."

I turn the pack of pills over in my hand. My heart beats faster as my mind starts running in multiple directions. I want kids, and I most definitely want them with her. If she tells me she doesn't want them, I'll be devastated. "Yes, I want kids. Having them with you would make me very happy."

"It would?" Her smile is so big and bright I can't help but kiss her.

"Yes, very much." I kiss her again and she relaxes in my arms. "Do you still want kids someday?"

She nods as she deepens the kiss. She cups my cheeks and takes me with her as she lays back on the bed. I smile against her lips before I take her tongue into my mouth. She tastes like wine and toothpaste and everything that's mine.

I run my hand down her arm, taking the strap of her nightgown with me. The soft, supple skin of her breast calls for my lips. I take one into my mouth and suck, making her writhe beneath me. While on our honeymoon, I spent a lot of time getting to know what makes her come. Sucking, licking, and biting her breasts while teasing her clit is one of them.

I grind my hard cock against her center while I lightly bite her pebbled nipple.

"Heath." Her voice is light and breathy.

"What, beautiful?" I ask between licks and nips of her breasts.

"I haven't taken my pill today." She manages between breaths. Her words cause me to stop, and I meet her lust-filled gaze. "I was thinking about not taking it. That is, if it's okay with you."

My cock gets harder as her words really sink in. "You're ready to make a baby with me now?"

"I am." Her smile is tentative and sweet. "Are you ready for that?"

"I'm more than ready." I kiss her hard before I finish my exploration of her breasts. I suck and nip at her breasts until she's begging me to make her come. By the time I strip her panties off her, she's soaking wet for me.

I run my finger up her center and swirl it around her clit, making her gasp. "Please, I need you inside me now." She begs.

"As you wish." I leave her long enough to discard my clothes. I lift her leg, opening her up to me. Her naked body is ripe and ready for me. I line my tip at her entrance and our eyes meet. "I think we're gonna need practice. Lots and lots of practice."

"Yes." She smiles as I slowly fill her with my thumb

pressed against her clit. I move slowly at first, then quicken my pace as her first climax nears. A sure way to make her come fast is touching her clit while fucking her hard. So I give her what she's begging me for.

Her climax hits her fast and hard. Her body clenches around me and squeezes as I move inside her. Normally I can hold off, make this last longer, but tonight I'm a goner. I come with her, and the world around us fades away.

There's only us and the promise of the family we're going to create.

BONUS SCENE

Emily

If one more guy comes up to me and gives me a cheesy pick-up line, I'll scream.

All I want is to drink my wine in peace and maybe eat a light dinner before I call it a night. Is that too much to ask?

Apparently.

Maybe it's California men. I never get lines like this back in New York. But I've been sitting at the bar in my hotel for about thirty minutes, and I've heard not one, not two, but six cheesy pick-up lines. Two from the same douchebag.

Aside from being sexy, what do you do for a living? Nope.

Are you a parking ticket? Because you've got FINE written all over you. Um, hell no.

I would like to treat you like a jet ski. Ride you hard and put you away wet. Gross.

But my personal favorite from tonight. *Do you want to play a game? It's called carpenter. It's where I pretend you're a piece of wood and I nail you.* Seriously? Who says that shit?

Do guys really think that works? Whatever happened to just saying hi. Hi works. I'll respond to hi. Preferably when they're looking me in the eyes and not at my chest. It's not like I've got a big rack to ogle in the first place. My barely there B-cup boobs don't exactly measure up to the busty tall blonde sitting on the other end of the bar. She hasn't been approached once. I wonder what her secret is that keeps the douche canoes away?

Alicia, my best friend and steamy romance author, says it's because I smile too much. She says it gives off the impression that I'm approachable. I guess I can see her point, but a smile shouldn't be just cause to act like a dick.

Life is better with a smile. I'm generally a happy person, and I sure as hell shouldn't have to change that about myself just because guys are pigs.

"Do you want another?" the bartender asks.

I look down at my empty wine glass, unaware I'd

drained it. "Yes, please. And can I see the menu?"

He tosses me a huge grin and nods. I hadn't really looked at him until now. He's cute, in a boy next door kind of way. Slightly shaggy blond hair, clean shaven, and a little dimple that only comes out with the big grins. I like dimples on men. They give off a boyish quality and a sense of vulnerability that I've always been drawn to.

He slides a menu in front of me, breaking the brief eye contact we'd made. He may be cute, but he's not my type. I prefer dark-haired men.

Not that I'm here to pick up a man tonight anyway. This trip is all about business. I co-own and run an upscale bar with my three brothers back in New York—Heath, Dexter, and Luke. In addition to the bar, we host events in the small room attached to the space. For larger events, we rent out the entire bar. The events side of the business has turned out to be quite lucrative and we're looking into expanding. We get more inquiries than we can accommodate, plus the events are starting to mean the bar is closed to the public more often than not.

We don't want to lose our regular patrons because we're always hosting private events, so we're looking for additional space. But if we do this, we're going all in. Weddings, anniversaries, birthdays, corporate business events, you name it. We want to be able to offer it all.

Which is what brought me to California to attend one of the largest events and hospitality conferences in the nation. If I'm going to lead this effort, I want to make sure I cover all my bases.

My brothers are already on board with this expansion, but educating ourselves and being on top of trends is why The Rock Room has been so successful. Expanding is always a risk, especially in this business. Maintaining a profitable bar and staying on trend is never easy in a city the size of New York—anywhere for that matter—but in New York, we're one of hundreds of options. We have to stand out and stay fresh if we want to remain on top.

The bartender brings me another glass of red wine, and I put in an order of pretzel bites. I see a man walk past me, pause, then turn back. I outwardly groan. *Here we go again.*

I know I shouldn't look at him. I should keep my head facing forward and pretend I don't see his large frame out of the corner of my eye. But that's not what I do. Nope. I glance over my shoulder and smile like a dumbass. Because that's the kind of stupid shit I do.

With a slightly crooked and very creepy grin on his face, his eyes shift to my chest. "Do you believe in love at first sight, or should I walk by again?" he asks.

He actually has the nerve to deliver that line while his eyes drift down to my bare legs, lingering for several uncomfortable beats.

I roll my eyes and struggle to hold back my smartass response, but it comes out anyway. "I do, actually. But you should keep walking because I'm not seeing it."

Instead of leaving like I expect, he chuckles and slides into the stool next to me. Usually I love a man in a suit and tie, but somehow, he makes it look bad. He's not a bad-looking man, but there's something about him that doesn't sit right with me. His smile looks animalistic—and not in a way that says I'm going to ravage you and make you come so hard you'll never forget my name, but more like a hyena that hasn't had a meal in weeks.

He leans in close, and I instantly pull back. He reeks of cheap cologne and based on the smell of his breath, he's had too much to drink.

"You're cute," he says.

"Uh, thanks." I cringe at my word choice. Why in the hell did I thank him? Not to mention my voice sounds weak and not nearly assertive enough to get this guy to go away.

He reaches across the bar and swirls a lock of my dark hair around his finger. He starts to pull it toward his nose like he's going to sniff it, but I slap his hand away.

"What in the hell do you think you're doing?"

He seems completely undeterred by my slap or outburst. Instead, his smile grows. "Taking you back to my room with me where I plan to get—"

"Do not finish that statement unless you want me to slap something other than your hand."

He laughs and swivels in his stool so he's facing me. He motions to his crotch and waggles his brows. "Cutie, I've got something you can slap."

My jaw drops. I'm speechless. Is this guy for real? I've met some real assholes in my life, but this is a first.

He lifts his hand again like he's going to touch my cheek, but another hand reaches from behind me and squeezes his hand hard enough that it makes him cry out.

"The lady is not interested in what you have to offer," a familiar deep voice growls from behind me.

My head whips around at the sound that I know all too well. "Evan?"

Evan Brooks should not be standing beside me. He should be in New York where he lives and works. I blink several times, thinking my eyes must be playing tricks on me. But he's not a mirage. His hand rests on my shoulder blade, and he leans down and kisses me lightly on the cheek. It's gentle and sweet and exactly what I'd expect from a man who's practically been like a fourth brother to me since the day I was born. He became best friends with my brother Dexter when they were in kindergarten. I wasn't anything more than a bump in my mom's belly at the time.

For the first several years of my life, he *was* a brother to me, no different than Dexter or Luke or Heath. But something shifted after I turned nine. He grew up to be this smart, sexy, sixteen-year-old man. Technically still a boy, but at nine, sixteen might as well be a man. Overnight, he stopped being a brother to me and turned into my Prince Charming.

I've had the biggest crush on Evan Brooks for almost twenty years, and it sucks. Because to him, I'm nothing more than a baby sister in need of rescuing.

"Hey." The creepy man who's still sitting too close to me glares up at Evan. "I found her first. Go find you another one."

Evan's eyes narrow and his hand on my back tenses. He leans forward and whispers something to the creep that I can't hear. Whatever it is, it's enough to make the man scramble off without a glance back in my direction.

I look up at Evan all wide-eyed with surprise. But he's not looking at me. He's tracking the man like a predator hunts his prey. There's a tense wrinkle in his forehead like he doesn't trust that the man won't return and try to pounce again. It's sexy and hot, and oh how I wish it meant something more than overly protective brotherly love.

Then he looks down at me with those dreamy deep brown eyes that I get lost in every time our eyes meet. I swoon. His expression softens, and he smiles. "You okay?"

I nod, still a little stunned to see him here. My expression must amuse him because he laughs, that deep throaty laugh that sends shivers down my spine every time I hear it. I shake my head and take a sip of my wine when I realize I'm staring at him. I can't help it sometimes. He's just so damn hot.

He's the kind of man that can rock the hell out of a suit. The suit doesn't make him look good. He makes the suit look good. It doesn't matter the cut, his body is sinfully sexy. Broad shoulders, defined biceps and forearms, muscular legs with the tightest ass known to man. His wool trousers do nothing to hide his cute ass dimples.

"Emily?" His hand tightens around my shoulder. His brow furrows, and I realize I'm staring. I shake my head, coming back to my senses. I've done an excellent job for all these years at hiding my true feelings for Evan. I can't let a moment of surprise allow me to reveal my secret crush.

"I'm fine." I manage. "What did you say to him?"

Evan takes the seat the man just vacated. He leans close to me, his expression serious—much more serious than I'm used to seeing on him. He's more of the fun-loving, smiley type than the serious, broody type. I lift my wine to my lips to hide my erratic breathing because I'm struggling to hide my lifelong crush on him right now.

"That you're *mine*. And that if he knew what was good for him, he'd leave," he says with an air of confidence that completely throws me off.

I suck in a breath just as the wine hits my throat. I immediately start coughing. The burning sensation in my lungs is intense as my coughing body tries to expel the wine from the organ it doesn't belong in. My eyes water, and I can't breathe. Evan jumps up and pats my back while waving to the bartender. I hear him say something about water, but all I can think about is clearing my lungs and breathing properly again.

Moments later Evan is shoving a glass in front of me. "Here, drink this."

I do, gulping down the water like I'm starving for it. After a couple of sips I start to feel normal again. I clear my throat, wipe my eyes, and force a chuckle. "Thanks. Who knew drinking and breathing at the same time was such a difficult task."

Evan's expression calms, and he smiles. It's his playful smile. The one that says he's ready to have fun, leave behind his responsibilities and cut loose for a bit. It's my favorite smile. The one that I have the hardest time hiding my silly schoolgirl crush around.

He's just so damn handsome when he smiles like that. With his short, perfectly trimmed beard, slightly wavy hair that he leaves long on top, and chestnut brown eyes, he's an irresistible man. A man that I want but will never have.

Evan

"What are you doing here?" Emily asks as she wipes her eyes dry.

I hate to see her coughing like this, but I can't stop the knowing smile that spreads across my face. My possessive words to that asshole did this to her. I've always enjoyed flustering her, but never at the expense of her health.

Instead of smiling, I should be scolding myself. It isn't fair to her to mess with her like this. She's my best friend's baby sister. No matter how old we get or how much I want her, I can never have her. Dexter would kill me if I messed around with Emily.

I take a sip of my whiskey before I set it on the bar between us. "A law conference. Heath asked me to help you guys with securing the new property for the expansion. There was a real estate and property law seminar I attended today. It's been a while since I worked in property law. I wanted to brush up."

"Oh." She looks surprised. Maybe even a little irritated. "Heath didn't tell me he talked to you. I haven't even started looking at properties yet."

"My attendance here is more pre-emptive than anything. I want to make sure I'm prepared when you're ready to make an offer." I do my best to keep my tone as calm and casual as possible. That last thing I want to do is piss Emily off. Especially after I just got rid of that asshole eying her like dinner. Her brothers are overprotective and have always made her feel like they think she needs their help, even with business. But Emily has one of the brightest business minds I know. She doesn't need her brothers' help—or mine for that matter—to pull off this expansion.

"But they want you to serve as our attorney on this?" she asks, her words more hesitant than irritated now.

Her hesitation I can handle and understand. I work in corporate law. While my years of experience is applicable, she'll need someone with a greater understanding of property law. I want to make sure that person is me.

It's a sadistic plan. I'm only torturing myself by considering this. I've been in love with her for longer than I care to remember but I've never made my feelings known. Not to her, at least. Dexter made it very clear when we were teenagers that if I ever laid a hand on his sister, it'd be the last thing my hand ever touched.

I take another sip of my whiskey before I answer her. "If I'm comfortable with it, yes. I'd like to be the one to help you when you're ready." I look up and hold my gaze on hers. "That is if you're okay with that."

"Of course." She nods a little too eagerly, like she's trying to compensate for her initial shock and irritation over hearing why I'm here. "There isn't anyone else I'd trust more to help us out."

Her smile returns and causes every nerve in my body to fire, creating an electrical charge inside me that has me squirming in my seat. All I want to do is touch her. I don't need much—a simple brush of her leg against mine or a friendly squeeze of her hand on my arm. I'm like a starving man who just needs one touch from her. That would be enough to sustain me for another year.

But I want so much more from her. I've imagined countless times what it would be like to take her hand in mine, or brush my fingertips down her arm, or better yet, cup her cheek and taste her lips.

Hell tasting her lips is the PG version of my fantasies. Where Emily Rockwell is concerned, I've imagined tasting every inch of her. My mouth waters at the very idea of swiping my tongue up her center and sucking her tight little clit between my lips. Fuck, what I wouldn't give to truly make her mine.

"Evan?" She rests her hand on my forearm, giving me exactly what I need while also feeding my lustful thoughts.

"I'm sorry, did you say something?" I clear my throat and shift in my seat. Being this close to Emily is never easy for me.

"I asked if you wanted any pretzel bites. I ordered this before you joined me."

I glance at the bar and there's a platter between us overflowing with pretzel bites and dipping sauces. "Um, sure. Thanks." I'm not really hungry, I ate dinner right before I entered the hotel bar, but I pick one up anyway. "So, I take it you're here for the event and hospitality conference I've seen advertised around the hotel?"

"Yep," she says just before she stuffs a bite in her mouth, fingers and all. Her lips wrap around her fingers and make a little sucking motion that forces me to swallow a groan. "I've actually learned a lot," she says around a mouth full of food. "Even discovered some new business sectors we can market event planning for."

"That's great." My voice squawks, and I fake a cough like it's my turn to choke on my food. *Get it together, Evan.*

Thank God she doesn't seem to notice the effect she has on me. Instead, she keeps eating and telling me about the seminars she attended today. She's excited and animated and it's so fucking adorable. I can't say I actually hear the words she says, but I nod and speak at all the right moments, so she doesn't seem to notice. I really should pay attention—I'm genuinely interested in her business and am a potential business partner—but the way she's eating is far too distracting.

I watch her intently as she takes another pretzel bite to her mouth. Her tongue pokes out between her plump lips and curls around the bottom of the pretzel. I take in a slow, labored breath. I can't help but imagine that tongue curling around my balls in the same way. Then she draws her fingers into her mouth and sucks the dip off her fingers. Fuck, what I wouldn't give to feel her lips suck on my cock like that.

This is a mistake. I shouldn't be sitting here with her like this. At least in New York, her brothers are usually in the same room with us. That alone keeps my mind out of the fucking gutter. But tonight, we're thousands of miles away from them.

I wonder what she'd say if I finally told her how I feel about her? I could easily tell her. If she rejected me, her brothers would never need to know. But what if she didn't reject me? The thought of that creates so much anxiety inside me, I have a strong urge to flee.

But I don't do any of that. Instead, we eat and drink and laugh about all the fun times we had growing up. We don't even touch each other once. No accidental fingers tangling as we reach for the same bite of food, no leaning into her side to get a whiff of her sweet perfume, and no brushing of my leg against hers.

My thoughts may be extremely crude, inappropriate and sexually charged, but my actions are those of a perfect gentleman. I'd never be anything else where Emily is concerned.

This is turning out to be both the best and worst night I've ever spent with her.

It's the best because she's herself with me tonight. I haven't seen this completely unguarded and relaxed version of Emily in a long time. Ever since she started The Rock Room with her brothers, she's been tense and serious, determined to prove herself as the grown and capable woman she's become.

It's the worst because I still can't touch her and make her mine.

A second platter of appetizers and one too many glasses of wine and whiskey later, and we're helping each other stumble to the elevator.

"Evan, you *really* shouldn't have let me drink that much. I can't remember the last time I had that much wine." She giggles as she leans into me for support. I instinctively wrap my arm around her and hold her close. She slips her arm around my waist and sighs.

"Me?" I chuckle. I should release her, but I don't. "I don't recall making you drink all that."

She extracts herself from my arms and punches the up button to call the elevator. I want to pull her back into me, but she falls against the wall opposite me and nibbles on her bottom lip like a vixen.

"Maybe not," she teases. I've done a great job keeping my eyes up all evening, but now I'm too drunk to stop myself. My eyes rake down her body taking in her gentle curves. Her black dress accentuates her body in all the right places. Her long dark hair is gathered to one side and draped over her shoulder. "But after all of these years, I've come to expect your protection."

I step closer to her—so close we're almost touching. "But I did protect you. If I'd been a moment later, I might have hurt that man who was clueless to your rejection."

"Yeah?" Her eyes darken and shift to my mouth. I lean in, dropping my head until I'm eye level with her. She's a good six inches shorter than me, but her heels eliminate almost half of that distance. My mouth inches closer to hers. Her chest rises and falls in quick movements. Just as her hands lift like she's going to cup my face, the elevator dings. We both pull apart and glance around like we expect to be charged at any minute by her three angry brothers.

The elevator doors open, and we both step inside.

"What floor?" she asks, her voice a little rough.

"Nine."

She lets out a ragged breath. "Me, too."

She presses the button. As soon as the door closes, she turns to me. "Evan?"

One look into her heated eyes and I'm done. Nothing on this earth can stop me from what I do next.

I cup her cheeks and walk her back until she's pinned between the elevator wall and me. Then my lips crash into hers.

~~~

The Rockwell's continue to fight for love in this friends to lovers, forbidden romance, best friend's sister, fun-filled and hot love story:

Emily and Evan fight for love in *Let Me Stay*: A Friends to Lovers, Best Friend's Sister Romantic Comedy (A Drunk Love Romantic Comedy, Book 2) release date May 2, 2022.

Visit https://www.amazon.com/dp/B09SGW1T93 to reserve your copy.

Connect with Me

Website:
http://ariabliss.com

Subscribe to my Newsletter:
https://ariabliss.com/sign-up/

Follow me on Amazon Author Central:
http://www.amazon.com/author/ariabliss.author

Follow me on Instagram:
http://www.instagram.com/ariabliss.author

Follow me on goodreads:
http://www.goodreads.com/ariablissauthor

Follow me on Bookbub:
https://www.bookbub.com/authors/aria-bliss

Join my Facebook Street Team:
https://www.facebook.com/groups/SassySuperFans/

Follow me on Facebook:
http://www.facebook.com/ariabliss.author/

Follow me on Twitter:
http://www.twitter.com/ariablissauthor

Books by Aria Bliss

A Drunk Love Romantic Comedy
Not For Me: Book 1
Let Me Stay: Book 2

Hearts of Watercress Falls
Healing Hearts: Book 1
Trusting Hearts: Book 2
Falling Hearts: Book 3
Laughing Hearts: Book 4
Forgiving Hearts: Book 5

An After-Hours Affair Collection
In Charge: Book 1
One Drink: Book 2
You're Mine: Book 3
Charm Me: Book 4
Stuck Together: Book 5 (A Holiday Romance)

~~~

Short Stories
Walk with Me

Author Bio

Sweet & Steamy Romance with a side order of Lust

Aria Bliss is the pen name of an award-winning and bestselling author. Aria writes steamy contemporary romance novels, novellas, and short stories. Her female leads are sassy and strong with a lot of spunk and drive for success. Their sensitive alpha male counterparts better be up to the challenge if they want to win their hearts. In Aria's first series, An After-hours Affair Collection, the career-focused women of New York City are drawn to a hot co-worker, business partner, or client that teaches them there's always time for a little romance. In her second series, Aria leaves the big city and heads to the mountains of Montana for some sexy, cowboy romance. *Walk with Me* is her first published short story. *In Charge* is her first book in the After-hours Affair collection.

Made in United States
North Haven, CT
04 February 2024